I feel as though my history is being rewritten, infinite paragraphs scratched out and hastily revised. Old and new images—memories—layer atop each other until the ink runs, rupturing the scenes into something new, something incomprehensible. Occasionally my thoughts feel like disturbing hallucinations, and the onslaught is so invasive I fear it's doing irreparable damage.

Because something is changing.

Every new memory is delivered with an emotional violence that drives into me, reorders my mind. I'd been feeling this pain in flickers—the sickness, the nausea, the disorientation—but I haven't wanted to question it too deeply. I haven't wanted to look too closely. The truth is, I didn't want to believe my own fears. But the truth is: I am a punctured tire. Every injection of air leaves me both fuller and flatter.

I am forgetting.

"Ella?"

Terror bubbles up inside of me, bleeds through my open eyes. It takes me a moment to remember that I am ~~Juliette~~ Ella. Each time, it takes me a moment longer.

BOOKS BY TAHEREH MAFI

Shatter Me: Series One

BOOK 1: *Shatter Me*

BOOK 2: *Unravel Me*

BOOK 3: *Ignite Me*

BOOK 4: *Restore Me*

BOOK 5: *Defy Me*

BOOK 6: *Imagine Me*

Shatter Me: Series One Novellas

BOOK 1.5: *Destroy Me*

BOOK 2.5: *Fracture Me*

BOOK 4.5: *Shadow Me*

BOOK 5.5: *Reveal Me*

BOOK 6.5: *Believe Me*

Shatter Me: Series One Novella Collections

Unite Me

Find Me

Shatter Me: Series Two

BOOK 1: *Watch Me*

BOOK 2: *Release Me*

The Woven Kingdom Series

BOOK 1: *This Woven Kingdom*

BOOK 2: *These Infinite Threads*

BOOK 3: *All This Twisted Glory*

BOOK 4: *Every Spiral of Fate*

An Emotion of Great Delight

A Very Large Expanse of Sea

IMAGINE ME

SHATTER ME: SERIES ONE
BOOK SIX

TAHEREH MAFI

STORYTIDE
An Imprint of HarperCollins*Publishers*

HarperCollins Children's Books,
a division of HarperCollins Publishers,
195 Broadway, New York, NY 10007

HarperCollins Publishers,
Macken House, 39/40 Mayor Street Upper,
Dublin 1, D01 C9W8, Ireland

Storytide is an imprint of HarperCollins Publishers.

Imagine Me

harpercollins.com

ISBN 978-0-06-349770-2

Typography by Ray Shappell
26 27 28 29 30 RTLO 10 9 8 7 6 5 4 3 2 1

SPECIAL EDITION, 2026

For Tara Weikum, for all these years

~~ELLA~~
JULIETTE

In the dead of night, I hear birds.

I hear them, I see them, I close my eyes and feel them, feathers shuddering in the air, bending the wind, wings grazing my shoulders when they ascend, when they alight. Discordant shrieks ring and echo, ring and echo—

How many?

Hundreds.

White birds, white with streaks of gold, like crowns atop their heads. They fly. They soar through the sky with strong, steady wings, masters of their destinies. They used to make me hope.

Never again.

I turn my face into the pillow, digging fingers into cotton flesh as the memories crash into me.

"Do you like them?" she says.

We're in a big, wide room that smells like dirt. There are trees everywhere, so tall they nearly touch the pipes and beams of the open ceiling. Birds, dozens of them, screech as they stretch their wings. Their calls are loud. A little scary. I try not to flinch as one of the large white birds swoops past me. It wears a bright, neon-green bracelet around one leg. They all do.

This doesn't make sense.

I remind myself that we're indoors—the white walls, the concrete floor under my feet—and I look up at my mother, confused.

I've never seen Mum smile so much. Mostly she smiles when Dad is around, or when she and Dad are off in the corner, whispering together, but right now it's just me and Mum and a bunch of birds and she's so happy I decide to ignore the funny feeling in my stomach. Things are better when Mum is in a good mood.

"Yes," I lie. "I like them a lot."

Her eyes brighten. "I knew you would. Emmaline didn't care for them, but you—you've always been a bit too fond of things, haven't you, darling? Not at all like your sister." Somehow, her words come out mean. They don't seem *mean, but they* sound *mean.*

I frown.

I'm still trying to figure out what's happening when she says—

"I had one as a pet when I was about your age. Back then, they were so common we could never be rid of them." She laughs, and I watch her as she watches a bird, midflight. "One of them lived in a tree near my house, and it called my name whenever I walked past. Can you imagine?" Her smile fades as she asks the question.

Finally, she turns to look at me.

"They're very nearly extinct now. You understand why I couldn't let that happen."

"Of course," I say, but I'm lying again. There is little I understand about Mum.

She nods. "These are a special sort of creature. Intelligent. They can speak, dance. And each of them wears a crown." She turns away again, staring at the birds the way she stares at all the things she makes for work: with joy. "The sulphur-crested cockatoo mates for life," she says. "Just like me and your father."

The sulphur-crested cockatoo.

I shiver, suddenly, at the unexpected sensation of a warm hand on my back, fingers trailing lightly along my spine.

"Love," he says, "are you all right?"

When I say nothing he shifts, the sheets rustling, and he tucks me into his hollows, his body curving around mine. He's warm and strong and as his hand slides down my torso I cant my head toward him, finding peace in his presence, in the safety of his arms. His lips touch my skin, a graze against my neck so subtle it sparks, hot and cold, right down to my toes.

"Is it happening again?" he whispers.

My mother was born in Australia.

I know this because she once told me so, and because now, despite my desperation to resist many of the memories now returned to me, I can't forget. She once told me that the sulphur-crested cockatoo was native to Australia. It was introduced to New Zealand in the nineteenth century, but Evie, my mother, didn't discover them there. She fell in love with the birds back home, as a child, when one of them, she claims, saved her life.

These were the birds that once haunted my dreams.

These birds, kept and bred by a crazy woman. I feel embarrassed to realize I'd held fast to nonsense, to the faded, disfigured impressions of old memories poorly discarded. I'd hoped for more. Dreamed of more. Disappointment lodges in my throat, a cold stone I'm unable to swallow.

And then

again

I feel it

I stiffen against the nausea that precedes a vision, the sudden punch to the gut that means there's more, there's more, there's always more.

Aaron pulls me closer, holds me tighter against his chest.

"Breathe," he whispers. "I'm right here, love. I'll be right here."

I cling to him, squeezing my eyes shut as my head swims. These memories were a gift from my sister, Emmaline. The sister I only just discovered, only just recovered.

And only because she fought to find me.

Despite my parents' relentless efforts to rid our minds of the lingering proof of their atrocities, Emmaline prevailed. She used her psychokinetic powers to return to me what was stolen from my memories. She gave me this gift—this gift of remembering—to help me save myself. To save *her*. To stop our parents.

To fix the world.

But now, in the wake of a narrow escape, this gift has become a curse. Every hour my mind is reborn. Altered. The memories keep coming.

And my dead mother refuses to be silenced.

"Little bird," she whispers, tucking a stray hair behind my ear. "It's time for you to fly away now."

"But I don't want to go," I say, fear making my voice shake. "I want to stay here, with you and Dad and Emmaline. I still don't understand why I have to leave."

"You don't have to understand," she says gently.

I go uncomfortably still.

Mum doesn't yell. She's never yelled. My whole life, she's never raised a hand to me, never shouted or called me names. Not like Aaron's dad. But Mum doesn't need to yell. Sometimes she just says things, things like you don't have to understand *and there's a warning there, a finality in her words that's always scared me.*

I feel tears forming, burning the whites of my eyes, and—

"No crying," she says. "You're far too old for that now."

I sniff, hard, fighting back the tears. But my hands won't stop shaking.

Mum looks up, nods at someone behind me. I turn around just in time to spot Paris, Mr. Anderson, waiting with my suitcase. There's no kindness in his eyes. No warmth at all. He turns away from me, looks at Mum. He doesn't say hello.

He says: "Has Max settled in yet?"

"Oh, he's been ready for days." Mum glances at her watch, distracted. "You know Max," she says, smiling faintly. "Always a perfectionist."

"Only when it comes to your wishes," says Mr. Anderson. "I've never seen a grown man so besotted with his wife."

Mum smiles wider. She seems about to say something, but I cut her off.

"Are you talking about Dad?" I ask, my heart racing. "Will Dad be there?"

My mother turns to me, surprised, like she'd forgotten I was there. She turns back to Mr. Anderson. "How's Leila doing, by the way?"

"Fine," he says. But he sounds irritated.

"Mum?" Tears threaten again. "Am I going to stay with Dad?"

But Mum doesn't seem to hear me. She's talking to Mr. Anderson when she says, "Max will walk you through everything when you arrive, and he'll be able to answer most of your questions. If there's something he can't answer, it's likely beyond your clearance."

Mr. Anderson looks suddenly annoyed, but he says nothing. Mum says nothing.

I can't stand it.

Tears are spilling down my face now, my body shaking so hard it makes my breaths rattle. "Mum?" I whisper. "Mum, please a-answer me—"

Mum clamps a cold, hard hand around my shoulder and I go instantly still. Quiet. She's not looking at me. She won't look at me. "You'll handle this, too," she says. "Won't you, Paris?"

Mr. Anderson meets my eyes then. So blue. So cold. "Of course."

A flash of heat courses through me. A rage so sudden it briefly replaces my terror.

I hate him.

I hate him so much that it does something to me when I look at him—and the abrupt surge of emotion makes me feel brave.

I turn back to Mum. Try again.

"Why does Emmaline get to stay?" I ask, wiping angrily at my wet cheeks. "If I have to go, can't we at least go toge—"

I cut myself off when I spot her.

My sister, Emmaline, is peeking out at me from behind the mostly closed door. She's not supposed to be here. Mum said so.

Emmaline is supposed to be doing her swimming lessons.

But she's here, her wet hair dripping on the floor, and she's staring at me, eyes wide as plates. She's trying to say something, but her lips move too fast for me to follow. And then, out of nowhere, a bolt of electricity runs up my spine and I hear her voice, sharp and strange—

Liars.

LIARS.

KILL THEM ALL

My eyes fly open and I can't catch my breath, my chest heaving, heart pounding. Warner holds me, making soothing sounds as he runs a reassuring hand up and down my arm.

Tears spill down my face and I swipe at them, hands shaking.

"I hate this," I whisper, horrified at the tremble in my voice. "I hate this so much. I hate that it keeps happening. I hate what it does to me," I say. *"I hate it."*

~~Warner~~ Aaron presses his cheek against my shoulder with a sigh, his breath teasing my skin.

"I hate it, too," he says softly.

I turn, carefully, in the cradle of his arms, and press my forehead to his bare chest.

It's been less than two days since we escaped Oceania. Two days since I killed my own mother. Two days since I met the residue of my sister, Emmaline. Only two days since my entire life was upended yet again, which feels impossible.

Two days and already things are on fire around us.

This is our second night here, at the Sanctuary, the locus of the rebel group run by Nouria—Castle's daughter—and her wife, Sam. We're supposed to be safe here. We're supposed to be able to breathe and regroup after the hell of the last few weeks, but my body refuses to settle. My mind is overrun, under attack. I thought the rush of new memories would eventually gutter out, but these last twenty-four hours have been an unusually brutal assault, and I seem to be the only one struggling.

Emmaline gifted all of us—all the children of the supreme commanders—with memories stolen by our parents. One by one we were awoken to the truths our parents had buried, and one by one we were returned to normal lives.

All but me.

The others have since moved on, reconciled their timelines, made sense of the betrayal. My mind, on the other hand, continues to falter. Spin. But then, none of the others lost as much as I did; they don't have as much to remember. Even Warner—*Aaron*—isn't experiencing so thorough a reimagining of his life.

It's beginning to scare me.

I feel as though my history is being rewritten, infinite paragraphs scratched out and hastily revised. Old and new images—memories—layer atop each other until the ink runs, rupturing the scenes into something new, something incomprehensible. Occasionally my thoughts feel like disturbing hallucinations, and the onslaught is so invasive I fear it's doing irreparable damage.

Because something is changing.

Every new memory is delivered with an emotional violence that drives into me, reorders my mind. I'd been feeling this pain in flickers—the sickness, the nausea, the disorientation—but I haven't wanted to question it too deeply. I haven't wanted to look too closely. The truth is, I didn't want to believe my own fears. But the truth is: I am a punctured tire. Every injection of air leaves me both fuller and flatter.

I am forgetting.

"Ella?"

Terror bubbles up inside of me, bleeds through my open eyes. It takes me a moment to remember that I am ~~Juliette~~ Ella. Each time, it takes me a moment longer.

Hysteria threatens—

I force it down.

"Yes," I say, forcing air into my lungs. "Yes."

~~Warner.~~ Aaron stiffens. "Love, what's wrong?"

"Nothing," I lie. My heart is pounding fast, too fast. I don't know why I'm lying. It's a fruitless effort; he can sense everything I'm feeling. I should just tell him. ~~I don't know why I'm not telling him.~~ I know why I'm not telling him.

I'm waiting.

I'm waiting to see if this will pass, if the lapses in my memory are only glitches waiting to be repaired. Saying it out loud makes it too real, and it's too soon to say these thoughts aloud, to give in to the fear. After all, it's only been a day since it started. It only occurred to me yesterday that something was truly wrong.

It occurred to me because I made a mistake.

Mistakes.

We were sitting outside, staring at the stars. I couldn't remember ever seeing the stars like that—sharp, clear. It was late, so late it wasn't night but infant morning, and the view was dizzying. I was freezing. A brave wind stole through a copse nearby, filling the air with steady sound. I was full of cake. Warner smelled like sugar, like decadence. I felt drunk on joy.

I don't want to wait, he said, taking my hand. Squeezing it. *Let's not wait.*

I blinked up at him. *For what?*

For what?

For what?

How did I forget what had happened just hours earlier? How did I forget the moment he asked me to marry him?

It was a glitch. It felt like a glitch. Where there was once a memory was suddenly a vacancy, a cavity held empty only until nudged into realignment.

I recovered, remembered. Warner laughed.

I did not.

I forgot the name of Castle's daughter. I forgot how we landed at the Sanctuary. I forgot, for a full two minutes, how I ever escaped Oceania. But my errors were temporary; they seemed like natural delays. I experienced only confusion as my mind buffered, hesitation as the memories resurfaced, waterlogged and vague. I thought maybe I was tired. Overwhelmed. I took none of it seriously, not until I was sitting under the stars and couldn't remember promising to spend the rest of my life with someone.

Mortification.

Mortification so acute I thought I'd expire from the full force of it. Even now fresh heat floods my face, and I find I'm relieved Warner can't see in the dark.

Aaron, not Warner.

Aaron.

"I can't tell just now whether you're afraid or embarrassed," he says, and exhales softly. It sounds almost like a laugh. "Are you worried about Kenji? About the others?"

I grab on to this half-truth with my whole heart.

"Yes," I say. "*Kenji.* James. Adam."

Kenji has been sick in bed since very early this morning. I squint at the slant of moon through our window and remember that it's long past midnight, which would mean that, technically, Kenji got sick yesterday morning.

Regardless, it was terrifying for all of us.

The drugs Nazeera forced into Kenji on their international flight from Sector 45 to Oceania were a dose too strong, and he's been reeling ever since. He finally collapsed—the twins, Sonya and Sara, have checked in on him and say he's going to be just fine—but not before we learned that Anderson has been rounding up the children of the supreme commanders.

Adam and James and Lena and Valentina and Nicolás are all in Anderson's custody.

James is in his custody.

It's been a devastating, awful couple of days. It's been a devastating, awful couple of weeks.

Months, really.

Years.

Some days, no matter how far back I go, I can't seem to find the good times. Some days, the occasional happiness I've known feels like a bizarre dream. An error. Hyperreal and unfocused, the colors too bright and the sounds too strong.

Figments of my imagination.

It was just days ago that clarity came to me, bearing gifts. Just days ago that the worst seemed behind me, that the world seemed full of potential, that my body was stronger than ever, my mind fuller, sharper, more capable than I'd ever known it.

But now

But now

But now I feel like I'm clinging to the blurring edges of sanity, that elusive, fair-weather friend always breaking my heart.

Aaron pulls me close and I melt into him, grateful for his warmth, for the steadiness of his arms around me. I take a deep, shuddering breath and let it all go, exhaling against him. I inhale the rich, heady scent of his skin, the faint aroma of gardenias he somehow carries with him always. Seconds pass in perfect silence and we listen to each other breathe.

Slowly, my heart rate steadies.

The tears dry up. The fears take five. Terror is distracted by a passing butterfly and sadness takes a nap.

For a little while it's just me and him and us and everything is untarnished, untouched by darkness.

I knew I loved ~~Warner.~~ Aaron before all this—before we were captured by The Reestablishment, before we were ripped apart, before we learned of our shared history—but that love was new, green, its depths uncharted, untested. In that brief, glimmering window during which the gaping holes in my memory felt fully accounted for, things between us changed. *Everything* between us changed. Even now, even with the noise in my head, I feel it.

Here.

This.

My bones against his bones. This is my home.

I feel him suddenly stiffen and I pull back, concerned. I can't see much of him in this perfect darkness, but I feel the delicate rise of goose bumps along his arms when he says,

"What are you thinking about?"

My eyes widen, comprehension dethroning concern. "I was thinking about you."

"Me?"

I close the gap between us again. Nod against his chest.

He says nothing, but I can hear his heart, racing in the quiet, and eventually I hear him exhale. It's a heavy, uneven sound, like he might've been holding his breath for too long. I wish I could see his face. No matter how much time we spend together, I still forget how much he can feel my emotions, especially at times like this, when our bodies are pressed together.

Gently, I run my hand down his back. "I was thinking about how much I love you," I say.

He goes uncommonly still, but only for a moment. And then he touches my hair, his fingers slowly combing the strands.

"Did you feel it?" I ask.

When he doesn't answer, I pull back again. I blink against the black until I'm able to make out the glint of his eyes, the shadow of his mouth.

"Aaron?"

"Yes," he says, but he sounds a little breathless.

"Yes, you felt it?"

"Yes," he says again.

"What does it feel like?"

He sighs. Rolls onto his back. He's quiet for so long that, for a while, I'm not sure he's going to answer. Then, softly, he says:

"It's hard to describe. It's a pleasure so close to pain I sometimes can't tell the two apart."

"That sounds awful."

"No," he says. "It's exquisite."

"I love you."

A sharp intake of breath. Even in this darkness I see the strain in his jaw—the tension there—as he stares at the ceiling.

I sit straight up, surprised.

Aaron's reaction is so unstudied I don't know how I never noticed it before. But then, maybe this is new. Maybe something really has changed between us. Maybe I never loved him this much before. That would make sense, I suppose. Because when I think about it, when I really think about how much I love him now, after everything we've—

Another sudden, sharp breath. And then he laughs, nervously.

"*Wow,*" I say.

He claps a hand over his eyes. "This is vaguely mortifying."

I'm smiling now, very nearly laughing. "Hey. It's—"

My body seizes.

A violent shudder rushes up my skin and my spine goes rigid, my bones held in place by invisible pins, my mouth frozen open and trying to draw breath.

Heat fills my vision.

I hear nothing but static, grand rapids, white water, ferocious wind. Feel nothing. Think nothing. Am nothing.

I am, for the most infinitesimal moment—

Free.

My eyelids flutter open *closed* open *closed* open *closed* I am a wing, two wings, a swinging door, five birds

Fire climbs inside of me, explodes.

Ella?

The voice appears in my mind with swift strength, sharp, like darts to the brain. Dully, I realize that I'm in pain—my jaw aches, my body still suspended in an unnatural position—but I ignore it. The voice tries again:

Juliette?

Realization strikes, a knife to the knees. Images of my sister fill my mind: bones and melted skin, webbed fingers, sodden mouth, no eyes. Her body suspended underwater, long brown hair like a swarm of eels. Her strange, disembodied voice pierces through me. And so I say, without speaking:

Emmaline?

Emotion drives into me, fingers digging in my flesh, sensation scraping across my skin. Her relief is tangible. I can taste it. She's relieved, relieved I recognized her, relieved she found me, relieved relieved relieved—

What happened? I ask.

A deluge of images floods my brain until it sinks, I sink. Her memories drown my senses, clog lungs. I choke as the feelings crash into me. I see Max, my father, inconsolable in the wake of his wife's murder; I see Supreme Commander Ibrahim, frantic and furious, demanding Anderson gather the other children before it's too late; I see Emmaline, briefly abandoned, seizing an opportunity—

I gasp.

Evie made it so that only she or Max could control Emmaline's powers, and with Evie dead, the fail-safes implemented were suddenly weakened. Emmaline realized that in the wake of our mother's death there would be a brief window of opportunity—a brief window during which she might be able to wrest back control of her own mind before Max remade the algorithms.

But Evie's work was too good, and Max's reaction too prompt. Emmaline was only partly successful.

Dying, she says to me.

Dying.

Every flash of her emotion is accompanied by torturous assault. My flesh feels bruised. My spine seems liquid, my eyes blind, searing. I feel Emmaline—her voice, her feelings, her visions—more strongly than before, because *she's* stronger than before. That she managed to regain enough power to find me is proof alone that she is at least partly untethered, unrestrained. Max and Evie had been experimenting on Emmaline to a reckless degree in the last several months, trying to make her stronger even as her body withered. This, *this,* is the consequence.

Being this close to her is nothing short of excruciating.

I think I've screamed.

Have I screamed?

Everything about Emmaline is heightened to a fever pitch; her presence is wild, breathtaking, and it shudders to life inside my nerves. Sound and sensation streak across my vision, barrel through me violently. I hear a spider scuttle across the wooden floor. Tired moths drag their wings along the wall. A mouse startles, settles, in its sleep. Dust motes fracture against a window, shrapnel skidding across the glass.

My eyes skitter, unhinged in my skull.

I feel the oppressive weight of my hair, my limbs, my flesh wrapped around me like cellophane, a leather casket. My tongue, my tongue is a dead lizard perched in my mouth, rough and heavy. The fine hairs on my arms stand and sway, stand and sway. My fists are so tightly clenched my fingernails pierce the soft flesh of my palms.

I feel a hand on me. Where? Am I?

Lonely, she says.

She shows me.

A vision of us, back in the laboratory where I first saw her, where I killed our mother. I see myself from Emmaline's point of view and it's startling. She can't see much more than a blur, but she can feel my presence, can make out the shape of my form, the heat emanating from my body. And then my words, my own words, hurled back into my brain—

there has to be another way
you don't have to die
we can get through this together
please
i want my sister back
i want you to live
Emmaline
i won't let you die here
Emmaline Emmaline
we can get through this together
we can get through this together
we can get through this
together

A cold, metallic sensation begins to bloom in my chest. It moves through me, up my arms, down my throat, pushes into my gut. My teeth throb. Emmaline's pain claws and slithers, clings with a ferocity I can't bear. Her tenderness, too, is desperate, terrifying in its sincerity. She's overcome by emotion, hot and cold, fueled by rage and devastation.

She's been looking for me, all this time.

In these last couple of days Emmaline has been searching the conscious world for my mind, trying to find safe harbor, a place to rest.

A place to die.

Emmaline, I say. *Please—*

Sister.

Something tightens in my mind, squeezes. Fear propels through me, punctures organs. I'm wheezing. I smell earth and damp, decomposing leaves and I feel the stars staring at my skin, wind pushing through darkness like an anxious parent. My mouth is open, catching moths. I am on the ground.

Where?

No longer in my bed, I realize, no longer in my tent, I realize, no longer protected.

But when did I walk?

Who moved my feet? Who pushed my body?

How far?

I try to look around but I'm blind, my head trapped in a vise, my neck reduced to fraying sinew. My breaths fill my ears, harsh and loud, harsh and loud, rough rough gasping efforts my head

swings

My fists unclench, nails scraping as my fingers uncurl, palms flattening, I smell heat, taste wind, hear dirt.

Dirt under my hands, in my mouth, under my fingernails. I'm screaming, I realize. Someone is touching me and I'm screaming.

Stop, I scream. *Please, Emmaline— Please don't do this—*

Lonely, she says.

l o n e l y

And with a sudden, ferocious agony—

I am displaced.

KENJI

It feels weird to call it luck.

It feels weird, but in some perverse, twisted way, this is luck. Luck that I'm standing in the middle of damp, freezing woodlands before the sun's bothered to lift its head. Luck that my bare upper body is half-numb from cold.

Luck that Nazeera's with me.

We pulled on our invisibility almost instantly, so she and I are at least temporarily safe here, in the half-mile stretch of untouched wilderness between regulated and unregulated territories. The Sanctuary was built on a couple of acres of unregulated land not far from where I'm standing, and it's masterfully hidden in plain sight only because of Nouria's unnatural talent for bending and manipulating light. Within Nouria's jurisdiction, the climate is somehow more temperate, the weather more predictable. But out here in the wild, the winds are relentless and combative. The temperatures are dangerous.

Still— We're lucky to be here at all.

Nazeera and I had been out of bed for a while, racing through the dark in an attempt at murdering one another. In the end it all turned out to be a complicated misunderstanding, but it was also a kind of kismet: If Nazeera hadn't snuck into my room at three o'clock in the morning and nearly killed me, I wouldn't have chased her through the forest, beyond the sight and soundproof protections of the Sanctuary. If we hadn't been so far from the Sanctuary, we never would've heard the distant, echoing screams of citizens crying out in terror. If we hadn't heard those cries, we never would've rushed toward the source. And if we hadn't done any of that, I never would've seen my best friend screaming her way into dawn.

I would've missed this. This:

J on her knees in the cold dirt, Warner crouched down beside her, both of them looking like death while the clouds literally melt out of the sky above them. The two of them are parked right outside the entrance to the Sanctuary, straddling the untouched stretch of forest that serves as a buffer between our camp and the heart of the nearest sector, number 241.

Why?

I froze when I saw them there, two broken figures entwined, limbs planted in the ground. I was paralyzed by confusion, then fear, then disbelief, all while the trees bent sideways and the wind snapped at my body, cruelly reminding me that I'd never had a chance to put on a shirt.

If my night had gone differently, I might've had that chance.

If my night had gone differently, I might've enjoyed, for the first time in my life, a romantic sunrise and an overdue reconciliation with a beautiful girl. Nazeera and I would've laughed about how she'd kicked me in the back and almost killed me, and how afterward I almost shot her for it. After that I would've taken a long shower, slept until noon, and eaten my weight in breakfast foods.

I had a plan for today: take it easy.

I wanted a little more time to heal after my most recent near-death experience, and I didn't think I was asking for much. I thought that, maybe, after everything I'd been through, the world might finally cut me some slack. Let me breathe between tragedies.

Nah.

Instead, I'm here, dying of frostbite and horror, watching the world fall to pieces around me. The sky, swinging wildly between horizontal and vertical horizons. The air, puncturing at random. Trees, sinking into the ground. Leaves, tap-dancing around me. I'm seeing it—I'm actively witnessing it—and still I can't believe it.

But I'm choosing to call it luck.

Luck that I'm seeing this, luck that I feel like I might throw up, luck that I ran all this way in my still-ill, injured body just in time to score a front-row seat to the end of the world.

Luck, fate, coincidence, serendipity—

I'll call this sick, sinking feeling in my gut a fucking magic trick if it'll help me keep my eyes open long enough to bear witness. To figure out how to help.

Because no one else is here.

No one but me and Nazeera, which seems crazy to an improbable degree. The Sanctuary is supposed to have security on patrol at all times, but I see no sentries, and no sign of incoming aid. No soldiers from the nearby sector, either. Not even curious, hysterical civilians. Nothing.

It's like we're standing in a vacuum, on an invisible plane of existence. I don't know how J and Warner made it this far without being spotted. The two of them look like they were literally dragged through the dirt; I have no idea how they escaped notice. And though it's possible J only just started screaming, I still have a thousand unanswered questions.

They'll have to wait.

I glance at Nazeera out of habit, forgetting for a moment that she and I are invisible. But then I feel her step closer, and I breathe a sigh of relief as her hand slips into mine. She squeezes my fingers. I return the pressure.

Lucky, I remind myself.

It's lucky that we're here right now, because if I'd been in bed where I should've been, I wouldn't have even known J was in trouble. I would've missed the tremble in my friend's voice as she cried out, begging for mercy. I would've missed the shattering colors of a twisted sunrise, a peacock in the middle of hell. I would've missed the way J clamped her head between her hands and sobbed. I would've missed the sharp scents of pine and sulfur in the wind, would've missed the dry ache in my throat, the tremor moving through my body. I would've missed the moment J mentioned her sister by name. I wouldn't have heard J *specifically* ask her sister not to do something.

Yeah, this is definitely luck.

Because if I hadn't heard any of that, I wouldn't have known who to blame.

Emmaline.

~~ELLA~~

~~JULIETTE~~

I have eyes, two, feel them, rolling back and forth, around and around in my skull I have lips, two, feel them, wet and and heavy, pry them open have teeth, many, tongue, one and fingers, ten, count them

onetwothreefourfive, again on the other side strange, ssstrange to have a tongue, sstrange it's a sssstrange ssort of thing, a strange ssssssssssortofthing

loneliness

  it creeps up on you
quiet
  and
still,

sits by your side in the dark, strokes your hair as you sleep wrapssitself around your bones squeezing sotightyoualmostcan't breathe almost can't hear the pulse racing in your blood as it rush, rushes up your

skin

touches its lips to the soft hairs at the back of your

neck

loneliness is a strangesortof thinga sstrangesortofthing an old friend standing beside you in the mirror screaming you're notenoughneverenough never ever enough

sssssometimes it just
won't

let

go

KENJI

I sidestep an eruption in the ground and duck just in time to avoid a cluster of vines growing in midair. A distant rock balloons to an astronomical size, and the moment it starts barreling in our direction I tighten my hold on Nazeera's hand and dive for cover.

The sky is ripping apart. The ground is fracturing beneath my feet. The sun flickers, strobing darkness, strobing light, everything stilted. And the clouds— There's something newly wrong with the clouds.

They're *disintegrating.*

Trees can't decide whether to stand up or lie down, gusts of wind shoot up from the ground with terrifying power, and suddenly the sky is full of birds. Full of fucking *birds.*

Emmaline is out of control.

We knew that her telekinetic and psychokinetic powers were godlike—beyond anything we've ever known—and we knew that The Reestablishment built Emmaline to control our experience of the world. But that was all, and that was just talk. Theory.

We'd never seen her like this.

Wild.

She's clearly doing something to J right now, ravaging her mind while lashing out at the world around us, because the acid trip I'm staring at is only getting worse.

"Go back," I cry out over the din. "Get help—bring the girls!"

A single shout of agreement and Nazeera's hand slips free from mine, her heavy boots on the ground my only indication that she's bolting toward the Sanctuary. But even now—especially now—her swift, certain actions fill me with no small measure of relief.

It feels good to have a capable partner.

I claw my way across the sparse forest, grateful to have avoided the worst of the obstacles, and when I'm finally close enough to properly discern Warner's face, I pull back my invisibility.

I'm shaking with exhaustion.

I'd only barely recovered from being drugged nearly to death, and yet here I am, already about to die again. But when I look up, half-bent, hands on my knees and trying to breathe, I realize I have no right to complain.

Warner looks even worse than I expected.

Raw, clenched, a vein straining at his temple. He's on his knees holding on to J like he's trying to hold back a riot, and I didn't realize until just this second that he might be here for more than just emotional support.

The whole thing is surreal: they're both practically naked, in the dirt, on their knees—J with her hands pressed flat against her ears—and I can't help but wonder what kind of hell brought them to this moment.

I thought I was the one having a weird night.

Something slams suddenly into my gut and I double over, hitting the ground hard. Arms shaking, I push up onto all fours and scan the immediate area for the culprit. When I spot it, I gag.

A dead bird, a couple feet away.

Jesus.

J is still screaming.

I shove my way through a sudden, violent gust of wind—and just when I've regained my balance, ready to clear the last fifty feet toward my friends—the world goes mute.

Sound, off.

No howling winds, no tortured screams, no coughs, no sneezes. This is not ordinary quiet. It's not stillness, not silence.

It's more than that.

It's nothing at all.

I blink, blink, my head turning in slow, excruciating motion as I scan the distance for answers, willing the explanations to appear. Hoping the sheer force of my mind is enough to sprout reason from the ground.

It isn't.

I've gone deaf.

Nazeera is no longer here, J and Warner are still fifty feet away, and I've gone deaf. Deaf to the sound of the wind, to the shuddering trees. Deaf to my own labored breathing, to the cries of citizens in the compounds beyond. I try to clench my fists and it takes forever, like the air has grown dense. Thick.

Something is wrong with me.

I'm slow, slower than I've ever been, like I'm running underwater. Something is purposely keeping me back, physically pushing me away from Juliette—and suddenly, it all makes sense. My earlier confusion dissolves. Of course no one else is here. Of course no one else has come to help.

Emmaline would never allow it.

Maybe I got this far only because she was too busy to notice me right away—to sense me here, in my invisible state. It makes me wonder what else she's done to keep this area clear of trespassers.

It makes me wonder if I'll survive.

It's growing harder to think. It takes forever to fuse thoughts. Takes forever to move my arms. To lift my head. To look around. By the time I manage to pry open my mouth, I've forgotten that my voice makes no sound.

A flash of gold in the distance.

I spot Warner, shifting so slowly I wonder whether we're both suffering from the same affliction. He's fighting desperately to sit up next to J—J who's still on her knees, bent forward, mouth open. Her eyes are squeezed shut in concentration, but if she's screaming, I can't hear it.

I'd be lying if I said I wasn't terrified.

I'm close enough to Warner and J to be able to make out their expressions, but it's no good; I have no idea whether they're injured, so I don't know the extent of what we're dealing with. I have to get closer, somehow. But when I take a single, painful step forward, a sharp keening explodes in my ears.

I cry out soundlessly, clapping my hands to my head as the silence is suddenly—*viciously*—compounded by pressure. The knifelike pain needles into me, pressure building in my ears with an intensity that threatens to crush me from the inside. It's like someone has overfilled my head with helium, like any minute now the balloon that is my brain will explode. And just when I think the pressure might kill me, just when I think I can't bear the pain any longer, the ground begins to rumble. Tremble.

There's a seismic *crack*—

And sound comes back online. Sound so violent it rips open something inside of me, and when I finally tear my hands away from my ears they're red, dripping. I stagger as my head pounds. Rings. Rings.

I wipe my bloody hands on my bare torso and my vision swims. I lunge forward in a stupor and land badly, my still-damp palms hitting the earth so hard the force of it shudders up my bones. The dirt beneath my feet has gone slick. Wet. I look up, squinting at the sky and the sudden, torrential rain. My head continues to swing on a well-oiled hinge. A single drop of blood drips down my ear, lands on my shoulder.

A second drop of blood drips down my ear, lands on my shoulder. A third drop of blood drips down my—

Name.

Someone calls my name.

The sound is large, aggressive. The word careens dizzily in my head, expanding and contracting. I can't pin it down.

Kenji

I turn around and my head rings, rings.

K e n j i

I blink and it takes days, revolutions around the sun.

Trusted

friend

Something is touching me, under me, hauling me up, but it's no good. I don't move.

Too

heavy

I try to speak but can't. I say nothing, do nothing as my mind is broken open, as cold fingers reach inside my skull and disconnect the circuitry within. I stand still. Stiffen. The voice echoes to life in the blackness behind my eyes, speaking words that feel more like memory than conversation, words I don't know, don't understand

the pain I carry, the fears I should've left behind. I sag under the weight of loneliness, the chains of disappointment. My heart alone weighs a thousand pounds. I'm so heavy I can no longer be lifted away from the earth. I'm so heavy I have no choice now but to be buried beneath it. I'm so heavy, too heavy

I exhale as I go down.

My knees crack as they hit the ground. My body slumps forward. Dirt kisses my face, welcomes me home.

The world goes suddenly dark.

Brave

My eyes flicker. Sound hums in my ears, something like dull, steady electricity. Everything is plunged into darkness. A blackout, a blackout in the natural world. Fear clings to my skin. Covers me.

but

w e a k

Knives bore holes into my bones that fill quickly with sorrow, sorrow so acute it takes my breath away.

I've never been so hopeful to cease existing.

I am floating.

Weightless and yet—weighted down, destined to sink forever. Dim light fractures the blackness behind my eyes and in the light, I see water. My sun and moon are the sea, my mountains the ocean. I live in liquid I never drink, drowning steadily in marbled, milky waters. My breathing is heavy, automatic, mechanic. I am forced to inhale, forced to exhale. The harsh, shuddering rasp of my own breath is my constant reminder of the grave that is my home.

I hear something.

It reverberates through the tank, dull metal against dull metal, arriving at my ears as if from outer space. I squint at the fresh set of shapes and colors, blurred forms. I clench my fists but my flesh is soft, my bones like fresh dough, my skin peeling in moist flakes. I'm surrounded by water but my thirst is insatiable and my anger—

My anger—

Something snaps. My head. My mind. My neck.

My eyes are wide, my breathing panicked. I'm on my knees, my forehead pressed into the dirt, my hands buried in wet earth.

I sit straight up and back, my head spinning.

"What the *fuck?*" I'm still trying to breathe. I look around. My heart is racing. "What— What—"

I was digging my own grave.

Slithering, terrifying horror moves through my body as I understand: Emmaline was in my head. She wanted to see if she could get me to kill myself.

And even as I think it—even as I look down at the miserable attempt I made to bury myself alive—I feel a dull, stabbing sympathy for Emmaline. Because I felt her pain, and it wasn't cruel.

It was desperate.

Like she was hoping that if I killed myself while she was in my head, somehow I'd be able to kill her, too.

J is screaming again.

I stagger to my feet, heart in my throat as the skies wrench open, releasing their wrath upon me. I'm not sure why Emmaline gave the inside of my head a shot—*brave but weak*—but I know enough to understand that whatever the hell is happening here is more than I can handle on my own. Right now, I can only hope that everyone in the Sanctuary is okay—and that Nazeera gets back here soon. Until then, my broken body will have to do its best.

I push forward.

Even as old, cold blood dries in my ears, across my chest, I push forward, steeling myself against the increasingly volatile weather conditions. The steady succession of earthquakes. The lightning strikes. The raging thunderstorm growing quickly into a hurricane.

Once I'm finally close enough, Warner looks up.

He seems stunned.

It occurs to me then that he's only just seeing me—after all this—he's only just realizing I'm here. A flicker of relief flashes through his eyes, too quickly replaced by pain.

And then he calls out two words—two words I never thought I'd inspire him to say:

"Help me."

The sentence is carried off in the wind, but the agony in his eyes remains. And from this vantage point, I finally understand the depth of what he's endured. At first I'd thought Warner was only holding her steady, trying to be supportive.

I was wrong.

J is vibrating with power, and Warner is only barely hanging on to her. Holding her still. Something—*someone*—is physically animating Juliette's body, articulating her limbs, trying to force her upright and possibly away from here, and it's only because of Warner that Emmaline hasn't succeeded.

I have no idea how he's doing it.

J's skin has gone translucent, veins bright and freakish in her pale face. She's nearly blue, ready to crack. A low-level hum emanates from her body, the crackle of energy, the buzz of power. I grab on to her arm and in the half second Warner shifts to distribute her weight between us, the three of us are flung forward. We hit the ground so hard I can hardly breathe, and when I'm finally able to lift my head I look at Warner, my own eyes wide with unmasked terror.

"Emmaline is doing this," I say, shouting the words at him.

He nods, his face grim.

"What can we do?" I cry. "How can she just keep screaming like this?"

Warner only looks at me.

He just *looks* at me, and the tortured expression in his eyes tells me everything I need to know. J *can't* keep screaming like this. She can't just be here on her knees screaming for a century. This shit is going to kill her. Jesus Christ. I knew it was bad, but for some reason I didn't think it was this bad.

J looks like she's going to die.

"Should we try to pick her up?" I don't even know why I ask. I doubt I could lift her arm above my head, much less her whole body. My own body is still shaking, so much so that I can barely do my part to keep this girl from lifting directly off the ground. I have no idea what kind of crazy shit is pumping through her veins right now, but J is on another planet. She looks half-alive, mostly alien. Her eyes are squeezed shut, her jaw unhinged. She's *radiating* energy. It's fucking terrifying.

And I can barely keep up.

The ache in my arms has begun to creep up my shoulders and down my back and I shiver, violently, when a sharp wind strikes my bare, overheated skin.

"Let's try," Warner says.

I nod.

Take a deep breath.

Beg myself to be stronger than I am.

I don't know how I do it, but through nothing short of a miracle, I make it to my feet. Warner and I manage to bind Juliette between us, and when I look over at him, I'm at least relieved to discover that he looks like he's struggling, too. I've never seen Warner struggle, not really, and I'm pretty sure I've never seen him sweat. But as much as I'd love to laugh a little right now, the sight of him straining so hard just to hold on to her only sends a fresh wave of fear through me. I have no idea how long he's been trying to restrain her all by himself. I have no idea what would've happened to her if he hadn't been there to hold on. And I have no idea what would happen to her right now, if we were to let go.

Something about that realization gives me renewed strength. It takes choice out of the situation. J needs us right now, period.

Which means I have to be stronger.

Standing upright like this has made us an easy target in all this madness, and I call out a warning as a piece of debris flies toward us. I pivot sharply to protect J, but take a hit to my spine, the pain so breathtaking I'm seeing stars. My back was already injured earlier tonight, and the bruises are bound to be worse now. But when Warner locks eyes with me in a sudden, terrified panic, I nod, letting him know I'm okay. I've got her.

Inch by agonizing inch, we move back toward the Sanctuary.

We're dragging J like she's Jesus between us, her head flung backward, feet dragging across the ground. She's finally stopped screaming, but now she's convulsing, her body seizing uncontrollably, and Warner looks like he's hanging on to his sanity by a single, fraying thread.

It feels like centuries pass before we see Nazeera again, but the rational part of my brain suspects it must've been only twenty, thirty minutes. Who knows. I'm sure she was trying her best to get back here with people who could help, but it feels like we're too late. Everything feels too late.

I have no idea what the hell is happening anymore.

Yesterday, this morning—an hour ago—I was worried about James and Adam. I thought our problems were simple and straightforward: get the kids back, kill the supreme commanders, have a nice lunch.

But now—

Nazeera and Castle and Brendan and Nouria rush to a sudden stop before us. They look between us.

They look beyond us.

Their eyes go round, their lips parting as they gasp. I crane my neck to see what they're seeing and realize that there's a tidal wave of fire headed straight toward us.

I think I'm going to collapse.

My body is worse than unsteady. By this point, my legs are made of rubber. I can barely support my own weight, and it's a miracle I'm holding on to J at all. In fact, a quick glance at Warner's clenched, insanely tense body is all it takes to realize that he's probably doing most of the work right now.

I don't know how any of us are going to survive this. I can't *move*. I sure as hell can't outrun a wave of fire.

And I don't really understand everything that happens next.

I hear an inhuman cry, and Stephan is suddenly rushing toward us. *Stephan*. He's suddenly in front of us, suddenly between us. He picks J up and into his arms like she might be a rag doll, and starts shouting at all of us to run. Castle hangs back to redirect water from a nearby well, and though his efforts at dousing the flames aren't entirely successful, it's enough to give us the edge we need to escape. Warner and I drag ourselves back to camp with the others, and the minute we cross the threshold into the Sanctuary, we're met with a frantic sea of faces. Countless figures surge forward, their shouts and cries and hysterical commotion fusing into a single, unbroken soundstorm. Logically, I understand why people are out here, worried, crying, shouting unanswered questions at each other—but right now I just want them all to get the hell out of my way.

Nouria and Sam seem to read my mind.

They bark orders into the crowd and the nameless bodies begin to clear out. Stephan is no longer running, but walking briskly, elbowing people out of his way as necessary, and I'm grateful. But when Sonya and Sara come sprinting toward us, shouting for us to follow them to the medical tent, I nearly launch myself forward and kiss them both.

I don't.

Instead, I take a moment to search for Castle, wondering if he made it out okay. But when I look back, scanning our stretch of protected land, I experience a sudden, sobering moment of realization. The disparity between *in here* and *out there* is unreal.

In here, the sky is clear.

The weather, settled. The ground seems to have sutured itself back together. The wall of fire that tried to chase us all the way back to the Sanctuary is now nothing but fading smoke. The trees are in their upright positions; the hurricane is little more than a fine mist. The morning looks almost pretty. For a second I could've sworn I heard a bird chirping.

I'm probably out of my mind.

I collapse in the middle of a well-worn path leading back to our tents, my face thudding against wet grass. The smell of fresh, damp earth fills my head and I breathe it in, all of it. It's a balm. A miracle. *Maybe*, I think. Maybe we're going to be okay. Maybe I can close my eyes. Take a moment.

Warner stalks past my prone body, his motions so intense I'm startled upright, into a sitting position.

I have no idea how he's still moving.

He's not even wearing shoes. No shirt, no socks, no shoes. Just a pair of sweatpants. I notice for the first time that he's got a huge gash across his chest. Several cuts on his arms. A nasty scratch on his neck. Blood is dripping slowly down his torso, and Warner doesn't even seem to notice. Scars all over his back, blood smeared across his front. He looks insane. But he's still moving, his eyes hot with rage and something else— Something that scares the shit out of me.

He catches up to Stephan, who's still holding J—who's still having seizures—and I crawl toward a tree, using the trunk to hoist myself off the ground. I drag myself after them, flinching involuntarily at a sudden breeze. I turn too fast, scanning the open woods for debris or a flying boulder, and find only Nazeera, who rests a hand on my arm.

"Don't worry," she says. "We're safe within the borders of the Sanctuary."

I blink at her. And then around, at the familiar white tents that cloak every solid, freestanding structure on the glorified campsite that is this place of refuge.

Nazeera nods. "Yeah—that's what the tents are for. Nouria enhanced all of her light protections with some kind of antidote that makes us immune to the illusions Emmaline creates. Both acres of land are protected, and the reflective material covering the tents provides more assured protection indoors."

"How do you know all of that?"

"I asked."

I blink at her again. I feel dumb. Numb. Like I broke something deep inside my brain. Deep inside my body.

"Juliette," I say.

It's the only word I've got right now, and Nazeera doesn't even bother to correct me, to tell me her real name is Ella. She just takes my hand and squeezes.

~~ELLA~~
~~JULIETTE~~

When I dream, I dream of sound.

Rain, taking its time, softly popping against concrete. Rain, gathering, drumming, until sound turns into static. Rain, so sudden, so strong, it startles itself. I dream of water dripping down lips and tips of noses, rain falling off branches into shallow, murky pools. I hear death when puddles shatter, assaulted by heavy feet.

I hear leaves—

Leaves, shuddering under the weight of resignation, yoked to branches too easily bent, broken. I dream of wind, lengths of it. Yards of wind, acres of wind, infinite whispers fusing to create a single breeze. I hear wind comb the wild grass of distant mountains, I hear wind howling confessions in empty, lonely plains. I hear the *sh sh sh* of desperate rivers trying to hush the world in a fruitless effort to hush itself.

But

    buried

in the din

is a single scream so steady it goes every day unheard. We see, but do not understand the way it stutters hearts, clenches jaws, curls fingers into fists. It's a surprise, always a surprise, when it finally stops screaming long enough to speak.

Fingers tremble.
Flowers die.
The sun flinches, the stars expire.
You are in a room, a closet, a vault, no key—
Just a single voice that says

Kill me

KENJI

J is sleeping.

She seems so close to death I can hardly look at her. Skin so white it's blue. Lips so blue they're purple. Somehow, in the last couple of hours, she lost weight. She looks like a little bird, young and small and fragile. Her long hair is fanned around her face and she's motionless, a little blue doll with her face pointed straight up at the ceiling. She looks like she could be lying in a casket.

I don't say any of this out loud, of course.

Warner seems pretty close to death himself. He looks pale, disoriented. Sickly.

And he's become impossible to talk to.

These past months of forced camaraderie nearly had me brainwashed; I'd almost forgotten what Warner used to be like.

Cold. Cutting. Eerily quiet.

He seems like an echo of himself right now, sitting stiffly in a chair next to her bed. We dragged J back here hours ago and he still won't really look at anyone. The cut on his chest looks even worse now, but he does nothing about it. He disappeared at one point, but only for a couple of minutes, and returned wearing his boots. He didn't bother to wipe the blood off his body. Didn't stop long enough to put on a shirt. He could easily steal Sonya's and Sara's powers to heal himself, but he makes no effort. He refuses to be touched. He refuses to eat. The few words out of his mouth were so scathing he made three different people cry. Nouria finally told him that if he didn't stop attacking her teammates she'd take him out back and shoot him. I think it was Warner's lack of protest that kept her from following through.

He's nothing but thorns.

Old Kenji would've shrugged it off and rolled his eyes. Old Kenji would've thrown a dart at Dickhead Warner and, honestly, would've probably been happy to see him suffer like this.

But I'm not that guy anymore.

I know Warner too well now. I know how much he loves J. I know he'd turn his skin inside out just to make her happy. He wanted to marry her, for God's sake. And I just watched him nearly kill himself to save her, suffering for hours through the worst levels of hell just to keep her alive.

Almost two hours, to be exact.

Warner said he'd been out there with J for nearly an hour before I showed up, and it was at least another forty-five minutes before the girls were able to stabilize her. He spent nearly two hours physically fighting to keep Juliette from harm, protecting her with his own body as he was lashed by fallen trees, flying rocks, errant debris, and violent winds. The girls said they could tell just by looking at him that he had at least two broken ribs. A fracture in his right arm. A dislocated shoulder. Probably internal bleeding. They raged at him so much that he finally sat down in a chair, wrapped his good hand around the wrist of his injured arm, and pulled his own shoulder back in place. The only proof of his pain was a single, sharp breath.

Sonya screamed, rushing forward, too late to stop him.

And then he broke open the seam at the ankle of his sweatpants, tore off a length of cotton, and made a sling for his freshly socketed arm. Only after that did he finally look up at the girls.

"Now leave me alone," he said darkly.

Sonya and Sara looked so frustrated—their eyes blazing with rare anger—I almost didn't recognize them.

I know he's being an asshole.

I know he's being stubborn and stupid and cruel. But I can't find the strength to be mad at him right now. I can't.

My heart is breaking for the guy.

We're all standing around J's bed, just staring at her. A monitor beeps softly in the corner. The room smells like chemicals. Sonya and Sara had to inject J with serious tranquilizers in order to get her body to settle, but it seemed to help: the moment she slowed down, the world outside did, too.

The Reestablishment was quick on the uptake, doing such seamless damage control I almost couldn't believe it. They capitalized on the problem, claiming that what happened this morning was a taste of future devastation. They claimed that they managed to get it under control before it got any worse, and they reminded the people to be grateful for the protections provided by The Reestablishment; that, without them, the world would be a lot worse. It fairly scared the shit out of everyone. Things feel a lot quieter now. The civilians seem subdued in a way they weren't before. It's stunning, really, how The Reestablishment managed to convince people that the sky collapsing while the sun just *disappeared* for a full minute were normal things that could happen in the world.

It's unbelievable that they feed people that kind of bullshit, and it's unbelievable that people eat it up.

But when I'm being super honest with myself, I'll admit that what scares me the most is that, if I didn't know any better, I might've eaten that shit up, too.

I sigh, hard. Drag a hand down my face.

This morning feels like a weird dream.

Surreal, like one of those melting clock paintings The Reestablishment destroyed. And I'm so wrung out, so tired, I don't even have the energy to be angry. I've only got enough energy to be sad.

We're all just really, really sad.

The few of us who could squeeze into this room: me, Castle, Nouria, Sam, Superman (my new nickname for Stephan), Haider, Nazeera, Brendan, Winston, Warner. All of us, sad, sorry sacks. Sonya and Sara left for a bit, but they'll be coming back soon, and when they do, they'll be sad, too.

Ian and Lily wanted to be here, but Warner kicked them out. He just straight up told them to get out, for reasons he didn't offer to disclose. He didn't raise his voice. Didn't even look at Ian. Just told him to turn around and leave. Brendan was so stunned his eyes nearly fell out of his head. But all of us were too afraid of Warner to say anything.

A small, guilty part of me wondered if maybe Warner knew that Ian talked shit about him that one time, that Warner knew (who knows how) that Ian didn't want to make the effort to go after him and J when we lost them at the symposium.

I don't know. It's just a theory. But it's obvious Warner is done playing the game. He's done with courtesy, done with patience, done with giving a single shit about anyone but J. Which means the tension in here is insane right now. Even Castle seems a little nervous around Warner, like he's not sure about him anymore.

The problem is, we all got too comfortable.

For a couple of months we forgot that Warner was scary. He smiled like four and a half times and we decided to forget that he was basically a psychopath with a long history of ruthless murder. We thought he'd been reformed. Gone soft. We forgot that he was only tolerating any of us because of Juliette.

And now, without her—

He no longer seems to belong.

Without her, we're fracturing. The energy in this room has palpably changed. We don't really feel like a team anymore, and it's scary how quickly it happened. If only Warner weren't so determined to be a dickhead. If only he weren't so eager to put on his old skin, to alienate everyone in this room. If only he'd muster the smallest bit of goodwill, we could turn this whole thing around.

Seems unlikely.

I'm not as terrified as the others, but I'm not stupid, either. I know his threats of violence aren't a bluff. The only people unperturbed are the supreme kids. They look right at home with this version of him. Haider, maybe most of all. That dude always seemed on edge, like he had no idea who Warner had turned into and he didn't know how to process the change. But now? No problem. Super comfortable with psycho Warner. Old pals.

Nouria finally breaks the silence.

Gently, she clears her throat. A couple of people lift their heads. Warner glares at the floor.

"Kenji," she says softly, "can I talk to you for a minute? Outside?"

My body stiffens.

I look around, uncertain, like she's got me confused with someone else. Castle and Nazeera turn sharply in my direction, surprise widening their eyes. Sam, on the other hand, is staring at her wife, struggling to hide her frustration.

"Um"—I scratch my head—"maybe we should talk in here," I say. "As a group?"

"Outside, Kishimoto." Nouria is on her feet, the softness gone from her voice, her face. "Now, please."

Reluctantly, I get to my feet.

I lock eyes with Nazeera, wondering if she has an opinion on the situation, but her expression is unreadable.

Nouria calls my name again.

I shake my head but follow her out the door. She leads me around a corner, into a narrow hallway.

It smells overwhelmingly like bleach.

J is posted up inside the *MT*—an obvious nickname for their medical tent—which feels like a misnomer, actually, because the tent element is entirely superficial. The inside of the building is a lot more like a proper hospital, with individual suites and operating rooms. It blew my mind a little the first time I first walked through here, because this space is super different from what we had at Omega Point and Sector 45. But then, before Sonya and Sara showed up, the Sanctuary had no healers. Their medical work was a lot more traditional: practiced by a handful of self-taught doctors and surgeons. There's something about their old-fashioned, life-threatening medical practices that makes this place feel a lot more like a relic of our old world. A building full of fear.

Out here, in the main corridor, I can hear more clearly the standard sounds of a hospital—machines beeping, carts rolling, occasional moans, shouts, pages over an intercom. I flatten myself against the wall as a team of people barrels past, pushing a gurney down the hallway. Its occupant is an elderly man hooked up to an IV, an oxygen mask on his face. When he sees Nouria, he lifts his hand in a weak wave. Attempts a smile.

Nouria gives him a bright smile in return, holding it steady until the man is wheeled into another room. The moment he's out of sight, she corners me. Her eyes flash, her dark brown skin glowing in the dim light like a warning. My spine straightens.

Nouria is surprisingly terrifying.

"What the hell happened out there?" she says. "What did you do?"

"Okay, first of all"—I hold up both hands—"I didn't *do* anything. And I already told you guys exactly what happened—"

"You never told me that Emmaline tried to access your mind."

That stops me up. "What? Yes I did. I literally told you that. I used those exact words."

"But you didn't provide the necessary details," she says. "How did it start? What did it feel like? Why did she let go?"

"I don't know," I say, frowning. "I don't understand what happened—all I've got are guesses."

"Then *guess,*" she says, narrowing her eyes. "Unless— She's not still in your head, is she?"

"What? No."

Nouria sighs, more irritation than relief. She touches her fingers to her temples in a show of resignation. "This doesn't make sense," she says, almost to herself. "Why would she try so hard to infiltrate Ella's mind? Why *yours?* I thought she was fighting against The Reestablishment. This feels more like she's working for them."

I shake my head. "I don't think so. When Emmaline was in my head it felt more to me like a desperate, last-ditch effort—like she was worried J wouldn't have the heart to kill her, and she was hoping I'd get it done faster. She called me brave, but weak. Like, I don't know, maybe this sounds crazy, but it felt almost like Emmaline thought—for a second—that if I'd made it that far in her presence, I might've been strong enough to contain her. But then she jumped in my head and realized she was wrong. I wasn't strong enough to hold her mind, and definitely not strong enough to kill her." I shrug. "So she bailed."

Nouria straightens. When she looks at me, she looks stunned. "You think she's really that desperate to die? You think she wouldn't put up a fight if someone tried to kill her?"

"Yeah, it's awful," I say, looking away. "Emmaline's in a really bad place."

"But she can exist, at least partially, in Ella's body." Nouria frowns. "Both consciousnesses in one person. How?"

"I don't know." I shrug again. "J said that Evie did a bunch of work on her muscles and bones and stuff while she was in Oceania—priming her for Operation Synthesis—to basically become Emmaline's new body. So I think, ultimately, J playing host to Emmaline is what Evie had planned all along."

"And Emmaline must've known," Nouria says quietly.

It's my turn to frown. "What are you getting at?"

"I don't know, exactly. But this situation complicates

things. Because if our goal was to kill Emmaline, and Emmaline is now living in Ella's body—"

"Wait." My stomach does a terrifying flip. "Is that why we're out here? Is this why you're being so secretive?"

"Lower your voice," Nouria says sharply, glancing at something behind me.

"I will not lower my fucking voice," I say. "What the hell are you thinking? What are you— Wait, what do you keep looking at?" I crane my neck but see only a blank wall behind my head. My heart is racing, my mind working too fast. I whip back around to face her.

"Tell me the truth," I demand. "Is this why you cornered me? Because you're trying to figure out if we can kill J while she's got Emmaline inside of her? Is that it? *Are you insane?*"

Nouria glares at me. "Is it insane to want to save the world? Emmaline is at the center of everything wrong with our universe right now, and she's trapped inside a body lying in a room just down the *hall*. Do you know how long we've been waiting for a moment like this? Don't get me wrong, I don't love this line of thinking, Kishimoto, but I'm not—"

"Nouria."

At the sound of her wife's voice, Nouria goes visibly still. She takes a step back from me, and I finally relax. A little.

We both turn around.

Sam's not alone. Castle is standing next to her, both of them looking more than a little pissed.

"Leave him alone," Castle says. "Kenji's been through enough already. He needs time to recuperate."

Nouria tries to respond, but Sam cuts her off. "How many times are we going to talk about this?" she says. "You can't just shut me out when you're stressed. You can't just go off on your own without telling me." Her blond hair falls into her eyes and, frustrated, she shoves the strands out of her face. "I'm your *partner.* This is our Sanctuary. Our life. We built it together, remember?"

"Sam." Nouria sighs, squeezing her eyes closed. "You know I'm not trying to shut you out. You know that's not—"

"You are literally shutting me out. You literally shut the door."

My eyebrows fly up my forehead. Castle and I connect glances: we seem to have walked into a private argument.

Good.

"Hey, Sam," I say, "did you know that your wife wants to kill Juliette?"

Castle gasps.

Sam's body goes slack. She stares at Nouria, stunned.

"Yeah," I say, nodding. "Nouria wants to murder her right now, actually, while she's still comatose. What do you think?" I tilt my head at Sam. "Good idea? Bad idea? Maybe sleep on it?"

"That can't be true," Sam says, still staring at her wife. "Tell me he's joking."

"It's not that simple," says Nouria, who shoots me a look so venomous I almost feel bad for being petty. I don't actually want Nouria and Sam to fight, but whatever. She can't casually suggest murdering my best friend and expect me to be nice about it. "I was just pointing out th—"

"Okay, enough."

I look up at the sound of Nazeera's voice. I have no idea when she showed up, but she's suddenly in front of us, arms crossed against her chest. "We're not doing this. No side conversations. No subgroups. We all need to talk about the impending shitstorm headed our way, and if we're going to have any chance of figuring out how to fight it, we have to stick together."

"Which impending shitstorm?" I ask. "Please be specific."

"I agree with Nazeera," Sam says, her eyes narrowing at her wife. "Let's all go back inside the room and talk. To each other. At the same time."

"Sam," Nouria tries again. "I'm not—"

"Bloody hell." Stephan stops short at the sight of us, his shoes squeaking on the tile. He seems to tower over our group, looking too polished and civilized to belong here. "What on earth are you lot doing out here?"

Then, quietly, to Nazeera: "And why've you left us alone with him? He's being a proper ass. Nearly made Haider cry just now."

Nazeera sighs, closing her eyes as she pinches the bridge of her nose. "Haider does this to himself. I don't understand why he's deluded himself into thinking Warner is his best friend."

"That, he might well be," Stephan says, frowning. "The bar is quite low, as you know."

Nazeera sighs again.

"If it makes Haider feel any better, Warner's being equally horrible to just about everyone," Sam says. She looks at Nouria. "Amir still won't tell me what Warner said to him, by the way."

"Amir?" Castle frowns. "The young man who oversees the patrol unit?"

Sam nods. "He quit this morning."

"No." Nouria blinks, stunned. "You're kidding."

"I wish I were. I had to give his job to Jenna."

"This is crazy." Nouria shakes her head. "It's only been three days and already we're falling apart."

"Three days?" says Stephan. "Three days since *we* arrived, is that it? That's not a very nice thing to say."

"We are not falling apart," Nazeera says suddenly. Angrily. "We can't afford to fall apart. Not right now. Not with The Reestablishment about to appear at our doorstep."

"Wait—what?" Sam frowns. "The Reestablishment has no idea where we—"

"God, this is so depressing," I groan, running both hands through my hair. "Why are we all at each other's throats right now? If Juliette were awake, she'd be so pissed at all of us. And she'd be super pissed at Warner for acting like this, for pushing us apart. Doesn't he realize that?"

"No," Castle says quietly. "Of course he doesn't."

A sharp *knock knock*—

And we all look up.

Winston and Brendan are peering around the corner at us, Brendan's closed fist held aloft an inch from the wall. He knocks once more against the plaster.

Nouria exhales loudly. "Can we help you?"

They march over to us, their expressions so different it's almost—*almost*—funny. Like light and dark, these two.

"Hello, everyone," Brendan says, smiling brightly.

Winston yanks the glasses off his face. Glowers. "What the hell is going on? Why are you all having a conference out here on your own? And why did you leave us alone with him?"

"We didn't," I try to say.

"We're not," Sam and Nazeera say at the same time.

Winston rolls his eyes. Shoves his glasses back on. "I'm getting too fucking old for this."

"You just need some coffee," Brendan says, gently patting Winston's shoulder. "Winston doesn't sleep very well at night," he explains to the rest of us.

Winston perks up. Goes instantly pink.

I smile.

I swear, it's all I do. I just smile, and in a fraction of a second Winston's locked eyes with me, his death stare screaming, *Shut your mouth, Kishimoto,* and I don't even have a chance to be offended before he turns abruptly away, his ears bright red.

An uncomfortable silence descends.

I wonder, for the first time, if it's really possible that

Brendan has no idea how Winston feels about him. He seems oblivious, but who knows. It's definitely not a secret to the rest of us.

"Well." Castle takes a sharp breath, claps his hands together. "We were about to go back inside the room to have a proper discussion. So if you gentlemen"—he nods at Winston and Brendan—"wouldn't mind turning back the way you came? We're getting a bit cramped in the hall."

"Right." Brendan glances quickly behind him. "But, um, do you think we might wait another minute or so? Haider was crying, you see, and I think he'd appreciate the privacy."

"Oh, for the love of God," I groan.

"What happened?" Nazeera asks, concern creasing her forehead. "Should I go in there?"

Brendan shrugs, his extremely white face glowing almost neon in this dark corridor. "He said something to Warner in Arabic, I believe. And I don't know exactly what Warner said back to him, but I'm pretty sure he told Haider to sod off, in one way or another."

"Asshole," Winston mutters.

"It's true, unfortunately." Brendan frowns.

I shake my head. "All right, okay, I know he's being a dick, but I think we can cut Warner a little slack, right? He's devastated. Let's not forget the hell he went through this morning."

"Pass." Winston crosses his arms, anger seeming to lift him out of embarrassment. "Haider is *crying*. Haider Ibrahim. Son of the supreme commander of Asia. He's sitting in a hospital chair *crying* because Warner hurt his feelings. I don't know how you can defend that."

"To be fair," Stephan interjects, "Haider's always been a bit delicate."

"Listen, I'm not defending Warner, I'm just—"

"Enough." Castle's voice is loud. Sharp. "That is quite enough." Something tugs gently at my neck, startling me, and I notice Castle's hands are up in the air. Like he just physically turned our heads to face him. He points back down the hall, toward J's recovery room. I feel a slight push at my back.

"Back inside. All of you. Now."

Haider doesn't seem any different when we step back inside the room. No evidence of tears. He's standing in a corner, alone, staring into the middle distance. Warner is in exactly the same position we left him in, sitting stiffly beside J.

Staring at her.

Staring at her like he might be able to will her back into consciousness.

Nazeera claps her hands together, hard. "All right," she says, "no more interruptions. We need to talk about strategy before we do anything else."

Sam frowns. "Strategy for what? Right now, we need to discuss Emmaline. We need to understand the events of the morning before we can even think about discussing the next steps forward."

"We *are* going to talk about Emmaline, and the events

of the morning," Nazeera says. "But in order to discuss the Emmaline situation, we'll need to talk about the Ella situation, which will necessitate a conversation about a larger, overarching strategy—one that will dovetail neatly with a plan to get the supreme kids back."

Castle stares at her, looking just as confused as Sam. "You want to discuss the supreme kids right now? Isn't it better if we star—"

"Idiots," Haider mutters under his breath.

We ignore him.

Well, most of us. Nazeera is shaking her head, giving the room at large that same look she gives me so often—the one that expresses her general exhaustion at being surrounded by idiots.

"How are you so unable to see how these things connect? The Reestablishment is looking for us. More specifically, they're looking for Ella. We were supposed to be in hiding, remember? But Emmaline's egregious display this morning just blew the cover on our location. We all saw the news—you all read the emergency reports. The Reestablishment did serious damage control to subdue the citizens. That means they know what happened here."

Again, more blank stares.

"Emmaline just led them directly to Ella," she says. She says this last sentence really slowly, like she fears for our collective intelligence. "Whether on purpose or by accident, The Reestablishment now has an approximate idea of our location."

Nouria looks stricken.

"Which means," Haider says, drawing the words out with his own irritating condescension, "they're much closer to finding us now than they were a few hours ago."

Everyone sits up straighter in their chairs. The air is suddenly different, intense in a new way. Nouria and Sam exchange worried glances.

It's Nouria who says, "You really think they know where we are?"

"I knew this would happen," Sam says, shaking her head.

Castle stiffens. "What's that supposed to mean?"

Sam bristles, but her words are calm when she says: "We took an enormous risk letting your team stay here. We risked our livelihood and the safety of our own men and women to allow you to take shelter among us. You're here for three days and already you've managed to disclose our location to the world."

"We haven't disclosed anything— And what happened today was no one's fault—"

Nouria lifts a hand. "Stop," she says, shooting a look at Sam, a look so brief I almost miss it. "We're losing our focus again. Nazeera was right when she said we were all in this together. In fact, we came together for the express purpose of defeating The Reestablishment. It's what we've always been working toward. We were never meant to live forever in self-made cages and communities."

"I understand that," Sam says, her steady voice belying the anger in her eyes. "But if they really know which sector to search, we could be discovered in a matter of days. The Reestablishment will be increasing their military presence within the hour, if they haven't done so already."

"They have done," Stephan says, looking just as exasperated as Nazeera. "Of course they have."

"So naive, these people," Haider says, shooting a dark look at his sister.

Nazeera sighs.

Winston swears.

Sam shakes her head.

"So what do you propose?" Winston says, but he's not looking at Nouria or Sam or Castle. He's looking at Nazeera.

Nazeera doesn't hesitate.

"We wait. We wait for Ella to wake up," she says. "We need to know as much as we can about what happened to her, and we need to prioritize her security above all else. There's a reason why Anderson wants her so desperately, and we need to find out what that reason is before we take any next steps."

"But what about a plan for getting the other kids back?" Winston asks. "If we wait for Ella to wake up before making a move to save them, we could be too late."

Nazeera shakes her head. "The plan for the other kids has to be tied up in the plan to save Ella," she says. "I'm certain that Anderson is using the kidnapping of the supreme kids as bait. A bullshit lure designed to draw us out into the open. Plus, he designed that scheme before he had any idea we'd accidentally out ourselves, which only further supports my theory that this was a bullshit lure. He was only hoping we'd step outside of our protections just long enough to give away our approximate location."

"Which we've now done," Brendan says, quietly horrified.

I drop my head in my hands. "*Shit.*"

"It seems clear that Anderson wasn't planning on doing any kind of honest trade for the hostages," Nazeera says. "How could he possibly? He never told us where he was. Never told us where to meet him. And most interestingly: he didn't even ask for the rest of the supreme kids. Whatever his plans are, he doesn't seem to require the full set of us. He didn't want Warner or me or Haider or Stephan. All he wanted was Ella, right?" She glances at Nouria. "That's what you said. That he only wanted Ella?"

"Yes," Nouria says. "That's true— But I still don't think I understand. You just laid out all the reasons for us to go to war, but your plan of attack involves doing nothing."

Nazeera can't hide her irritation. "We should still be making plans to fight," she says. "We'll need a plan to find the kids, steal them back, and then, eventually, murder our parents. But I'm proposing we wait for Ella until we make any moves. I'm suggesting we do a full and complete lockdown here at the Sanctuary until Ella is conscious. No going in or out until she wakes up. If you need emergency supplies, Kenji and I can use our stealth to go on discreet missions to find what you need. The Reestablishment will have soldiers posted up everywhere, monitoring every movement in this area, but as long as we remain isolated, we should be able to buy ourselves some time."

"But we have no idea how long it'll take for Ella to wake up," Sam says. "It could be weeks—it could be *never*—"

"Our mission," Nazeera says, cutting her off, "has to be about protecting Ella at all costs. If we lose her, we lose everything. That's it. That's the whole plan right now. Keeping Ella alive and safe is the priority. Saving the kids is secondary. Besides, the kids will be fine. Most of us have been through worse in basic training simulations."

Haider laughs.

Stephan makes an amused sound of agreement.

"But what about James?" I protest. "What about Adam? They're not like you guys. They've never been prepared for this shit. For God's sake, James is only ten years old."

Nazeera looks at me then, and for a moment, she falters. "We'll do our best," she says. And though her words sound genuinely sympathetic, that's all she gives me. *Our best.*

That's it.

I feel my heart rate begin to spike.

"So we're just supposed to risk letting them die?" Winston asks. "We're just supposed to gamble on a ten-year-old's life? Let him remain imprisoned and tortured at the hands of a sociopath and hope for the best? Are you serious?"

"Sometimes sacrifices are necessary," Stephan says.

Haider merely shrugs.

"No way, no way," I say, panicking. "We need another plan. A better plan. A plan that saves everyone, and quickly."

Nazeera looks at me like she feels sorry for me.

That's enough to straighten my spine.

I spin around, my panic transforming quickly into anger. I home in on Warner, sitting in the corner like a useless sack of meat. "What about you?" I say to him. "What do you think about this? You're okay with letting your own brothers die?"

The silence is suddenly suffocating.

Warner doesn't answer me for a long time, and the room is too stunned at my stupidity to interfere. I just broke a tacit agreement to pretend Warner doesn't exist, but now that I've provoked the beast, everyone wants to see what happens next.

Eventually, Warner sighs.

It's not a calm, relaxing sound. It's a harsh, angry sound that only seems to leave him more tightly wound. He doesn't even lift his head when he says, "I'm okay with a lot of things, Kishimoto."

But I'm too far gone to turn back now.

"That's bullshit," I say, my fists clenching. "That's bullshit, and you know it. You're better than this."

Warner says nothing. He doesn't move a muscle, doesn't stop staring at the same spot on the floor. And I know I shouldn't antagonize him—I *know* he's in a fragile state right now—but I can't help it. I can't let this go, not like this.

"So that's it? After everything—that's it? You're just

going to let James die?" My heart is pounding, hard and heavy in my chest. I feel my frustration peaking, spiraling. "What do you think J would say right now, huh? How do you think she'd feel about you letting someone murder a child?"

Warner stands up.

Fast, too fast. Warner is on his feet and I'm suddenly sorry. I was feeling a little brave but now I'm feeling nothing but regret. I take an uncertain step back. Warner follows. Suddenly he's standing in front of me, studying my eyes, but it turns out I can't hold his gaze for longer than a second. His eyes are such a pale green they're disorienting to look at on his good days. But today— Right now—

He looks insane.

I notice, when I turn away, that he's still got blood on his fingers. Blood smeared across his throat. Blood streaking through his gold hair.

"Look at me," he says.

"Um, no thanks."

"Look at me," he says again, quietly this time.

I don't know why I do it. I don't know why I give in. I don't know why there's still a part of me that believes in Warner and hopes to see something human in his eyes. But when I finally look up, I lose that hope. Warner looks cold. Detached. All wrong.

I don't understand it.

I mean, I'm devastated, too. I'm upset, *too,* but I didn't turn into a completely different person. And right now, Warner seems like a completely different person. Where's the guy who was going to propose to my best friend? Where's the guy having a panic attack on his bedroom floor? Where's the guy who laughed so hard his cheeks dimpled? Where's the guy I thought was my friend?

"What happened to you, man?" I whisper. "Where'd you go?"

"Hell," he says. "I've finally found hell."

~~ELLA~~

~~JULIETTE~~

I wake in waves, consciousness bathing me slowly. I break the surface of sleep, gasping for air before I'm pulled under

another current

another current

another

Memories wrap around me, bind my bones. I sleep. When I sleep, I dream I am sleeping. In those dreams, I dream I am dead. I can't tell real from fiction, can't tell dreams from truth, can't tell time anymore it might've been days or years who knows who knows I begin to

s

t

i

r

I dream even as I wake, dream of red lips and slender fingers, dream of eyes, hundreds of eyes, I dream of air and anger and death.

I dream Emmaline's dreams.

She's here.

She went quiet once she settled here, in my mind. She stilled, retreated. Hid from me, from the world. I feel heavy with her presence but she does not speak, she only decays, her mind decomposing slowly, leaving compost in its wake. I am heavy with it, heavy with her refuse. I am incapable of carrying this weight, no matter how strong Evie made me I am incapable, incompatible. I am not enough to hold our minds, combined. Emmaline's powers are too much. I drown in it, I drown in it, I

gasp

when my head breaks the surface again.

I drag air into my lungs, beg my eyes to open and they laugh. Eyes laughing at lungs gasping at pain ricocheting up my spine.

Today, there is a boy.

Not one of the regular boys. Not Aaron or Stephan or Haider. This is a new boy, a boy I've never met before.

I can tell, just by standing next to him, that he's terrified.

We stand in the big, wide room filled with trees. We stare at the white birds, the birds with the yellow streaks and the crowns on their heads. The boy stares at the birds like he's never seen anything like them. He stares at everything with surprise. Or fear. Or worry. It makes me realize that he doesn't know how to hide his emotions. Whenever Mr. Anderson looks at him, he sucks in his breath. Whenever I look at him, he goes bright red. Whenever Mum speaks to him, he stutters.

"What do you think?" Mr. Anderson says to Mum. He tries to whisper, but this room is so big it echoes a little.

Mum tilts her head at the boy. Studies him. "He's what, six years old now?" But she doesn't wait for him to answer. Mum just shakes her head and sighs. "Has it really been that long?"

Mr. Anderson looks at the boy. "Unfortunately."

I glance at him, at the boy standing next to me, and watch as he stiffens. Tears spring to his eyes, and it hurts to watch. It hurts so much. I hate Mr. Anderson so much. I don't know why Mum likes him. I don't know why anyone likes him. Mr. Anderson is an awful person, and he hurts Aaron all the time. In fact— Now that I think about it, there's something about this boy that reminds me of Aaron. Something about his eyes.

"Hey," I whisper, and turn to face him.

He swallows, hard. Wipes at his tears with the edge of his sleeve.

"Hey," I try again. "I'm Ella. What's your name?"

The boy looks up, then. His eyes are a deep, dark blue. He's the saddest boy I've ever met, and it makes me sad just to look at him.

"I'm A-Adam," he says quietly. He turns red again.

I take his hand in mine. Smile at him. "We're going to be friends, okay? Don't worry about Mr. Anderson. No one likes him. He's mean to all of us, I promise."

Adam laughs, but his eyes are still red. His hand trembles in mine, but he doesn't let go.

"I don't know," he whispers. "He's pretty mean to me."

I squeeze his hand. "Don't worry," I say. "I'll protect you."

Adam smiles at me then. Smiles a real smile. But when we finally look up again, Mr. Anderson is staring at us.

He looks angry.

There's a buzzing building inside of me, a mass of sound that consumes thought, devours conversation.

We are flies—gathering, swarming—bulging eyes and fragile bones flittering nervously toward imagined destinies. We hurl our bodies at the panes of tantalizing windows, aching for the world promised on the other side. Day after day we drag injured wings and eyes and organs around the same four walls; open or closed, the exits elude us. We hope to be rescued by a breeze, hoping for a chance to see the sun.

Decades pass. Centuries stack together.

Our bruised bodies still careen through the air. We continue to hurl ourselves at promises. There is madness in the repetition, in the repetition, in the repetition that underscores our lives. It is only in the desperate seconds before death that we realize the windows against which we broke our bodies were only mirrors, all along.

KENJI

It's been four days.

Four days of nothing. J is still sleeping. The twins are calling it a coma, but I'm calling it sleeping. I'm choosing to believe J is just really, really tired. She just needs to sleep off some stress and she'll be fine. This is what I keep telling everyone.

She'll be fine.

"She's just tired," I say to Brendan. "And when she wakes up she'll be glad we waited for her to go get James. It'll be fine."

We're in the Q, which is short for the quiet tent, which is stupid because it's never quiet in here. The Q is the default common room. It's a gathering space slash game room where people at the Sanctuary get together in the evenings and relax. I'm in the kitchen area, leaning against the insubstantial counter. Brendan and Winston and Ian and I are waiting for the electric kettle to boil.

Tea.

This was Brendan's idea, of course. For some reason, we could never get our hands on tea back at Omega Point. We only had coffee, and it was seriously rationed. Only after we moved onto base in Sector 45 did Brendan realize we could get our hands on tea, but even then he wasn't so militant about it.

But here—

Brendan's made it his mission to force hot tea down our throats every night. He doesn't even need the caffeine—his ability to manipulate electricity always keeps his body charged—but he says he likes it because he finds the ritual soothing. So, whatever. Now we gather in the evenings and drink tea. Brendan puts milk in his tea. Winston adds whiskey. Ian and I drink it black.

"Right?" I say, when no one answers me. "I mean, a coma is basically just a really long nap. J will be fine. The girls will get her better, and then she'll be fine, and everything will be fine. And James and Adam will be fine, obviously, because Sam's seen them and she says they're fine."

"Sam saw them and said they were unconscious," Ian says, opening and closing cabinets. When he finds what he's looking for—a sleeve of cookies—he rips the package open. He doesn't even have a chance to pull one free before Winston's swiped it.

"Those cookies are for our tea," he says sharply.

Ian glowers.

We all glance at Brendan, who seems oblivious to the sacrifices being made in his honor. "Yes, Sam said that they were unconscious," he says, collecting small spoons from a drawer. "But she also said they looked stable. Alive."

"Exactly," I say, pointing at Brendan. "Thank you. *Stable. Alive.* These are the critical words."

Brendan takes the rescued sleeve of cookies from Winston's proffered hand, and begins arranging dishes and flatware with a confidence that baffles us all. He doesn't look up when he says, "It's really kind of amazing, isn't it?"

Winston and I share a confused look.

"I wouldn't call it amazing," Ian says, plucking a spoon from the tray. He examines it. "But I guess forks and shit are pretty cool, as far as inventions go."

Brendan frowns. Looks up. "I'm talking about Sam. Her ability to see across long distances." He retrieves the spoon from Ian's hand and replaces it on the tray. "What a remarkable skill."

Sam's preternatural ability to see across long distances was what convinced us of Anderson's threats to begin with. Several days ago—when we first got the news about the kidnapping—she'd used both data and sheer determination to pinpoint Anderson's location to our old base at Sector 45. She'd spent a straight fourteen hours searching, and though she hadn't been able to get a visual on the other supreme kids, she'd been able to see flickers of James and Adam, who are the only ones I care about anyway. Those flickers of life—unconscious, but alive and stable—aren't much in the way of assurances, but I'm willing to take anything at this point.

"Anyway, yeah. Sam is great," I say, stretching out against the counter. "Which brings me back to my original point: Adam and James are going to be fine. And J is going to wake up soon and be fine. The world owes me at least that much, right?"

Brendan and Ian exchange glances. Winston takes off his glasses and cleans them, slowly, with the hem of his shirt.

The electric kettle pops and steams. Brendan drops a couple of tea bags into a proper teapot and fills its porcelain belly with the hot water from the kettle. He then wraps the teapot in a towel and hands it to Winston, and the two of them carry everything over to the little corner of the room we've been claiming for ourselves lately. It's nothing major, just a cluster of seats with a couple of low tables in the middle. The rest of the room is abuzz with activity. Lots of talking and mingling.

Nouria and Sam are alone in a corner, deep in conversation. Castle is talking quietly with the girls, Sonya and Sara. We've all been spending a lot of time here—pretty much everyone has—ever since the Sanctuary was declared officially on lockdown. We're all in this weird limbo right now; there's so much happening, but we're not allowed to leave the grounds. We can't go anywhere or do anything about anything. Not yet, anyway. Just waiting for J to wake up.

Any minute now.

There are a ton of other people here, too—but only some I'm beginning to recognize. I nod hello to a couple of people I know only by name, and drop into a soft, well-worn armchair. It smells like coffee and old wood in here, but I'm starting to like it. It's becoming a familiar routine. Brendan, as usual, finishes setting everything up on the coffee table. Teacups, spoons, little plates and triangle napkins. A little pitcher for milk. He's really, really into this whole thing. He readjusts the cookies he'd already arranged on a plate, and smooths out the paper napkins. Ian stares at him with the same expression every night—like Brendan is crazy.

"Hey," Winston says sharply. "Knock it off."

"Knock what off?" Ian says, incredulous. "Come on, man, you don't think this is a little weird? Having tea parties every night?"

Winston lowers his voice to a whisper. "I'll kill you if you ruin this for him."

"All right, enough. I'm not deaf, you know." Brendan narrows his eyes at Ian. "And I don't care if you lot think it's weird. I've little left of England, save this."

That shuts us up.

I stare at the teapot. Brendan says it's steeping.

And then, suddenly, he claps his hands together. He stares straight at me, his ice-blue eyes and white-blond hair giving me Warner vibes. But somehow, even with all his bright, white, cold hues, Brendan is the opposite of Warner. Unlike Warner, Brendan glows. He's warm. Kind. Naturally hopeful and super smiley.

Poor Winston.

Winston, who's secretly in love with Brendan and too afraid of ruining their friendship to say anything about it. Winston thinks he's too old for Brendan, but the thing is—he's not getting any younger, either. I keep telling Winston that if he wants to make a move, he should do it now, while he's still got his original hips, and he says, *Ha ha I'll murder you, asshole,* and reminds me he's waiting for the right moment. But I don't know. Sometimes I think he'll keep it inside forever. And I'm worried it might kill him.

"So, listen," Brendan says carefully. "We wanted to talk to you."

I blink, refocusing. "Who? Me?"

I glance around at their faces. Suddenly, they all look serious. Too serious. I try to laugh when I ask, "What's going on? Is this some kind of intervention?"

"Yes," Brendan says. "Sort of."

I go suddenly stiff.

Brendan sighs.

Winston scratches a spot on his forehead.

Ian says, "Juliette is probably going to die, you know that, right?"

Relief and irritation flood through me simultaneously. I manage to roll my eyes and shake my head at the same time. "Stop doing this, Sanchez. Don't be that guy. It's not funny anymore."

"I'm not trying to be funny."

I roll my eyes again, this time looking to Winston for support, but he just shakes his head at me. His eyebrows furrow so hard his glasses slip down his nose. He tugs them off his face.

"This is serious," he says. "She's not okay. And even if she does wake up again— I mean, whatever happened to her—"

"She's not going to be the same," Brendan finishes for him.

"Says who?" I frown. "The girls said—"

"Bro, the girls said that something about her chemistry changed. They've been running tests on her for days. Emmaline did something weird to her—something that's, like, physically altered her DNA. Plus, her brain is fried."

"I know what they said," I snap, irritated. "I was there when they said it. But the girls were just being cautious. They think it's *possible* that whatever happened to her might've left some damage, but—this is Sonya and Sara we're talking about. They can heal anything. All we need to do is wait for J to wake up."

Winston shakes his head again. "They wouldn't be able to heal something like that," he says. "The girls can't repair that kind of neurological devastation. They might be able to keep her alive, but I'm not sure they'll be able t—"

"She might not even wake up," Ian says, cutting him off. "Like, ever. Or, best-case scenario, she could be in a coma for *years*. Listen, the point here is that we need to start making plans without her. If we're going to save James and Adam, we need to go now. I know Sam's been checking on them, and I know she says they're stable for now, but we can't wait anymore. Anderson doesn't know what happened to Juliette, which means he's still waiting for us to give her up. Which means Adam and James are still at risk— Which means we're running out of time. And, for once," he says, taking a breath, "I'm not the only one who feels this way."

I sit back, stunned. "You're messing with me, right?"

Brendan pours tea.

Winston pulls a flask out of his pocket and weighs it in his hand before holding it out to me. "Maybe you should have this tonight," he says.

I glare at him.

He shrugs, and empties half the flask into his teacup.

"Listen," Brendan says gently. "Ian is a beast with no bedside manner, but he's not wrong. It's time to think of a new plan. We all still love Juliette, it's just—" He cuts himself off, frowns. "Wait, is it Juliette or Ella? Was there ever a consensus?"

I'm still scowling when I say, "I'm calling her Juliette."

"But I thought she wanted to be called Ella," Winston says.

"She's in a fucking coma," Ian says, and takes a loud sip of tea. "She doesn't care what you call her."

"Don't be such a brute," Brendan says. "She's our friend."

"*Your* friend," he mutters.

"Wait— Is that what this is about?" I sit forward. "Are you jealous she never best-friended you, Sanchez?"

Ian rolls his eyes, looks away.

Winston is watching with fascinated interest.

"All right, drink your tea," Brendan says, biting into a biscuit. He gestures at me with the half-eaten cookie. "It's getting cold."

I shoot him a tired look, but I take an obligatory sip and nearly choke. It tastes weird tonight. And I'm about to push it away when I realize Brendan is still staring at me, so I take a long, disgusting pull of the dark liquid before replacing the cup in the saucer. I try not to gag.

"Okay," I say, slamming my palms down on my thighs. "Let's put it to a vote: Who here thinks Ian is annoyed that J didn't fall in love with him when she showed up at Point?"

Winston and Brendan share a look. Slowly, they both lift their hands.

Ian rolls his eyes again. "*Pendejos,*" he mutters.

"The theory holds at least a little water," Winston says.

"I have a girlfriend, dumbasses." And as if on cue, Lily looks up from across the room, locks eyes with Ian. She's sitting with Alia and some other girl I don't recognize.

Lily waves.

Ian waves back.

"Yes, but you're used to a certain level of attention," Winston says, reaching for a biscuit. He looks up, scans the room. "Like those girls, right over there," he says, gesturing with his head. "They've been staring at you since you walked in."

"They have not," Ian says, but he can't help but glance over.

"It's true." Brendan shrugs. "You're a handsome guy."

Winston chokes on his tea.

"Okay, enough." Ian holds up his hands. "I know you guys think this is hilarious, but I'm being serious. At the end of the day, Juliette is *your* friend. Not mine."

I exhale dramatically.

Ian shoots me a look. "When she first showed up at

Point, I tried reaching out to her, to offer her my friendship, and she never followed up. And even after we were taken hostage by Anderson"—he nods an acknowledgment at Brendan and Winston—"she took her sweet time trying to get information out of Warner. She never gave a shit about the rest of us, and all we've ever done is put everything on the line to protect her."

"Hey, that's not fair," Winston says, shaking his head. "She was in an awful position—"

"Whatever," Ian mutters. He looks down, into his tea. "This whole situation is some kind of bullshit."

"Cheers to that," Brendan says, refilling his cup. "Now have more tea."

Ian mutters a quiet, angry thank-you, and lifts the cup to his lips. Suddenly, he stiffens. "And then there's this," he says, raising an eyebrow. As if all that weren't enough, we have to deal with *this* douche bag." Ian gestures, with the teacup, toward the entrance.

Shit.

Warner is here.

"She brought him here," Ian is saying, but he has the sense, at least, to keep his voice down. "It's because of her that we have to tolerate this asshole."

"To be fair, that was originally Castle's idea," I point out.

Ian flips me off.

"What's he doing here?" Brendan asks quietly.

I shake my head and take another unconscious sip of my disgusting tea. There's something about the grossness that's beginning to feel familiar, but I can't put my finger on it.

I look up again.

I haven't spoken a word to Warner since that first day—The day J got attacked by Emmaline. He's been a ghost since then. No one has really seen him, no one but the supreme kids, I think.

He went straight back to his roots.

It looks like he finally took a shower, though. No blood. And I'm guessing he healed himself, though there's no way to be sure, because he's fully clothed, wearing an outfit I can only assume was borrowed from Haider. A lot of leather.

I watch, for only a few seconds, as he stalks clear across the room—straight through people and conversations and apologizing to no one—toward Sonya and Sara, who are still talking to Castle.

Whatever.

Dude doesn't even look at me anymore. Doesn't even acknowledge my existence. Not that I care. It's not like we were actually friends.

At least, that's what I keep telling myself.

Somehow I've already drained my teacup, because Brendan's refilled it. I throw back the fresh cup in a couple of quick gulps and shove a dry biscuit in my mouth. And then I shake my head. "All right, we're getting distracted," I say, and the words feel just a little too loud, even to my own ears. "Focus, please."

“Right,” Winston says. “Focus. What are we focusing on?”

“New mission,” Ian says, sitting back in his chair. He counts off on his fingers: “Save Adam and James. Kill the other supreme commanders. Finally get some sleep.”

“Nice and easy,” Brendan says. “I like it.”

“You know what?” I say. “I think I should go talk to him.”

Winston raises an eyebrow. “Talk to who?”

“Warner, obviously.” My brain feels warm. A little fuzzy. “I should go talk to him. No one talks to him. Why are we just letting him revert back into an asshole? I should talk to him.”

“That’s a great idea,” Ian says, smiling as he sits forward. “Go for it.”

“Don’t you dare listen to him,” Winston says, shoving Ian back into his chair. “Ian just wants to watch you get murdered.”

“Fucking rude, Sanchez.”

Ian shrugs.

“On an unrelated note,” Winston says to me. “How does your head feel?”

I frown, gingerly touching my fingers to my skull. “What do you mean?”

“I mean,” Winston says, “that this is probably a good time to tell you I’ve been pouring whiskey in your tea all night.”

“What the hell?” I sit up too fast. Bad idea. “Why?”

“You seemed stressed.”

"I'm not stressed."

Everyone stares at me.

"All right, whatever," I say. "I'm stressed. But I'm not drunk."

"No." He peers at me. "But you probably need all the brain cells you can spare if you're going to talk to Warner. I would. I'm not too proud to admit that I find him genuinely terrifying."

Ian rolls his eyes. "There's nothing terrifying about that guy. His only problem is that he's an arrogant son of a *puta* with his own head stuck so far up his ass he ca—"

"Wait," I say, blinking. "Where'd he go?"

Everyone spins around, looking for him.

I swear, five seconds ago he was standing right there. I swivel my head back and forth like a cartoon character, understanding only vaguely that I'm moving both a little too fast and a little too slow due to Winston, number one idiot slash well-meaning friend. But in the process of scanning the room for Warner, I spot the one person I'd been making an effort to avoid:

Nazeera.

I fling myself back down in my chair too hard, nearly knocking myself out. I hunch over, breathing a little funny, and then, for no rational reason, I start laughing. Winston, Ian, and Brendan are all staring at me like I'm insane, and I don't blame them. I don't know what the hell is wrong with me. I don't even know why I'm hiding from Nazeera. There's nothing scary about her, not exactly. Nothing more scary than the fact that we haven't really discussed the last emotional conversation we had, shortly after she kicked me in the back and I nearly murdered her for it.

She told me I was her first kiss.

And then the sky melted and Juliette was possessed by her sister and the romantic moment was forever interrupted. It's been about five days since she and I had that conversation, and ever since then it's just been super stress and work and more stress and Anderson is an asshole and James and Adam are being held hostage.

Also: I've been pissed at her.

There's a part of me that would really, really like to just carry her away to a private corner somewhere, but there's another part of me that won't allow it. Because I'm mad at her. She knew how much it meant to me to go after James, and she just shrugged it off with little to no sympathy. A little sympathy, I guess. But not much. Anyway, am I thinking too much? I think I'm thinking too much.

"What the hell is wrong with you?" Ian is staring at me, stunned.

"Nazeera is here."

"So?"

"So, I don't know, Nazeera is here," I say, keeping my voice low. "And I don't want to talk to her."

"Why not?"

"Because my head is stupid right now, that's why not." I glare at Winston. "You did this to me. You made my head stupid, and now I have to avoid Nazeera, because if I don't, I will almost certainly do and or say something extremely stupid and fuck everything up. So I need to hide."

"Damn," Ian says, and shrugs. "That's too bad, because she's heading straight here."

I stiffen. Stare at him. And then, to Brendan: "Is he lying?"

Brendan shakes his head. "I'm afraid not, mate."

"Shit. Shit. Shit shit shit."

"It's nice to see you, too, Kenji."

I look up. She's smiling.

Ugh, so pretty.

"Hi," I say. "How are you?"

She looks around. Fights back a laugh. "I'm good," she says. "How . . . are you?"

"Fine. Fine. Thanks for asking. It was nice seeing you."

Nazeera glances from me to the other guys and back again. "I know you hate it when I ask you this, but— Are you drunk?"

"No," I say too loudly. I slump down farther in my seat. "Not drunk. Just a little . . . fuzzy." The whiskey is starting to settle now, warm, liquid fingers reaching up around my brain and squeezing.

She raises an eyebrow.

"Winston did it," I say, and point.

He shakes his head and sighs.

"All right," Nazeera says, but I can hear the mild

irritation in her voice. “Well, this is not the ideal situation, but I’m going to need you on your feet.”

“What?” I crane my head. Look at her. “Why?”

“There’s been a development with Ella.”

“What kind of development?” I sit straight up, feeling suddenly sober. “Is she awake?”

Nazeera tilts her head. “Not exactly,” she says.

“Then what?”

“You should come see for yourself.”

~~ELLA~~

~~JULIETTE~~

Adam feels close.

I can almost see him in my mind, a blurred form, watercolors bleeding through membrane, staining the whites of my eyes. He is a flooded river, blues in lakes so dark, water in oceans so heavy I sag, surrendering to the heft of the sea.

I take a deep breath and fill my lungs with tears, feathers of strange birds fluttering against my closed eyes. I see a flash of dirty-blond hair and darkness and stone I see blue and green and

Warmth, suddenly, an exhalation in my veins—

Emmaline.

Still here, still swimming.

She has grown quiet of late, the fire of her presence reduced to glowing embers. She is sorry for taking me from myself. Sorry for the inconvenience. Sorry to have disturbed my world so deeply. Still, she does not want to leave. She likes it here, likes stretching out inside my bones. She likes the dry air and the taste of real oxygen. She likes the shape of my fingers, the sharpness of my teeth. She is sorry, but not sorry enough to go back, so she is trying to be very small and very quiet. She hopes to make it up to me by taking up as little space as possible.

I don't know how I understand this so clearly, except that her mind seems to have fused with mine. Conversation is no longer necessary. Explanations, redundant.

In the beginning, she inhaled everything.

Excited, eager—she took it all. New skin. Eyes and mouth. I felt her marvel at my anatomy, at the systems drawing in air through my nose. I seemed to exist here almost as an afterthought, blood pumping through an organ beating merely to pass the time. I was little more than a passenger in my own body, doing nothing as she explored and decayed in starts and sparks, steel scraping against itself, stunning contractions of pain like claws digging, digging. It's better now that she's settled, but her presence has faded to all but an aching sadness. She seems desperate to find purchase as she disintegrates, unwittingly taking with her bits and pieces of my mind. Some days are better than others. Some days the fire of her existence is so acute I forget to draw breath.

But most days I am an idea, and nothing more.

I am foam and smoke moonlighting as skin. Dandelions gather in my rib cage, moss growing steadily along my spine. Rainwater floods my eyes, pools in my open mouth, dribbles down the hinges holding together my lips.

I

continue

to

sink.

And then—

why now?

suddenly

surprisingly

chest heaving, lungs working, fists clenching, knees bending, pulse racing, blood pumping

I float

"Ms. Ferrars— That is, Ella—"

"Her name is Juliette. Just call her Juliette, for God's sake."

"Why don't we call her what she *wants* to be called?"

"Right. Exactly."

"But I thought she wanted to be called Ella."

"There was never a consensus. Was there a consensus?"

Slowly, my eyelids flutter open.

Silence explodes, coating mouths and walls and doors and dust motes. It hangs in the air, cloaking everything, for all of two seconds.

Then

Shouts, screams, a million sounds. I try to count them all and my head spins, swims. My heart is pounding hard and fast in my chest, recklessly shaking me, shaking my hands, ringing my skull. I look around fast, too fast, head whipping back and forth and everything swings around and around and

So many faces, blurred and strange.

I'm breathing too hard, spots dotting my vision, and I place two hands down on the—I look down—bed below me and squeeze my eyes shut

What am I

Who am I

Where am I

Silence again, swift and complete, like magic, magic, a hush falls over everyone, everything, and I exhale, panic draining out of me and I sit back, soaking in the dregs when

Warm hands

touch mine.

Familiar.

I go suddenly still. My eyes stay closed. Feeling moves through me like a wildfire, flames devouring the dust in my chest, the kindling in my bones. Hands become arms around me and the fire blazes. My own hands are caught between us and I feel the hard lines of his body through the soft cotton of his shirt.

A face appears, disappears, behind my eyes.

There's something so safe here in the feel of him, in the scent of him—something entirely his own. Being near him does something to me, something I can't even explain, can't control. I know I shouldn't, know I shouldn't, but I can't help but drag the tips of my fingers down the perfect lines of his torso.

I hear his breath catch.

Flames leap through me, jump up my lungs and I inhale, dragging oxygen into my body that only fans the flames further. One of his hands clasps the back of my head, the other grasps at my waist. A flash of heat roars up my spine, reaches into my skull. His lips are at my ear whispering, whispering

Come back to life, love
I'll be here when you wake up

My eyes fly open.

The heat is merciless. Confusing. Consuming. It calms me, settles my raging heart. His hands move along my body, light touches along my arms, the sides of my torso. I claw my way back to him by memory, my shaking hands tracing the familiar shape of his back, my cheek still pressed against the familiar beat of his heart. The scent of him, so familiar, so familiar, and then I look up—

His eyes, something about his eyes

Please, he says, *please don't shoot me for this*

The room comes into focus by degrees, my head settling onto my neck, my skin settling onto my bones, my eyes staring into the very desperately green eyes that seem to know too much, too well. Aaron Warner Anderson is bent over me, his worried eyes inspecting me, his hand caught in the air like he might've been about to touch me.

He jerks back.

He stares, unblinking, chest rising and falling.

"Good morning," I assume. I'm unsure of my voice, of the hour and this day, of these words leaving my lips and this body that contains me.

His smile looks like it hurts.

"Something's wrong," he whispers. He touches my cheek. Soft, so soft, like he's not sure if I'm real, like he's afraid if he gets too close I'll just oh, look she's gone, she's just disappeared. His four fingers graze the side of my face, slowly, so slowly before they slip behind my head, caught in that in-between spot just above my neck. His thumb brushes the apple of my cheek.

My heart implodes.

He keeps looking at me, looking into my eyes for help, for guidance, for some sign of a protest like he's so sure I'm going to start screaming or crying or running away but I won't. I don't think I could even if I wanted to because I don't want to. I want to stay here. Right here. I want to be paralyzed by this moment.

He moves closer, just an inch. His free hand reaches up to cup the other side of my face.

He's holding me like I'm made of feathers. Like I'm a bird. White with streaks of gold like a crown atop its head.

I will fly.

A soft, shuddering breath leaves his body.

"Something's wrong," he says again, but distantly, like he might be talking to someone else. "Her energy is different. Tainted."

The sound of his voice coils through me, spirals around my spine. I feel myself straighten even as I feel strange, jet-lagged, like I've traveled through time. I pull myself into a seated position and Warner shifts to accommodate me. I'm tired and weak from hunger, but other than a few general aches, I seem to be fine. I'm alive. I'm breathing and blinking and feeling human and I know exactly why.

I meet his eyes. "You saved my life."

He tilts his head at me.

He's still studying me, his gaze so intense I flush, confused, and turn away. The moment I do, I nearly jump out of my skin. Castle and Kenji and Winston and Brendan and a ton of other people I don't recognize are all staring at me, at Warner's hands on me, and I'm suddenly so mortified I don't even know what to do with myself.

"Hey, princess." Kenji waves. "You okay?"

I try to stand and Warner tries to help me and the moment his skin brushes mine another sudden, destabilizing bolt of feeling runs me over. I stumble, sideways, into his arms and he pulls me in, his heat setting fire to my body all over again. I'm trembling, heart pounding, nervous pleasure pulsing through me.

I don't understand.

I'm overcome by a sudden, inexplicable need to touch him, to press my skin against his skin until the friction sets fire to us both. Because there's something about him—there's *always* been something about him that's intrigued me and I don't understand it. I pull away, startled by the intensity of my own thoughts, but his fingers catch me under the chin. He tilts my face toward him.

I look up.

His eyes are such a strange shade of green: bright, crystal clear, piercing in the most alarming way. His hair is thick, the richest slice of gold. Everything about him is meticulous. Pristine. His breath is cool and fresh. I can feel it on my face.

My eyes close automatically. I breathe him in, feeling

suddenly giddy. A bubble of laughter escapes my lips.

"Something's definitely wrong," someone says.

"Yeah, she doesn't look like she's okay." Someone else.

"Oh, okay, so we're all just saying really obvious things out loud? Is that what we're doing?" Kenji.

Warner says nothing. I feel his arms tighten around me and my eyes flicker open. His gaze is fixed on mine, his eyes green flames that will not extinguish and his chest is rising and falling so fast, so fast, so fast. His lips are there, right there above mine.

"Ella?" he whispers.

I frown.

My eyes flick up, to his eyes, then down, to his lips.

"Love, do you hear me?"

When I don't answer, his face changes.

"Juliette," he says softly, "can you hear me?"

I blink at him. I blink and blink and blink at him and find I'm still fascinated by his eyes. Such a startling shade of green.

"We're going to need everyone to clear the room," someone says suddenly. Loudly. "We need to begin running tests immediately."

The girls, I realize. It's the girls. They're here. They're trying to get him away from me, trying to get him to break away from me. But Warner's arms are like steel bands around my body.

He refuses.

"Not yet," he says urgently. "Not just yet."

And for some reason they listen.

Maybe they see something in him, see something in his face, in his features. Maybe they see what I see from this disjointed, foggy perspective. The desperation in his expression, the anguish carved into his features, the way he looks at me, like he might die if I do.

Tentatively, I reach up, touch my fingers to his face. His skin is smooth and cold. Porcelain. He doesn't seem real.

"What's wrong?" I say. "What happened?"

Impossibly, Warner goes paler. He shakes his head and presses his face to my cheek. "Please," he whispers. "Come back to me, love."

"Aaron?"

I hear the small hitch in his breath. The hesitation. It's the first time I've used his name so casually.

"Yes?"

"I want you to know," I tell him, "that I don't think you're crazy."

"What?" He startles.

"I don't think you're crazy," I say. "And I don't think you're a psychopath. I don't think you're a heartless murderer. I don't care what anyone else says about you. I think you're a good person."

Warner is blinking fast now. I can hear him breathing.

In and out.

Unevenly.

A flash of stunning, searing pain, and my body goes

suddenly slack. I see the glint of metal. I feel the burn of the syringe. My head begins to swim and all the sounds begin to melt together.

"Come on, son," Castle says, his voice expanding, slowing down, "I know this is hard, but we need you to step back. We have t—"

An abrupt, violent sound gives me a sudden moment of clarity.

A man I don't recognize is at the door, one hand on the doorframe, gasping for breath. "They're here," he says. "They've found us. They're here. Jenna is dead."

KENJI

The guy gasping at the doorframe is still finishing his sentence when everyone jumps into action. Nouria and Sam rush past him into the hall, shouting orders and commands—something about initiating protocol for System Z, something about gathering the children, the elderly, and the sick. Sonya and Sara press something into Warner's hands, glance one last time at J's limp, unconscious figure, and chase Nouria and Sam out the door.

Castle crouches to the ground, closing his eyes as he flattens his hands against the floor, listening. Feeling.

"Eleven—no twelve, bodies. About five hundred feet out. I'd guess we have about two minutes before they reach us. I'll do my best to slow them down until we can clear out of here." He looks up. "Mr. Ibrahim?"

I don't even realize Haider is here with us until he says, "That's more than enough time."

He stalks across the room to the wall opposite Juliette's bed, running his hands along the smooth surface, ripping down picture frames and monitors as he goes. Glass and wood shatter in a heap on the floor. Nazeera gasps, goes suddenly still. I turn, terrified, to face her and she says—

"I need to tell Stephan."

She dashes out the door.

Warner is unhooking Juliette from the bed, removing her needles, bandaging her wounds. Once she's free, he wraps her sleeping body in the soft blue robe hanging nearby, and at nearly the exact same moment, I hear the telltale ticking of a bomb.

I glance back, at the wall where Haider still stands. Two carefully spaced explosives are now affixed to the plaster, and I hardly even have time to digest this before Haider bellows at us to move out into the hall. Warner is already halfway out the door, holding the carefully wrapped bundle of J in his arms. I hear Castle's voice—a sudden cry—and my own body is lifted and thrown out the door, too.

The room explodes.

The walls shake so hard it rattles my teeth, but when the tremors settle, I rush back into the room.

Haider blew off a single wall.

A perfect, exact rectangle of wall. Gone. I didn't even know such a feat was possible. Pieces of brick and wood and drywall are scattered on the open ground beyond J's room, and cold night winds rush in, slapping me awake. The moon is excessively full and bright tonight, a spotlight shining directly into my eyes.

I'm stunned.

Haider explains without prompting: "The hospital is too big, too complicated—we needed an efficient exit. The Reestablishment won't care about collateral damage when they come for us—in fact, they might be craving it—but if we're to have any hope of sparing innocent lives, we have to remove ourselves as far from the central buildings and common spaces as possible. Now move out," he shouts. "Let's go."

But I'm reeling.

I blink at Haider, still recovering from the blast, the lingering whisper of whiskey in my brain, and now this:

proof that Haider Ibrahim has a conscience.

He and Warner stalk past me, through the open wall, and start running into the gleaming woods, Warner with J in his arms. Neither of them bothers to explain what they're thinking. Where they're going. What the hell is going to happen next.

Well, actually, I think that last part is obvious.

What's going to happen next is that Anderson is going to show up and try to murder us.

Castle and I lock eyes—we're the last people still standing in what remains of J's hospital room—and we chase after Warner and Haider toward a clearing at the far end of the Sanctuary, as far away from the tents as possible. At one point Warner breaks off from our group, disappearing down a path so dark I can't see the end of it. When I move to follow, Haider barks at me to leave him alone. I don't know what Warner does with Juliette, but when he rejoins us, she's no longer in his arms. He says something, briefly, to Haider, but it sounds like French. Not Arabic. *French.*

Whatever. I don't have time to think about it.

It's already been five minutes, by my estimate. Five

minutes, which means they should be here any second now. There are twelve bodies incoming. There are only four of us here.

Me, Haider, Castle, Warner.

I'm freezing.

We're standing quietly in the darkness, waiting for death, and the individual seconds seem to tick by with excruciating slowness. The smell of wet earth and decaying vegetation fills my head and I look down, feeling but not seeing the thick pile of leaves underfoot. They're soft and slightly damp, rustling a little when I shift my weight.

I try not to move.

Every sound unnerves me. A sudden shudder of branches. An innocent breeze. My own ragged breaths.

It's too dark.

Even the bright, robust moon isn't enough to properly penetrate these woods. I don't know how we're going to fight anyone if we can't see what's coming. The light is uneven, scattering through branches, shattering across the soft earth. I look down, examining a narrow shaft of light illuminating the tops of my boots, and watch as a spider scuttles up and around the obstacle of my feet.

My heart is pounding.

There's no time. If only we had more time.

It's all I can think. Over and over again. They caught us off guard, we weren't prepared, it didn't have to go down like this. My head is spinning with *what-ifs* and *maybes* and *it could've beens* even as I face down the reality right in front of me. Even as I stare straight into the black hole devouring my future, I can't help but wonder if we could've done this differently.

The seconds build. Minutes pass.

Nothing.

The rapid beating of my heart slows into a sick stutter of dread. I've lost perspective—my sense of time is warped in the dark—but I swear it feels like we've been here for too long.

"Something is wrong," Warner says.

I hear a sharp intake of breath. Haider.

Warner says softly, "We miscalculated."

"No," Castle cries.

That's when I hear the screams.

We run without hesitation, all four of us, hurtling ourselves toward the sounds. We tear through branches, sprain ankles on overgrown roots, propel ourselves into the darkness with the force of pure, undiluted panic. *Rage.*

Sobs rend the sky. Violent cries echo into the distance. Inarticulate voices, guttural moans, goose bumps rising along my flesh. We are sprinting toward death.

I know we're close when I see the light.

Nouria.

She's cast an ethereal glow above the scene, bringing the remains of a battlefield into sharp focus.

We slow down.

Time seems to expand, fracturing apart as I bear witness to a massacre. Anderson and his men made a detour. We hoped they'd come straight for Warner, straight for Juliette. We hoped. We tried. We took a gamble.

We bet wrong.

And we know The Reestablishment well enough to understand that they were punishing these innocent people for harboring us. Slaughtering entire families for providing us aid and relief. Nausea hits me with the force of a blade, stunning me, knocking me sideways. I slump against a tree. I can feel my mind disconnecting, threatening unconsciousness, and somehow I force myself not to pass out from horror. Terror. Heartbreak.

I keep my eyes open.

Sam and Nouria are on their knees, holding broken, bleeding bodies close to their chests, their tortured cries piercing the strange half night. Castle stands beside me, his body slack. I hear his half-choked sob.

We knew it was possible—Haider said they might do this—but somehow I still can't believe my eyes. I desperately want this to be a nightmare. I would cut off my right arm for a nightmare. But reality persists.

The Sanctuary is little more than a graveyard.

Unarmed men and women mowed down. From where I'm standing I count six children, dead. Eyes open, mouths agape, fresh blood still dripping down limp bodies. Ian is on his knees, vomiting. Winston stumbles backward, hits a tree. His glasses slide down his face and he only remembers to catch them at the last moment. Only the supreme kids still seem to have their heads on straight, and there's something about that realization that strikes fear into my heart. Nazeera, Haider, Warner, Stephan. They walk calmly through the wreckage, faces unchanged and solemn. I don't know what they've seen—what they've been a part of—that makes them able to stand here, still relatively cool in the face of so much human devastation, and I don't think I want to know.

I offer Castle my hand and he takes it, steadies himself. We exchange a single glance before diving into the fray.

Anderson is easy to spot, standing tall in the midst of hell, but hard to reach. His Supreme Guard swarms us, weapons drawn. Still, we move closer. No matter what comes next, we fight to the death. That was always the plan, from the first. And it's what we'll do now.

Round two.

The still-living fighters on the field straighten at our approach, at the scene forming, and steal glances at one another. We're surrounded by firepower, that's true, but nearly everyone here has a supernatural gift. There's no reason we shouldn't be able to put up a fight. A crowd gathers slowly around us—half Sanctuary, half Point—hale bodies breaking away from the wreckage to form a new battalion. I feel the fresh hope moving through the air. The tantalizing *maybe*. Carefully, I pull free a gun from my side holster.

And just as I'm about to make a move—

"Don't."

Anderson's voice is loud. Clear. He breaks through his wall of soldiers, stalking toward us casually, looking as polished as always. I don't understand, at first, why so many people gasp at his approach. I don't see it. I don't notice the body he's dragging with him, and when I finally notice the body, I don't recognize it. Not right away.

It's not until Anderson jerks the small figure upright, nudging his head back with a gun, that I feel the blood exit my heart. Anderson presses the gun to James's throat, and my knees nearly give out.

"This is very simple," Anderson says. "You will hand over the girl, and in return, I won't execute the boy."

We're all frozen.

"I should clarify, however, that this is not an exchange. I'm not offering to return him to you. I'm only offering not to murder him here, on the spot. But if you hand over the girl now, without a fight, I will consider letting most of you disappear into the shadows."

"Most of us?" I say.

Anderson's eyes glance off my face and the faces of several others. "Yes, most of you," he says, his gaze lingering on Haider. "Your father is very disappointed in you, young man."

A single gunshot explodes without warning, ripping open a hole in Anderson's throat. He grabs at his neck and falls, with a choked cry, on one knee, looking around for his assailant.

Nazeera.

She materializes in front of him just in time to jump up, into the sky. The supreme soldiers start shooting upward, releasing round after round with impunity, and though I'm terrified for Nazeera, I realize she took that risk for me. For James.

We'll do our best, she'd said. I didn't realize her best included risking her life for that kid. For *me*. God, I fucking love her.

I go invisible.

Anderson is struggling to stanch the flow of blood at his throat while keeping his grip on James, who appears to be unconscious.

Two guards remain at his side.

I fire two shots.

They both go down, crying out and clutching limbs, and Anderson nearly roars. He starts clawing at the air in front of him, then fumbles for his gun with one red hand, blood still seeping from his lips. I take that opportunity to punch him in the face.

He rears back, more surprised than injured, but Brendan moves in quickly, clapping his hands together to create a twisting, crackling bolt of electricity he wraps around Anderson's legs, temporarily paralyzing him.

Anderson drops James.

I catch him before he hits the floor, and bolt toward Lily, who's waiting just outside of Nouria's ring of light. I unload his unconscious body into her arms and Brendan builds an electric shield around their bodies. A beat later, they're gone.

Relief floods through me.

Too quickly. It unsteadies me. My invisibility falters for less than a second, and in less than a second I'm attacked from behind.

I hit the ground, hard, air leaving my lungs. I struggle to flip over, to stand up, but a supreme soldier is already pointing a rifle at my face. He shoots.

Castle comes out of nowhere, knocking the soldier off his feet, stopping the bullets with a single gesture. He redirects the ammunition meant for my body, and I don't even realize what's happened until I see the dude drop to his knees. He's a human sieve, bleeding out the last of his life right in front of me, and it all feels suddenly surreal.

I drag myself up, my head pounding in my throat. Castle is already moving, ripping a tree from its roots as he goes. Stephan is using his superstrength to pummel as many soldiers as he can, but they won't stop shooting, and he's moving slowly, blood staining nearly every inch of his clothing. I watch him sway. I run toward him, try to shout a warning, but my voice gets lost in the din, and my legs won't move fast enough. Another soldier charges at him, unloading rounds, and this time, I scream.

Haider comes running.

He dives in front of his friend with a cry, knocking Stephan to the ground, protecting his body with his own, throwing something into the air as he goes.

It explodes.

I'm thrown backward, my skull ringing. I lift my head, delirious, and spot Nazeera and Warner, each locked in hand-to-hand combat. I hear a bloodcurdling scream and force myself up, toward the sound.

It's Sam.

Nouria beats me to her, falling to her knees to lift her wife's body off the ground. She wraps blinding bands of light around the two of them, the protective spirals so bright they're excruciating to look at. A nearby soldier throws his arm over his eyes as he shoots, crying out and holding steady even as the force of Nouria's light begins to melt the flesh off his hands.

I put a bullet through his teeth.

Five more guards appear out of nowhere, coming at me from all sides, and for half a second I can't help but be surprised. Castle said there were only twelve bodies, two of which belonged to Anderson and James, and I thought we'd taken out at least several of the others by now. I glance around the battlefield, at the dozens of soldiers still actively attacking our team, and then back again, at the five heading my way.

My head swims with confusion.

And then, when they all begin to shoot—terror.

I go invisible, stealing through the single foot of space between two of them, turning back just long enough to open fire. A couple of my shots find their marks; the others are wasted. I reload the clip, tossing the now-empty one to the ground, and just as I'm about to shoot again, I hear her voice.

"Hang on," she whispers.

Nazeera wraps her arms around my waist and jumps.

Up.

A bullet whizzes past my calf. I feel the burn as it grazes skin, but the night sky is cool and bracing, and I allow myself to take a steadying breath, to close my eyes for a full and complete second. Up here, the screams are muted, the blood could be water, the screams could be laughter.

The dream lasts for only a moment.

Our feet touch the ground again and my ears refill with the sounds of war. I squeeze Nazeera's hand by way of thanks, and we split up. I charge toward a group of men and women I only vaguely recognize—people from the Sanctuary—and throw myself into the bloodshed, urging one of the injured fighters to pull back and take shelter. I'm soon lost in the motions of battle, defending and attacking, guns firing. Guttural moaning. I don't even think to look up until I feel the ground shake beneath my feet.

Castle.

His arms are pointed upward, toward a nearby building. The structure begins to shake violently, nails flying, windows shuddering. A cluster of supreme guards reaches for their guns but stop short at the sound of Anderson's voice. I can't hear what he says, but he seems to be nearly himself again, and his command appears to be shocking enough to inspire a moment of hesitation in his soldiers. For no reason I can fathom, the guards I'd been fighting suddenly slink away.

Too late.

The roof of the nearby building collapses with a scream,

and with a final, violent shove, Castle tears off a wall. With one arm he shoves aside the few of our teammates standing in harm's way, and with the other he drops the ton of wall to the ground, where it lands with an explosive crash. Glass flies everywhere, wooden beams groaning as they buckle and break. A few supreme soldiers escape, diving for cover, but at least three of them get caught under the rubble. We all brace for a retaliatory attack—

But Anderson holds up a single arm.

His soldiers go instantly still, weapons going slack in their hands. Almost in unison, they stand at attention.

Waiting.

I glance at Castle for a directive, but he's got eyes on Anderson just like the rest of us. Everyone seems paralyzed by a delirious hope that this war might be over. I watch Castle turn and lock eyes with Nouria, who's still cradling Sam to her chest. A moment later, Castle raises his arm. A temporary standstill.

I don't trust it.

Silence coats the night as Anderson staggers forward, his lips a violent, liquid red, his hand casually holding a handkerchief to his neck. We'd heard about this, of course—about his ability to heal himself—but seeing it actually happen in real time is something else altogether. It's *wild.*

When he speaks, his voice shatters the quiet. Breaks the spell. "Enough," he says. "Where is my son?"

Murmurs move through the crowd of bloodied fighters, a red sea slowly parting at his approach. It's not long before

Warner appears, striding forward in the silence, his face spattered in red. A machine gun is locked in his right hand.

He looks up at his father. He says nothing.

"What did you do with her?" Anderson says softly, and spits blood on the ground. He wipes his lips with the same cloth he's using to contain the open wound on his neck. The whole scene is disgusting.

Warner continues to say nothing.

I don't think any of us know where he hid her. J seems to have *disappeared,* I realize.

Seconds pass in a silence so intense we all begin to worry about the fate of our standstill. I see a few of the supreme soldiers lift their guns in Warner's direction, and not a second later a single lightning bolt fractures the sky above us.

Brendan.

I glance at him, then at Castle, but Anderson once again lifts his arm to stall his soldiers. Once again, they stand down.

"I will only ask you one more time," Anderson says to his son, his voice trembling as it grows louder. *"What did you do with her?"*

Still, Warner stares impassively.

He's spattered in unknown blood, holding a machine gun like it might be a briefcase, and staring at his father like he might be staring at the ceiling. Anderson can't control his temper the way Warner can—and it's obvious to everyone that this is a battle of wills he's going to lose.

Anderson already looks half out of his mind.

His hair is matted and sticking up in places. Blood is congealing on his face, his eyes shot through with red. He looks so deranged—so unlike himself—that I honestly have no idea what's going to happen next.

And then he lunges for Warner.

He's like a belligerent drunk, wild and angry, unhinged in a way I've never seen before. His swings are wild but strong, unsteady but studied. He reminds me, in a sudden, frightening flash of understanding, of the father Adam so often described to me. A violent drunk fueled by rage.

Except that Anderson doesn't appear to be drunk at the moment. No. This is pure, unadulterated anger.

Anderson seems to have lost his mind.

He doesn't just want to shoot Warner. He doesn't want someone else to shoot Warner. He wants to beat him to a pulp. He wants physical satisfaction. He wants to break bones and rupture organs with his own hands. Anderson wants the pleasure of knowing that he and he alone was able to destroy his own son.

But Warner isn't giving him that satisfaction.

He meets Anderson blow for blow in fluid, precise movements, ducking and sidestepping and twisting and defending. He never misses a beat.

It's almost like he can read Anderson's mind.

I'm not the only one who's stunned. I've never seen Warner move like this, and I almost can't believe I've never seen it before. I feel a sudden, unbidden surge of respect for him as I watch him block attack after attack. I keep waiting for him to knock the dude out, but Warner makes no effort to hit Anderson; he only defends. And only when I see the increasing fury on Anderson's face do I realize that Warner is doing this on purpose.

He's not fighting back because he knows it's what Anderson wants. The cool, emotionless expression on Warner's face is driving Anderson insane. And the more he fails to rattle his son, the more enraged Anderson gets. Blood still trickles, slowly, from the half-healed wound on his neck when he cries out, angrily, and pulls free a gun from inside his jacket pocket.

"*Enough*," he shouts. "That is enough."

Warner takes a careful step back.

"Give me the girl, Aaron. Give me the girl and I will spare the rest of these idiots. I only want the girl."

Warner is an immovable object.

"Fine," Anderson says angrily. "Seize him."

Six supreme guards begin advancing on Warner, and he doesn't so much as flinch. I exchange glances with Winston and it's enough; I throw my invisibility over Winston just as he throws his arms out, his ability to stretch his limbs knocking three of them to the ground. In the same moment, Haider pulls a machete from somewhere inside the bloodied chain mail he's wearing under his coat, and tosses it to Warner, who drops the machine gun and catches the blade by the hilt without even looking.

A fucking *machete*.

Castle is on his knees, arms toward the sky as he breaks

off more pieces of the half-devastated building, but this time Anderson's men don't give him the chance. I run forward, too late to help as Castle is knocked out from behind, and still I throw myself into the fight, battling for ownership of the soldier's gun with skills I developed as a teenager: a single, solid punch to the nose. A clean uppercut. A hard kick to the chest. A good old-fashioned strangulation.

I look up, gasping for breath, hoping for good news—

And do a double take.

Ten men have closed in on Warner, and I don't understand where they came from. I thought we were down to three or four. I spin around, confused, turning back just in time to watch Warner drop to one knee and swing up with the machete in a sudden, perfect arc, gutting the man like a fish. Warner turns, another strong swing slicing through the guy on his left, disconnecting the dude's spine in a move so horrific I have to look away. In the second it takes me to turn back, another guard has already charged forward. Warner pivots sharply, shoving the blade directly up the guy's throat and into his open, screaming mouth. With a final tug, Warner pulls the blade free, and the man falls to the ground with a single, soft thud.

The remaining members of the Supreme Guard hesitate.

I realize then, that—whoever these new soldiers are—they've been given specific orders to attack Warner, and no one else. The rest of us are suddenly without an obvious task, free to sink into the ground, disappear into exhaustion.

Tempting.

I search for Castle, wanting to make sure he's okay, and realize he looks stricken.

He's staring at Warner.

Warner, who's staring at the blood pooling beneath his feet, his chest heaving, his fist still clenched around the shank of the machete. All this time, Castle really thought Warner was just a nice boy who'd made some simple mistakes. The kind of kid he could bring back from the brink.

Not today.

Warner looks up at his father, his face more blood than skin, his body shaking with rage.

"Is this what you wanted?" he cries.

But even Anderson seems surprised.

Another guard moves forward so silently I don't even see the gun he's aimed in Warner's direction until the soldier screams and collapses to the ground. His eyes bulge as he clutches at his throat, where a shard of glass the size of my hand is caught in his jugular.

I whip my head around to face Warner. He's still staring at Anderson, but his free hand is now dripping blood.

Jesus Christ.

"Take me, instead," Warner says, his voice piercing the quiet.

Anderson seems to come back to himself. "What?"

"Leave her. Leave them all. Give me your word that you will leave her alone, and I will come back with you."

I go suddenly still. And then I look around, eyes wild, for any indication that we're going to stop this idiot from doing something reckless, but no one meets my eyes. Everyone is riveted.

Terrified.

But when I feel a familiar presence suddenly materialize beside me, relief floods through my body. I reach for her hand at the same time she reaches for mine, squeezing her fingers once before breaking the brief connection. Right now, it's enough to know she's here, standing next to me.

Nazeera is okay.

We all wait in silence for the scene to change, hoping for something we don't even know how to name.

It doesn't come.

"I wish it were that simple," Anderson says finally. "I really do. But I'm afraid we need the girl. She is not so easily replaced."

"You said that Emmaline's body was deteriorating." Warner's voice is low, but clear. Miraculously steady. "You said that without a strong enough body to contain her, she'd become volatile."

Anderson visibly stiffens.

"You need a replacement," Warner says. "A new body. Someone to help you complete Operation Synthesis."

"No," Castle cries. "No— Don't do this—"

"Take me," Warner says. "I will be your surrogate."

Anderson's eyes go cold.

He sounds almost convincingly calm when he says, "You would be willing to sacrifice yourself—your youth and your health and your entire life—to let that damaged, deranged girl continue to walk the earth?" Anderson's voice begins to rise in pitch. He seems suddenly on the verge of another breakdown.

"Do you even understand what you're saying? You have every opportunity—all the potential—and you'd be willing to throw it all away? In exchange for *what*?" he cries. "Do you even know the kind of life to which you'd be sentencing yourself?"

A dark look passes over Warner's face. "I think I would know better than most."

Anderson pales. "Why would you do this?"

It becomes clear to me then that even now, despite everything, Anderson doesn't actually want to lose Warner. Not like this.

But Warner is unmoved.

He says nothing. Betrays nothing. He only blinks as someone else's blood drips down his face.

"Give me your word," Warner finally says. "Your word that you will leave her alone forever. I want you to let her disappear. I want you to stop tracking her every move. I want you to forget she ever existed." He pauses. "In exchange, you can have what's left of my life."

Nazeera gasps.

Haider takes a sudden, angry step forward and Stephan grabs his arm, somehow still strong enough to restrain Haider even as his own body bleeds out. "This is his choice," Stephan gasps, wrapping his free arm around a tree for support. "Leave him."

"This is a stupid choice," Haider cries. "You can't do this, *habibi*. Don't be an idiot."

But Warner doesn't seem to hear anyone anymore. He stares only at Anderson, who seems genuinely distraught.

"I will stop fighting you," Warner says. "I will do exactly as you ask. Whatever you want. Just let her live."

Anderson is silent for so long it sends a chill through me. Then:

"No."

Without warning, Anderson raises his arm and fires two shots. The first, at Nazeera, hitting her square in the chest. The second—

At me.

Several people scream. I stumble, then sway, before collapsing.

Shit.

"Find her," Anderson says, his voice booming. "Burn the whole place to the ground if you have to."

The pain is blinding.

It moves through me in waves, electric and searing. Someone is touching me, moving my body. *I'm okay,* I try to say. I'm okay. I'm okay. But the words don't come. He's hit me in my shoulder, I think. Just shy of my chest. I'm not sure. But Nazeera— Someone needs to get to Nazeera.

"I had a feeling you'd do something like this," I hear Anderson say. "And I know you used one of these two"—I imagine him pointing to my prone body, to Nazeera's—"in order to make it happen."

Silence.

"Oh, I see," Anderson says. "You thought you were clever. You thought I didn't know you had any powers at all." Anderson's voice seems suddenly loud, too loud. He laughs. "You thought *I* didn't know? As if you could hide something like that from me. I knew it the day I found you in her holding cell. You were sixteen. You think I didn't have you tested after that? You think I haven't known, all these years, what you yourself didn't realize until six months ago?"

A fresh wave of fear washes over me.

Anderson seems too pleased and Warner's gone quiet again, and I don't know what any of that means for us. But just as I'm beginning to experience full-blown panic, I hear a familiar cry.

It's a sound of such horrific agony I can't help but try to see what's happening, even as flashes of white blur my vision.

I catch a mottled glimpse:

Warner standing over Anderson's body, his right hand clenched around the handle of the machete he's buried in his father's chest. He plants his right foot on his father's gut, and, roughly, pulls out the blade.

Anderson's moan is so animal, so pathetic I almost feel sorry for him. Warner wipes the blade on the grass, and tosses it back to Haider, who catches it easily by the hilt even as he stands there, stunned, staring at—*me*, I realize. Me and Nazeera. I've never seen him so unmasked. He seems paralyzed by fear.

"Watch him," Warner shouts to someone. He examines a gun he stole from his father, and, satisfied, he's off, running after the Supreme Guard. Shots ring out in the distance.

My vision begins to go spotty.

Sounds bleed together, shifting focus. For moments at a time all I hear is the sound of my own breathing, my heart beating. At least, I hope that's the sound of my heart beating. Everything smells sharp, like rust and steel. I realize then, in a sudden, startling moment, that I can't feel my fingers.

Finally I hear the muffled sounds of nearby movement, of hands on my body, trying to move me.

"Kenji?" Someone shakes me. "Kenji, can you hear me?" Winston.

I make a sound in my throat. My lips seem fused together.

"Kenji?" More shaking. "Are you okay?"

With great difficulty, I pry my lips apart, but my mouth makes no sound. Then, all at once: "Heyyyyybuddy."

Weird.

"He's conscious," Winston says, "but disoriented. "We don't have much time. I'll carry these two. See if you can find a way to transport the others. Where are the girls?"

Someone says something back to him, and I don't catch it. I reach out suddenly with my good hand, clamping down on Winston's forearm.

"Don't let them get J," I try to say. "Don't let—"

~~ELLA~~
~~JULIETTE~~

When I open my eyes, I feel steel.

Strapped and molded across my body, thick, silver stripes pressed against my pale skin. I'm in a cage the exact size and shape of my silhouette. I can't move. Can hardly part my lips or bat an eyelash; I only know what I look like because I can see my reflection in the stainless steel of the ceiling.

Anderson is here.

I see him right away, standing in a corner of the room, staring at the wall like he's both pleased and angry, a strange sneer plastered to his face. There's a woman here, too, someone I've never seen before. Blond, very blond. Tall and freckled and willowy. She reminds me of someone I've seen before, someone I can't presently remember.

And then, suddenly—

My mind catches up to me with a ferociousness that's nearly paralyzing. James and Adam, kidnapped by Anderson. Kenji, falling ill. New memories from my own life, continuing to assault my mind and taking with them, bits and pieces of me.

And then, Emmaline.

Emmaline, stealing into my consciousness. Emmaline,

her presence so overwhelming I was forced into near oblivion, coaxed to sleep. I remember waking, eventually, but my recollection of that moment is vague. I remember confusion, mostly. Distorted reels.

I take a moment to check in with myself. My limbs. My heart. My mind. Intact?

I don't know.

Despite a bit of disorientation, I feel almost fully myself. I can still sense pockets of darkness in my memories, but I feel like I've finally broken the surface of my own consciousness. And it's only then that I realize I no longer feel even a whisper of Emmaline.

Quickly, I close my eyes again. I feel around for my sister in my head, seeking her out with a desperate panic that surprises me.

Emmaline? Are you still here?

In response, a gentle warmth rushes through me. A single, soft shudder of life. She must be close to the end, I realize.

Nearly gone.

Pain shoots through my heart.

My love for Emmaline is at once new and ancient, so complicated I don't even know how to properly articulate my feelings about it. I only know that I have nothing but compassion for her. For her pain, her sacrifices, her broken spirit, her longing for all that her life could've been. I feel no anger or resentment toward her for infiltrating my mind, for violently disrupting my world to make room for herself in my skin. Somehow I understand that the brutality of her act was nothing more than a desperate plea for companionship in the last days of her life.

She wants to die knowing she was loved.

And I, I love her.

I was able to see, when our minds were fused, that Emmaline had found a way to split her consciousness, leaving a necessary bit of it behind to play her role in Oceania. The small part of her that broke off to find me—that was the small part of her that still felt human, that felt the world acutely. And now, it seems, that human piece of her is beginning to fade away.

The callused fingers of grief curve around my throat.

My thoughts are interrupted by the sharp staccato of heels against stone. Someone is moving toward me. I'm careful not to flinch.

"She should've been awake by now," the female voice says. "This is odd."

"Perhaps the sedative you gave her was stronger than you thought." Anderson.

"I'm going to assume your head is still full of morphine, Paris, which is the only reason I'm going to overlook that statement."

Anderson sighs. Stiffly, he says: "I'm sure she'll be awake any minute now."

Fear trips the alarms in my head.

What's happening? I ask Emmaline. *Where are we?*

The dregs of a gentle warmth become a searing heat that blazes up my arms. Goose bumps rise along my skin.

Emmaline is afraid.

Show me where we are, I say.

It takes longer than I'm used to, but very slowly Emmaline fills my head with images of my room, of steel walls and glittering glass, long tables laid out with all manner of tools and blades, surgical equipment. Microscopes as tall as the wall. Geometric patterns in the ceiling glow with warm, bright light. And then there's me.

I am mummified in metal.

I'm lying supine on a gleaming table, thick horizontal stripes holding me in place. I am naked but for the carefully placed restraints keeping me from full exposure.

Realization dawns with painful speed.

I recognize these rooms, these tools, these walls. Even the smell—stale air, synthetic lemon, bleach and rust. Dread creeps through me slowly at first, and then all at once.

I am back on base in Oceania.

I feel suddenly ill.

I am a world away. An international flight away from my chosen family, back again in the house of horrors I grew up in. I have no recollection of how I got here, and I don't know what devastation Anderson left in my wake. I don't know where my friends are. I don't know what's become of Warner. I can't remember anything useful. I only know that something must be terribly, terribly wrong.

Even so, my fear feels different.

My captors—Anderson? This woman?—have obviously done something to me, because I can't feel my powers the way I normally do, but there's something about this horrible, familiar pattern that's almost comforting. I've woken up in chains more times than I can remember, and every time, I've found my way out. I'll find my way out of this, too.

And at least this time, I'm not alone.

Emmaline is here. As far as I'm aware, Anderson has no idea she's with me, and it gives me hope.

The silence is broken by a long-suffering sigh.

"Why do we need her to be awake, anyway?" the woman says. "Why can't we perform the procedure while she's asleep?"

"They're not my rules, Tatiana. You know as well as I do that Evie set this all in motion. Protocol states that the subject must be awake when the transfer is initiated."

I take it back.

I take it back.

Pure, unadulterated terror spikes through me, dispelling my earlier confidence with a single blow. It should've occurred to me right away that they'd try to do to me what Evie didn't get right the first time. Of course they would.

My sudden panic nearly gives me away.

"Two daughters with the exact same DNA fingerprint,"

Tatiana says suddenly. "Anyone else would think it was a wild coincidence. But Evie was always careful about having a backup plan, wasn't she?"

"From the very beginning," Anderson says quietly. "She made sure there was a spare."

The words are a blow I couldn't have anticipated.

A spare.

That's all I ever was, I realize. A spare part kept in captivity. A backup weapon in the case that all else failed.

Shatter me.

Break glass in case of emergency.

It takes everything I've got to remain still, to fight back the urge to swallow the sudden swell of emotion in my throat. Even now, even from the grave, my mother manages to wound me.

"How lucky for us," the woman says.

"Indeed," Anderson says, but there's tension in his voice. Tension I'm only just beginning to notice.

Tatiana starts rambling.

She begins talking about how clever Evie was to realize that someone had interfered with her work, how clever she was to have realized right away that Emmaline was the one who'd tampered with the results of the procedure she'd performed on me. Evie always knew, Tatiana is saying, that there was a risk in bringing me back to base in Oceania—and the risk, she says, was Emmaline's physical closeness.

"After all," Tatiana says, "the two girls hadn't been in such close proximity in nearly a decade. Evie was worried

Emmaline would try to make contact with her sister." A pause. "And she did."

"What is your point?"

"My point," Tatiana says slowly, like she's talking to a child, "is that this seems dangerous. Don't you think it's more than a little unwise to put the two girls under the same roof again? After what happened last time? Doesn't this seem a little . . . reckless?"

Stupid hope blooms in my chest.

Of course.

Emmaline's body is nearby. Maybe Emmaline's voice disappearing from my mind has nothing to do with her impending death—maybe she feels farther away simply because she *moved.* It's possible that upon reentry to Oceania the two parts of her consciousness reconnected. Maybe Emmaline feels distant now only because she's reaching out to me from her tank—the way she did the last time I was here.

Sharp, searing heat flashes behind my eyes, and my heart leaps at her response.

I am not alone, I say to her. *You are not alone.*

"You know as well as I do that this was the only way," Anderson says to Tatiana. "I needed Max's help. My injuries were too serious."

"You seem to be needing Max's help quite a lot these days," she says coldly. "And I'm not the only one who thinks your needs are becoming liabilities."

"Don't push me," he says quietly. "This isn't the day."

"I don't care. You know as well as I do that it would've been safer to initiate this transfer back at Sector 45, thousands of miles away from Emmaline. We had to transport the boy, too, remember? Extremely inconvenient. That you so desperately needed Max to assist with your vanity is an altogether different issue, one that concerns both your failings and your ineptitude."

Silence falls, heavy and thick.

I have no idea what's happening above my head, but I can only imagine the two of them are glaring each other into the ground.

"Evie had a soft spot for you," Tatiana says finally. "We all know that. We all know how willing she was to overlook your mistakes. But Evie is dead now, isn't she? And her daughter would be two for two if it weren't for Max's constant efforts to keep you alive. The rest of us are running out of patience."

Before Anderson has a chance to respond, a door slams open.

"Well?" A new voice. "Is it done?"

For the first time, Tatiana seems subdued. "She's not yet awake, I'm afraid."

"Then wake her up," the voice demands. "We're out of time. All the children have been tainted. We still have to get the rest of them under control and clear their minds as soon as possible."

"But not before we figure out what they know," Anderson says quickly, "and who they might've told."

Heavy footsteps move into the room, fast and hard. I hear a rustle of movement, a sudden brief gasp. "Haider told me something interesting when your men dragged him back here," the man says quietly. "He says you shot my daughter."

"It was a practical decision," Anderson says. "She and Kishimoto were possible targets. I had no choice but to take them both out."

It takes every ounce of my self-control to keep from screaming.

Kenji.

Anderson shot Kenji.

Kenji, and this man's daughter. He must be talking about Nazeera. Oh my God. Anderson shot Kenji and Nazeera. Which would make this man—

"Ibrahim, it was for the best." Tatiana's heels click against the floor. "I'm sure she's fine. They've got those healer girls, you know."

Supreme Commander Ibrahim ignores her.

"If my daughter is not returned to me alive," he says angrily, "I will personally remove your brain from your skull."

The door slams shut behind him.

"Wake her up," Anderson says.

"It's not that simple— There's a process—"

"I won't say it again, Tatiana." Anderson is shouting now, his temperature spiking without warning. "Wake her up now. I want this over with."

"Paris, you have to calm d—"

"I tried to kill her *months* ago." Metal slams against metal. "I told all of you to finish the job. If we're in this position right now—if Evie is dead—it's because no one listened to me when they should have."

"You are unbelievable." Tatiana laughs, but the sound is flat. "That you ever assumed you had the authority to murder Evie's daughter tells me everything I need to know about you, Paris. You're an idiot."

"Get out," he says, seething. "I don't need you breathing down my neck. Go check in on your own insipid daughter. I'll take care of this one."

"Feeling fatherly?"

"Get. Out."

Tatiana says nothing more. I hear the sound of a door opening and closing. The soft, distant clangs and chimes of metal and glass. I have no idea what Anderson is doing, but my heart is beating wildly. Angry, indignant Anderson is nothing to take lightly.

I would know.

And when I feel a sudden, ruthless spike of pain, I scream. Panic forces my eyes open.

"I had a feeling you were faking it," he says.

Roughly, he yanks the scalpel out of my thigh. I choke back another scream. I've hardly had a chance to catch my breath when, again, he buries the scalpel in my flesh—deeper this time. I cry out in agony, my lungs constricting. When he finally wrenches the tool free I nearly pass out from the pain. I'm making labored, gasping sounds, my chest so tightly bound I can't breathe properly.

"I was hoping you'd hear that conversation," Anderson says calmly, pausing to wipe the scalpel on his lab coat. The blood is dark. Thick. My vision fades in and out. "I wanted you to know that your mother wasn't stupid. I wanted you to know that she was aware that something had gone wrong. She didn't know the exact failings of the procedure—but she suspected the injections hadn't done everything they were meant to do. And when she suspected foul play, she made a contingency plan."

I'm still gasping for air, my head spinning. The pain in my leg is searing, clouding my mind.

"You didn't think she was that stupid, did you? Evie Sommers?" Anderson almost laughs. "Evie Sommers hasn't been stupid a day in her life. Even on the day she died, she died with a plan in place to save The Reestablishment, because she'd dedicated her life to this cause. This was it," he says, prodding at my wound. "You.

"You and your sister. You were her life's work, and she wasn't about to let it all go up in flames without a fight."

I don't understand, I try to say.

"I know you don't understand," he says. "Of course you don't understand. You never did inherit your mother's genius, did you? You never had her mind. No, you were only ever meant to be a tool, from the very beginning. So here's everything you need to understand: you now belong to me."

"No," I gasp. I struggle, uselessly, against the restraints. "No—"

I feel the sting and the fire at the same time. Anderson has stuck me with something, something that blazes through me with a pain so excruciating my heart hardly remembers to beat. My skin breaks out in an all-consuming sweat. My hair begins to stick to my face. I feel at once paralyzed and as if I'm falling, free-falling, sinking into the coldest depths of hell.

Emmaline, I cry.

My eyelids flutter. I see Anderson, flashes of Anderson, his eyes dark and troubled. He looks at me like he's finally got me exactly where he wants me, where he's always wanted me, and I understand then, without understanding why, exactly, that he's excited. I sense his happiness. I don't know how I know. I can just tell from the way he stands, the way he stares. He's feeling joyous.

It terrifies me.

My body makes another effort to move but the action is futile. There's no point in moving, no point in struggle.

This is over, something tells me.

I have lost.

I've lost the battle and the war. I've lost the boy. I've lost my friends. I've lost my will to live, the voice says to me.

And then I understand: Anderson is in my head.

My eyes are not open. My eyes might never again open.

Wherever I am is not in my control. I belong to Anderson now. I belong to The Reestablishment, where I've always belonged, *where you've always belonged,* he says to me, *where you will remain forever. I've been waiting for this moment for a very, very long time,* he says to me, *and now, finally, there's nothing you can do about it.*

Nothing.

Even then, I don't understand. Not right away. I don't understand even as I hear the machines roar to life. I don't understand even as I see the flash of light behind my eyelids. I hear my own breath, loud and strange and reverberating in my skull. I can feel my hands shaking. I can feel the metal sinking into the soft flesh of my body. I am here, strapped into steel against my will and there is no one to save me.

Emmaline, I cry.

A whisper of heat moves through me in response, a whisper so subtle, so quickly extinguished, I fear I might've imagined it.

Emmaline is nearly dead, Anderson says. *Once her body is removed from the tank, you will take her place. Until then, this is where you'll live. Until then, this is where you'll exist. This is all you were ever meant for,* he says to me.

This is all you will ever be.

KENJI

No one comes to the funeral.

It took two days to bury all the bodies. Castle tired his mind nearly to sickness digging up so much dirt. The rest of us used shovels. But there weren't many of us to do the work then, and there aren't enough of us to attend a funeral now.

Still, I sit here at dawn, perched atop a boulder, sitting high above the valley where we buried our friends. Teammates. My left arm is in a sling, my head hurts like a bitch, my heart is permanently broken.

I'm okay, otherwise.

Alia comes up behind me, so quiet I hardly even notice her. I hardly *ever* notice her. But there are too few bodies for her to hide behind now. I scoot over on the rock and she settles down beside me, the two of us staring out at the sea of graves below. She's holding two dandelions. Offers one to me. I take it.

Together, we drop the flowers, watching them as they float gently into the chasm. Alia sighs.

"You okay?" I ask her.

"No."

"Yeah." I nod.

Seconds pass. A gentle breeze pushes the hair out of my

face. I stare directly into the newborn sun, daring it to burn my eyes out.

"Kenji?"

"Yeah?"

"Where's Adam?"

I shake my head. Shrug.

"Do you think we'll find him?" she asks, her voice practically a whisper.

I look up.

There's a yearning there—something more than general concern in her tone. I turn fully to meet her eyes, but she won't look at me.

She's suddenly blushing.

"I don't know," I say to her. "I hope so."

"Me too," she says softly.

She rests her head on my shoulder. We stare out, into the distance. Let the silence devour our bodies.

"You did an amazing job, by the way." I nod at the valley below. "This is beautiful."

Alia really outdid herself. She and Winston.

The monuments they designed are simple and elegant, made from stone sourced from the land itself.

And there are two.

One for the lives lost here, at the Sanctuary, two days ago. The other for the lives lost *there,* at Omega Point, two months ago. The list of names is long. The injustice of it all roars through me.

Alia takes my hand. Squeezes.

I realize I'm crying.

I turn away, feeling stupid, and Alia lets go, gives me space to pull myself together. I wipe at my eyes with excessive force, angry with myself for falling apart. Angry with myself for being disappointed. Angry with myself for ever allowing hope.

We lost J.

We're not even sure exactly how it happened. Warner has been virtually comatose since that day, and getting information out of him has been near impossible. But it sounds like we never really stood a chance, in the end. One of Anderson's men had the preternatural ability to clone himself, and it took us too long to figure it out. We couldn't understand why their defense would suddenly double and triple just as we thought we were wearing them down. But it turns out Anderson had an inexhaustible supply of dummy soldiers. Warner couldn't get over it. It was the one thing he kept repeating, over and over—

I should've known, I should've known

—and despite the fact that Warner's been killing himself for the oversight, Castle says it was precisely because of Warner that any of us are still alive.

There weren't supposed to be *any* survivors. That was Anderson's decree. The command he gave after I went down.

Warner figured out the trick just in time.

His ability to harness the soldier's powers and use it

against him was our one saving grace, apparently, and when the dude realized he had competition, he took what he could get and ran.

Which means he managed to snag an unconscious Haider and Stephan. It means Anderson escaped.

And J, of course.

It means they got J.

"Should we head back?" Alia says quietly. "Castle was awake when I left. He said he wanted to talk to you."

"Yeah." I nod, get to my feet. Pull myself together. "Any update on James, by the way? Is he cleared for visitors yet?"

Alia shakes her head. Stands up, too. "Not yet," she says. "But he'll be awake soon. The girls are optimistic. Between his healing powers and theirs, they feel certain they'll be able to get him through it."

"Yeah," I say, taking a deep breath. "I'm sure you're right."

Wrong.

I'm not sure of anything.

The wreckage left in the wake of Anderson's attack has laid all of us low. Sonya and Sara are working around the clock. Sam was severely injured. Nazeera is still unconscious. Castle is weak. Hundreds of others are trying to heal.

A serious darkness has descended upon us all.

We fought hard, but we took too many hits. We were too few to begin with. There was only so much any of us could do.

These are the things I keep telling myself, anyway.

We start walking.

"This feels worse, doesn't it?" Alia says. "Worse than last time." She stops, suddenly, and I follow her line of sight, study the scene before us. The torn-down buildings, the detritus along the paths. We did our best to clean up the worst of it, but if I look in the wrong place at the wrong time, I can still find blood on broken tree branches. Shards of glass.

"Yeah," I say. "Somehow, this is so much worse."

Maybe because the stakes were higher. Maybe because we've never lost J before. Maybe because I've never seen Warner this lost or this broken. Angry Warner was better than this. At least angry Warner had some fight left in him.

Alia and I part ways when we enter the dining tent. She's been volunteering her time, going from cot to cot to check on people, offering food and water where necessary, and this dining tent is currently her place of work. The massive space has been made into a sort of convalescent home. Sonya and Sara are prioritizing major injuries; minor wounds are being treated the traditional way, by what's left of the original staff of doctors and nurses. This room is stacked, end to end, with those of us who are either healing from minor injuries, or resting after major intervention.

Nazeera is here, but she's sleeping.

I drop down in a seat next to her cot, checking up on her the way I do every hour. Nothing's changed. She's still lying here, still as stone, the only proof of life coming from a nearby monitor and the gentle movements of her breathing. Her wound was a lot worse than mine. The girls say she's going to be okay, but they think she'll be asleep until at least tomorrow. Even so, it kills me to look at her. Watching that girl go down was one of the hardest things I've ever had to witness.

I sigh, dragging a hand down my face. I still feel like shit, but at least I'm awake. Few of us are.

Warner is one of them.

He's still covered in dry blood, refusing to be helped. He's conscious, but he's been lying on his back, staring at the ceiling since the day he was dragged in here. If I didn't know any better, I'd think he was a corpse. I've been checking, too, every once in a while—making sure I caught that gentle rise and fall of his chest—just to be certain he was still breathing.

I think he's in shock.

Apparently, once he realized J was gone, he tore the remaining soldiers to pieces with his bare hands.

Apparently.

I don't buy it, of course, because the story sounds just a little to the left of what I consider credible, but then, I've been hearing all kinds of shit about Warner these last couple of days. He went from being only relatively consequential to becoming genuinely terrifying to assuming superhero status—in thirty-six hours. In a plot twist I never could've expected, people here are suddenly obsessed with him.

They think he saved our lives.

One of the volunteers checking my wound yesterday told me that she heard someone else say that they saw Warner uproot an entire tree with only one hand.

Translation: He probably broke off a tree branch.

Someone else told me that they'd heard from a friend that some girl had seen him save a cluster of children from friendly fire.

Translation: He probably shoved a bunch of kids to the ground.

Another person told me that Warner had single-handedly murdered nearly all the supreme soldiers.

Translation—

Okay, that last one is kind of true.

But I know Warner wasn't trying to do anyone around here a favor. He doesn't give a shit about being a hero.

He was only trying to save J's life.

"You should talk to him," Castle says, and I startle so badly he jumps back, freaking out for a second, too.

"Sorry, sir," I say, trying to slow my heart rate. "I didn't see you there."

"That's quite all right," Castle says. He's smiling, but his eyes are sad. Exhausted. "How are you doing?"

"As well as can be expected," I say. "How's Sam?"

"As well as can be expected," he says. "Nouria is struggling, of course, but Sam should be able to make a full recovery. The girls say it was mostly a flesh wound. Her skull was fractured, but they're confident they can get it nearly back to the way it was." He sighs. "They'll be all right, both of them. In time."

I study him for a moment, suddenly seeing him like I've never seen him before:

Old.

Castle's dreads are untied, hanging loose about his face, and something about the break from his usual style—locs tied neatly at the base of his neck—makes me notice things I'd never seen before. New gray hairs. New creases around his eyes, his forehead. It takes him a little longer to stand up straight like he used to. He seems worn out. Looking like he's been kicked down one too many times.

Kind of like the rest of us.

"I hate that this is the thing that seems to have conquered the distance between us," he says after a stretch of silence. "But now Nouria and I—both resistance leaders—have each suffered great losses. The whole thing has been hard for her, just as it was for me. She needs more time to recover."

I take a sharp breath.

Even the mention of that dark time inspires an ache in my heart. I don't allow myself to dwell for too long on the husk of a person Castle became after we lost Omega Point. If I do, the feelings overwhelm me so completely I pivot straight to anger. I know he was hurting. I know there was so much else going on. I know it was hard for everyone. But for me, losing Castle like that—however temporarily—was worse than losing everyone else. I needed him, and it felt like he'd abandoned me.

"I don't know," I say, clearing my throat. "It's not really the same thing, is it? What we lost— I mean, we lost literally everything in the bombing. Not only our people and our home, but years of research. Priceless equipment. Personal treasures." I hesitate, try to be delicate. "Nouria and Sam only lost half of their people, and their base is still standing. This loss isn't nearly as great."

Castle turns, surprised. "It's not as if it's a competition."

"I know that," I say. "It's just th—"

"And I wouldn't want my daughter to know the kind of grief we've experienced. You have no idea the depth of what she's already suffered in her young life. She certainly doesn't need to experience more pain to be deserving of your compassion."

"I didn't mean it like that," I say quickly, shaking my head. "I'm only trying to point out th—"

"Have you seen James yet?"

I gape at him, my mouth still shaped around an unspoken word. Castle just changed the subject so quickly it nearly gave me whiplash. This isn't like him. This isn't like *us*.

Castle and I never used to have trouble talking. We never avoided hard topics and sensitive conversations. But things have felt off for a little while now, if I'm being honest. Maybe ever since I realized Castle had been lying to me, all these years, about J. Maybe I've been a little less respectful lately. Crossed lines. Maybe all this tension is coming from me— maybe I'm the one pushing him away without realizing it.

I don't know.

I want to fix whatever is happening between us, but right now, I'm just too wrung out. Between J and Warner and James and unconscious Nazeera— My head is in such a weird place I'm not sure I have the bandwidth for much else.

So I let it go.

"No, I haven't seen James," I say, trying to sound upbeat. "Still waiting on that green light." Last I checked, James was in the medical tent with Sonya and Sara. James has his own healing abilities, so he should be fine, physically—I know that—but he's been through so much lately. The girls wanted to make sure he was fully rested and fed and hydrated before he had any visitors.

Castle nods.

"Warner is gone," he says after a moment, a non sequitur if there ever was one.

"What? No I just saw him. He—" I cut myself off as I glance up, expecting to find the familiar sight of him lying on his cot like a carcass. But Castle's right. He's gone.

I whip my head around, scanning the room for his retreating figure. I get nothing.

"I still think you should talk to him," Castle says, returning to his opening statement.

I bristle.

"You're the adult," I point out. "You're the one who wanted him to take refuge among us. You're the one who believed he could change. Maybe you should be the one to talk to him."

"That's not what he needs, and you know it." Castle sighs. Glances across the room. "Why is everyone so afraid of him? Why are *you* so afraid of him?"

"Me?" My eyes widen. "I'm not afraid of him. Or, I mean, whatever, I'm not the only one afraid of him. Though let's be real," I mutter, "anyone with two brain cells to rub together should be afraid of him."

Castle raises an eyebrow.

"Except for you, of course," I add hastily. "What reason would you have to be afraid of Warner? He's such a nice guy. Loves children. Big talker. Oh, and bonus: He no longer murders people professionally. No, now murdering people is just a fulfilling hobby."

Castle sighs, visibly annoyed.

I crack a smile. "Sir, all I'm saying is that we don't really know him, right? When Juliette was around—"

"Ella. Her name is Ella."

"Uh-huh. When she was around, Warner was tolerable. Barely. But now she's not around, and he's acting just like the guy I remember when I enlisted, the guy he was when he was working for his dad and running Sector 45. What reason does he have to be loyal or kind to the rest of us?"

Castle opens his mouth to respond, but just then arrives my salvation: lunch.

A smiling volunteer comes by, handing out simple salads in bowls of foil. I take the proffered food and plastic silverware with an overenthusiastic *thanks*, and promptly rip the lid off the container.

"Warner has been dealt a punishing blow," Castle says. "He needs us now more than ever."

I glance up at Castle. Shove a forkful of salad in my mouth. I chew slowly, still deciding how to respond, when I'm distracted by movement in the distance.

I look up.

Brendan and Winston and Ian and Lily are in the corner gathered around a small, makeshift table, all of them holding tinfoil lunch bowls. They're waving us over.

I gesture with a forkful of salad. Speak with my mouth full. "You want to join us?"

Castle sighs even as he stands, smoothing out invisible wrinkles in his black pants. I glance over at Nazeera's sleeping figure as I collect my things. I know, rationally, that she's going to be fine, but she's recovering from a full blow to the chest—not unlike J once did—and it hurts to see her so vulnerable. Especially for a girl who once laughed in my face at the prospect of ever being overpowered.

It scares me.

"Coming?" Castle says, glancing over his shoulder. He's already a few steps away, and I have no idea how long I've been standing here, staring at Nazeera.

"Oh, yeah," I say. "Right behind you."

The minute we sit down at their table, I know something is off. Brendan and Winston are sitting stiffly, side by side, and Ian doesn't do more than glance at me when I sit down. I find this reception especially strange, considering the fact that *they* flagged *me* down. You'd think they'd be happy to see me.

After a few minutes of uncomfortable silence, Castle speaks. "I was just telling Kenji," he says, "that he should be the one to talk to Warner."

Brendan looks up. "That's a great idea."

I shoot him a dark look.

"No, really," he says, carefully choosing a piece of potato to spear. Wait—where did they get potatoes? All I got was salad. "Someone definitely needs to talk to him."

"*Someone* definitely does," I say, irritated. I narrow my eyes at Brendan's potatoes. "Where'd you get those?"

"This is just what they gave me," Brendan says, looking up in surprise. "Of course, I'm happy to share."

I move quickly, jumping out of my seat to spear a chunk of potato from his bowl. I shove the whole piece in my mouth before I even sit back down, and I'm still chewing when I thank him.

He looks mildly repulsed.

I guess I am a bit of a caveman when Warner isn't around to keep me decent.

"Anyway, Castle's right," Lily says. "You should talk to him, and soon. I think he's kind of a loose cannon right now."

I stab a piece of lettuce, roll my eyes. "Can I maybe eat my lunch before everyone starts jumping down my throat? This is the first real meal I've had since I got shot."

"No one is jumping down your throat." Castle frowns.

"And I thought Nouria said the normal dining hours went back into effect yesterday morning."

"They did," I say.

"But you were shot three days ago," Winston says. "Which means—"

"All right, okay, calm down, Detective Winston. Can we change the subject, please?" I take another bite of lettuce. "I don't like this one."

Brendan puts down his knife and fork. Hard.

I straighten.

"Go talk to him," he says again, this time with an air of finality that surprises me.

I swallow my food. Too fast. Nearly choke.

"I'm serious," Brendan says, frowning as I cough up a lung. "This is a wretched time for all of us, and you've more of a connection with him than anyone else here. Which means you have a moral responsibility to find out what he's thinking."

"A moral responsibility?" My cough turns into a laugh.

"Yes. A moral responsibility. And Winston agrees with me."

I look up, raising my eyebrows at Winston. "I bet he does. I bet Winston agrees with you all the time."

Winston adjusts his glasses. He stabs blindly at his food and mutters, "I hate you," under his breath.

"Oh yeah?" I gesture between Winston and Brendan with my fork. "What the hell is going on here? This energy is super weird."

When no one answers me I kick Winston under the table. He turns away, mumbling nonsense before taking a long pull from his water glass.

"Okay," I say slowly. I pick up my own water glass. Take a sip. "Seriously. What's going on? You two playing footsie under the table or someshit?"

Winston goes full tomato.

Brendan picks up his utensils and, looking down at his plate, says, "Go ahead. Tell him."

"Tell me what?" I say, glancing between the two of them. When no one responds, I look over at Ian like, *What the hell?*

Ian only shrugs.

Ian's been quieter than usual. He and Lily have been spending a lot more time together lately, which is understandable, but it also means I haven't really seen him much in the last couple of days.

Castle suddenly stands.

He claps me on the back. "Talk to Mr. Warner," he says. "He's vulnerable right now, and he needs his friends."

"Are you—?" I make a show of looking around, over my shoulders. "I'm sorry, which friends are you referring to? Because as far as I know, Warner doesn't have any."

Castle narrows his eyes at me. "Don't do this," he says. "Don't deny your own emotional intelligence in favor of petty grievances. You know better. Be better. If you care about him at all, you will sacrifice your pride to reach out to him. Make sure he's okay."

"Why do you have to make it sound so dramatic?" I say,

looking away. "It's not that big of a deal. He'll survive."

Castle rests his hand on my shoulder. Forces me to meet his eyes. "No," he says to me. "He might not."

I wait until Castle is gone before I finally set down my fork. I'm irritated, but I know he's right. I mumble a general good-bye to my friends as I push away from the table, but not before I notice Brendan smiling triumphantly in my direction. I'm about to give him shit for it, but then I notice, with a start, that Winston has turned a shade of pink so magnificent you could probably see it from space.

And then, there it is: Brendan is holding Winston's hand under the table.

I gasp, audibly.

"Shut up," Winston says. "I don't want to hear it."

My enthusiasm withers. "You don't want to hear me say congratulations?"

"No, I don't want to hear you say *I told you so*."

"Yes, but I did fucking tell you so, didn't I?" A wave of happiness moves through me, conjures a smile. I didn't know I still had it in me.

Joy.

"I'm so happy for you guys," I say. "Truly. You just made this shitty day so much better."

Winston looks up, suspicious. But Brendan beams at me.

I stab a finger in their direction. "But if you two turn into Adam and Juliette clones I swear to God I will lose my mind."

Brendan's eyes go wide. Winston turns purple.

"Kidding!" I say. "I'm just kidding! Obviously I'm super

happy for you two!" After a dead beat, I clear my throat. "No but seriously, though."

"Fuck off, Kenji."

"Yup." I shoot a finger gun at Winston. "You got it."

"*Kenji*," I hear Castle call out. "Language."

I swivel around, surprised. I thought Castle was gone. "It wasn't me!" I shout back. "For the first time, I swear, it wasn't me!"

I see only the back of Castle's head as he turns away, but somehow, I can tell he's still annoyed.

I shake my head. I can't stop smiling.

It's time to regroup.

Pick up the pieces. Keep going. Find J. Find Adam. Tear down The Reestablishment, once and for all. And the truth is—we're going to need Warner's help. Which means Castle is right, I need to talk to Warner. Shit.

I look back at my friends.

Lily's got her head on Ian's shoulder, and he's trying to hide his smile. Winston flips me off, but he's laughing. Brendan pops another piece of potato in his mouth and shoos me away.

"Go on, then."

"All right, all right," I say. But just as I'm about to take the necessary steps forward, I'm saved yet again.

Alia comes running toward me, her face lit in an expression of happiness I rarely see on her. It's transformative. Hell, she's glowing. It's easy to lose track of Alia, who's quiet in both voice and presence. But when she smiles like that—

She looks beautiful.

"James is awake," she says, nearly out of breath. She's squeezing my arm so hard it's cutting off my circulation.

I don't care.

I'd been carrying this tension for almost two weeks now. Worrying, all this time, about James and whether he was okay. When I saw him for the first time the other day, bound and gagged by Anderson, I felt my knees give out. We had no idea how he was doing or what kind of trauma he'd sustained. But if the girls are letting him have visitors—

That's got to be a good sign.

I send up silent thanks to anyone who might be listening. Mom. Dad. Ghosts. I'm grateful.

Alia is half dragging me down the hall, and even though her physical effort isn't necessary, I let her do it. She seems so excited I don't have the heart to stop her.

"James is officially up and ready for visitors," she says, "and he asked to see *you*."

~~ELLA~~
JULIETTE

When I wake, I am cold.

I dress in the dark, pulling on crisp fatigues and polished boots. I pull my hair back in a tight ponytail and perform a series of efficient ablutions at the small sink in my chamber.

Teeth brushed. Face washed.

After three days of rigorous training, I was selected as a candidate for supreme soldier, honored with the prospect of serving our North American commander. Today is my opportunity to prove I deserve the position.

I lace my boots, knotting them twice.

Satisfied, I pull the release latch. The lock exhales as it comes open, and the seam around my door lets through a ring of light that cuts straight across my vision. I turn away from the glare only to be met by my own reflection in a small mirror above the sink. I blink, focusing.

Pale skin, dark hair, odd eyes.

I blink again.

A flash of light catches my eye in the mirror. I turn. The monitor adjacent to my sleep pod has been dark all night, but now it flashes with information:

Juliette Ferrars, report
Juliette Ferrars, report

My hand vibrates.

I glance down, palm up, as a soft blue light beams through the thin skin at my wrist.

report

I push open the door.

Cool morning air rushes in, shuddering against my face. The sun is still rising. Golden light bathes everything, briefly distorting my vision. Birds chirp as I climb my way up the side of the steep hill that protects my private chamber against the howling winds. I haul myself over the edge.

Immediately, I spot the compound in the distance.

Mountains stagger across the sky. A massive lake glitters nearby. I push against tangles of wild, ferocious gusts of wind as I hike toward base. For no reason at all, a butterfly lands on my shoulder.

I come to a halt.

I pluck the insect off my shirt, pinching its wings between my fingers. It flutters desperately as I study it, scrutinizing its hideous body as I turn it over in my hand. Slowly, I increase the intensity of my touch, and its flutters grow more desperate, wings snapping against my skin.

I blink. The butterfly thrashes.

A low hum drums up from its insect body, a soft buzz

that passes for a scream. I wait, patiently, for the creature to die, but it only beats its wings harder, resisting the inevitable. Irritated, I close my fingers, crushing it in my fist. I wipe its remains against an overgrown stalk of wheat and soldier on.

It's the fifth of May.

This is technically fall weather in Oceania, but the temperatures are erratic, inconsistent. Today the winds are particularly angry, which makes it unseasonably cold. My nose grows numb as I forge my way through the field; when I find a paltry slant of sunlight I lean into it, warming under its rays. Every morning and evening, I make this two-mile hike to base. My commander says it's necessary.

He did not explain why.

When I finally reach headquarters, the sun has shifted in the sky. I glance up at the dying star as I push open the front door, and the moment I step foot in the entry, I'm assaulted by the scent of burnt coffee. Quietly, I make my way down the hall, ignoring the sounds and stares of workers and armed soldiers.

Once outside his office, I stop. It's only a couple of seconds before the door slides open.

Supreme Commander Anderson looks up at me from his desk.

He smiles.

I salute.

"Step inside, soldier."

I do.

"How are you adjusting?" he says, closing a folder on his desk. He does not ask me to sit down. "It's been a few days since your transfer from 241."

"Yes, sir."

"And?" He leans forward, clasps his hands in front of him. "How are you feeling?"

"Sir?"

He tilts his head at me. Picks up a mug of coffee. The acrid scent of the dark liquid burns my nose. I watch him take a sip and the simple action conjures a stutter of emotion inside of me. Feeling presses against my mind in flashes of memory: a bed, a green sweater, a pair of black glasses, then nothing. Flint failing to spark a flame.

"Are you missing your family?" he asks.

"I have no family, sir."

"Friends? A boyfriend?"

Vague irritation rises up inside of me; I push it aside. "None, sir."

He relaxes in his chair, his smile growing wider. "It's better that way, of course. Easier."

"Yes, sir."

He gets to his feet. "Your work these past couple of days has been remarkable. Your training has been even more successful than we expected." He glances up at me then, waiting for a reaction.

I merely stare.

He takes another sip of the coffee before setting the cup down beside a sheaf of papers. He walks around the desk and stands in front of me, assessing. One step closer and the smell of coffee overwhelms me. I inhale the bitter, nutty scent and it floods my senses, leaving me vaguely nauseated. Still, I stare straight ahead.

The closer he gets, the more aware of him I become.

His physical presence is solid. Categorically male. He's a wall of muscle standing before me, and even the suit he wears can't hide the subtle, sculpted curves of his arms and legs. His face is hard, the line of his jaw so sharp I can see it even out of focus. He smells like coffee and something else, something clean and fragrant. It's unexpectedly pleasant; it fills my head.

"Juliette," he says.

A needle of unease pierces my mind. It is more than unusual for the supreme commander to call me by my first name.

"Look at me."

I obey, lifting my head to meet his eyes.

He stares down at me, his expression fiery. His eyes are a strange, stark shade of blue, and there's something about him—his heavy brow, his sharp nose—that stirs up ancient feelings inside my chest. Silence gathers around us, unspoken curiosities pulling us together. He searches my face for so long that I begin to search him, too. Somehow I know that this is rare; that he might never again give me the opportunity to look at him like this.

I seize it.

I catalog the faint lines creasing his forehead, the

starbursts around his eyes. I'm so close I can see the grain of his skin, rough but not yet leathery, his most recent shave evidenced in a microscopic nick at the base of his jaw. His brown hair is full and thick, his cheekbones high and his lips a dusky shade of pink.

He touches a finger to my chin, tilts up my face. "Your beauty is excessive," he says. "I don't know what your mother was thinking."

Surprise and confusion flare through me, but it does not presently occur to me to be afraid. I do not feel threatened by him. His words seem perfunctory. When he speaks, I catch a glimpse of a slight chip on his bottom incisor.

"Today," he says. "Things will change. You will shadow me from here on out. Your duty is to protect and serve my interests, and mine alone."

"Yes, sir."

His lips curve, just slightly. There's something there behind his eyes, something more, something else. "You understand," he says, "that you belong to me now."

"Yes, sir."

"My rule is your law. You will obey no other."

"Yes, sir."

He steps forward. His irises are so blue. A lock of dark hair curves across his eyes. "I am your master," he says.

"Yes, sir."

He's so close I can feel his breath against my skin. Coffee and mint and something else, something subtle, fermented. Alcohol, I realize.

He steps back. "Get on your knees."

I stare at him, frozen. The command was clear enough, but it feels like an error. "Sir?"

"On your knees, soldier. Now."

Carefully, I comply. The floor is hard and cold and my uniform is too stiff to make this position comfortable. Still, I remain on my knees for so long that a curious spider scuttles forward, peering at me from underneath a chair. I stare at Anderson's polished boots, the muscled curves of his calves noticeable even through his pants. The floor smells like bleach and lemon and dust.

When he commands me to, I look up.

"Now say it," he says softly.

I blink at him. "Sir?"

"Tell me that I am your master."

My mind goes blank.

A dull, warm sensation washes over me, a searching paralysis that locks my tongue, jams my mind. Fear propels through me, drowning me, and I fight to break the surface, clawing my way back to the moment.

I meet his eyes.

"You are my master," I say.

His stiff smile bends, curves. Joy catches fire in his eyes. "Good," he says softly. "Very good. How strange that you might turn out to be my favorite yet."

KENJI

I stop short at the door.

Warner is here.

Warner and James, together.

James was given his own private section of the MT—which is otherwise full and cramped—and the two of them are here, Warner sitting in a chair beside James's bed, James propped up against a stack of pillows. I'm so relieved to see him looking okay. His dirty-blond hair is a little too long, but his light, bright blue eyes are open and animated. Still, he looks more than a little tired, which probably explains the IV hooked up to his body.

Under normal circumstances, James should be able to heal himself, but if his body is drained, it makes the job harder. He must've arrived malnourished and dehydrated. The girls are probably doing what they can to help speed up the recovery process. I feel a rush of relief.

James will be better soon. He's such a strong kid. After everything he's been through—

He'll get through this, too. And he won't be alone.

I glance again at Warner, who looks only marginally better than the last time I saw him. He really needs to wash that blood off his body. It's not like Warner to overlook basic rules of hygiene—which should be proof enough that the guy is close to a full-on breakdown—but for now, at least, he seems okay. He and James appear to be deep in conversation.

I remain at the door, eavesdropping. It only belatedly occurs to me that I should give them privacy, but by then I'm too invested to walk away. I'm almost positive Anderson told James the truth about Warner. Or, I don't know, exactly. I can't actually imagine a scenario in which Anderson would gleefully reveal to James that Warner is his brother, or that Anderson is his dad. But somehow I can just tell that James knows. *Someone* told him. I can tell by the look on his face.

This is the come-to-Jesus moment.

This is the moment where Warner and James finally come face-to-face not as strangers, but as brothers. Surreal.

But they're speaking quietly, and I can only catch bits and pieces of their conversation, so I decide to do something truly reprehensible: I go invisible, and step farther into the room.

The moment I do, Warner stiffens.

Shit.

I see him glance around, his eyes alert. His senses are too sharp.

Quietly, I back up a few steps.

"You're not answering my question," James says, poking Warner in the arm. Warner shakes him off, his eyes narrowed at a spot a mere foot from where I'm standing.

"Warner?"

Reluctantly, Warner turns to face the ten-year-old. "Yes," he says, distracted. "I mean— What were you saying?"

"Why didn't you ever tell me?" James says, sitting up straighter. The bedsheets fall down, puddle in his lap. "Why didn't you say anything to me before? That whole time we lived together—"

"I didn't want to scare you."

"Why would I be scared?"

Warner sighs, stares out the window when he says, quietly, "Because I'm not known for my charm."

"That's not fair," James says. He looks genuinely upset, but his visible exhaustion is keeping him from reacting too strongly. "I've seen a lot worse than you."

"Yes. I realize that now."

"And *no one* told me. I can't believe no one told me. Not even Adam. I've been so mad at him." James hesitates. "Did everyone know? Did Kenji know?"

I stiffen.

Warner turns again, this time staring precisely in my direction when he says, "Why don't you ask him yourself?"

"Son of a bitch," I mutter, my invisibility melting away.

Warner almost smiles. James's eyes go wide.

This was not the reunion I was hoping for.

Still, James's face breaks into the biggest smile, which—I'm not going to lie—does wonders for my self-esteem. He throws off the covers and tries to jump out of bed, barefoot and oblivious to the needle stuck in his arm, and in those two and a half seconds I manage to experience both joy and terror.

I shout a warning, rushing forward to stop him from ripping open the flesh of his forearm, but Warner beats me to it. He's already on his feet, not so gently pushing the kid back down.

"Oh." James blushes. "Sorry."

I tackle him anyway, pulling him in for a long, excessive hug, and the way he clings to me makes me think I'm the first to do it. I try to fight back a rush of anger, but I'm unsuccessful. He's a ten-year-old kid, for God's sake. He's been through hell. How has no one given him the physical reassurance he almost certainly needs right now?

When we finally break apart, James has tears in his eyes. He wipes at his face and I turn away, trying to give him privacy, but when I take a seat at the foot of James's bed I catch a flash of pain steal in and out of Warner's eyes. It lasts for only half a second, but it's enough to make me feel bad for the guy. And it's enough to make me think he might be human again.

"Hey," I say, speaking to Warner directly for the first time. "So what, uh— What are you doing here?"

Warner looks at me like I'm an insect. His signature look. "What do you think I'm doing here?"

"Really?" I say, unable to hide my surprise. "That's so decent of you. I didn't think you'd be so . . . emotionally . . . responsible." I clear my throat. Smile at James. He's studying us curiously. "But I'm happy to be wrong, bro. And I'm sorry I misjudged you."

"I'm here to gather information," Warner says coldly. "James is one of the only people who might be able to tell us where my father is located."

My compassion quickly turns to dust.

Catches fire.

Turns to rage.

"You're here to interrogate him?" I say, nearly shouting. "Are you insane? The kid has only barely recovered from unbelievable trauma, and you're here trying to mine him for information? He was probably *tortured*. He's a freaking *child*. What the hell is wrong with you?"

Warner is unmoved by my theatrics. "He was not tortured."

That stops me cold.

I turn to James. "You weren't?"

James shakes his head. "Not exactly."

"Huh." I frown. "I mean, don't get me wrong—I'm thrilled—but if he didn't torture you, what did Anderson do with you?"

James shrugs. "He mostly left me in solitary confinement. They didn't beat me," he says, rubbing absently at his ribs, "but the guards were pretty rough. And they didn't feed me much." He shrugs again. "But honestly, the worst part was not seeing Adam."

I pull James into my arms again, hold him tight. "I'm

so sorry," I say gently. "That sounds horrible. And they wouldn't let you see Adam at all? Not even once?" I pull back. Look him in the eye. "I'm so, so sorry. I'm sure he's okay, little man. We'll find him. Don't worry."

Warner makes a sound. A sound that seems almost like a laugh.

I spin around angrily. "What the hell is wrong with you?" I say. "This isn't funny."

"Isn't it? I find the situation hilarious."

I'm about to say something to Warner I really shouldn't say in front of a ten-year-old, but when I glance back at James, I pull up short. James is rapidly shaking his head at me, his bottom lip trembling. He looks like he's about to cry again.

I turn back to Warner. "Okay, what is going on?"

Warner almost smiles when he says, "They weren't kidnapped."

My eyebrows fly up my forehead. "Say what now?"

"They weren't kidnapped."

"I don't understand."

"Of course you don't."

"This is not the time, bro. Tell me what's going on."

"Kent tracked down Anderson on his own," Warner says, his gaze shifting to James. "He offered his allegiance in exchange for protection."

My entire body goes slack. I nearly fall off the bed.

Warner goes on: "Kent wasn't lying when he said he would try for amnesty. But he left out the part about being a traitor."

"No. No way. No fucking way."

"There was never an abduction," Warner says. "No kidnapping. Kent bartered himself in exchange for James's protection."

This time, I actually fall off the bed. "Barter himself—how?" I manage to drag myself up off the floor, stumbling to my feet. "What does Adam even have to barter with? Anderson already knows all our secrets."

It's James who says quietly, "He gave them his power."

I stare at the kid, blinking like an idiot.

"I don't understand," I say. "How can you give someone your power? You can't just give someone your power. Right? It's not like a pair of pants you can just take off and hand over."

"No," Warner says. "But it's something The Reestablishment knows how to harvest. How else do you think my father took Sonya's and Sara's healing powers?"

"Adam told them what he can d-do," James says, his voice breaking. "He told them that he can use his power to turn other people's powers off. He thought it m-might be useful to them."

"Imagine the possibilities," Warner says, affecting awe. "Imagine how they might weaponize a power like that for global use—how they could make such a thing so powerful they could effectively shut down every single rebel group in the world. Reduce their *Unnatural* opposition to zero."

"Jesus fucking Christ."

I think I'm going to pass out. I actually feel faint. Dizzy.

Like I can't breathe. Like this is impossible. "No way," I'm saying. I'm practically breathing the words. "No way. Not possible."

"I once said that Kent's ability was useless," Warner says quietly. "But I see now that I was a fool."

"He didn't want to do it," James says. He's actively crying now, the silent tears moving down his face. "I swear he only did it to save me. He offered the only thing he had—the only thing he thought they'd want—to keep me safe. I know he didn't want to do it. He was just desperate. He thought he was doing the right thing. He kept telling me he was going to keep me safe."

"By running into the arms of the man who abused him his whole life?" I'm clutching my hair in my hands. "This doesn't make any sense. How does this— *How—? How?*"

I look up suddenly, realizing.

"And then look what he did," I say, stunned. "After everything, Anderson still used you as bait. He brought you here as leverage. He would've *killed* you, even after everything Adam gave up."

"Kent was a desperate idiot," Warner says. "That he was ever willing to trust my father with James's well-being tells you exactly how far gone he was."

"He was desperate, but he's not an idiot," James says angrily, his eyes refilling with tears. "He loves me and he was just trying to keep me safe. I'm so worried about him. I'm so scared something happened to him. And I'm so scared Anderson did something awful to him." James swallows, hard. "What are we going to do now? How are we going to get Adam and Juliette back?"

I squeeze my eyes shut, try to take deep breaths. "Listen, don't stress about this, okay? We're going to get them back. And when we do, I'm going to murder Adam myself."

James gasps.

"Ignore him," Warner says. "He doesn't mean it."

"Yes, I damn well do mean it."

Warner pretends not to hear me. "According to the information I gathered just moments before you barged in here," he says calmly, "it sounds like my father was holding court back in Sector 45, just as Sam predicated. But he won't be there now, of that I'm certain."

"How can you be certain of *anything* right now?"

"Because I know my father," he says. "I know what matters most to him. And I know that when he left here, he was severely, gruesomely injured. There's only one place he'd go in a state like that."

I blink at him. "Where?"

"Oceania. Back to Maximillian Sommers, the only person capable of piecing him back together."

That stops me dead. "*Oceania?* Please tell me you're joking. We have to go back to Oceania?" I groan. "Dammit. That means we have to steal another plane."

"*We*," he says, irritated, "aren't doing anything."

"Of course we—"

Just then, the girls walk in. They come up short at the sight of me and Warner. Two sets of eyes blink at us.

"What are you doing here?" they ask at the same time.

Warner is on his feet in an instant. "I was just leaving."

"I think you mean *we* were just leaving," I say sharply.

Warner ignores me, nods at James, and heads for the door. I'm following him out of the room before I remember, suddenly—

"James," I say, spinning around. "You're going to be okay, you know that, right? We're going to find Adam and bring him home and make all of this okay. Your job from here on out is to relax and eat chocolate and sleep. All right? Don't worry about anything. Do you understand?"

James blinks at me. He nods.

"Good." I step forward to plant a kiss on the top of his head. "Good," I say again. "You're going to be just fine. Everything is going to be fine. I'm going to make sure everything is fine, okay?"

James stares up at me. "Okay," he says, wiping away the last of his tears.

"Good," I say for the third time, and nod, still staring at his small, innocent face. "Okay, I'm going to go make that happen now. Cool?"

Finally, James smiles. "Cool."

I smile back, giving him everything I've got, and then dart out the door, hoping to catch Warner before he tries to rescue J without me.

~~ELLA~~ JULIETTE

It is a relief not to speak.

Something changed between us this morning, something broke. Anderson seems relaxed in front of me in a way that seems unorthodox, but it's not my business to question him. I'm honored to have this position, to be his most trusted supreme soldier, and that's all that matters. Today is my first official day of work, and I'm happy to be here, even when he ignores me completely.

In fact, I enjoy it.

I find comfort in pretending to disappear. I exist only to shadow him as he moves from one task to another. I stand aside, staring straight ahead. I do not watch him as he works, but I feel him, constantly. He takes up all available space. I am attuned to his every movement, his every sound. It is my job now to know him completely, to anticipate his needs and fears, to protect him with my life, and to serve his interests entirely.

So I listen, for hours, to the details.

The creak of his chair as he leans back, considering. The sighs that escape him as he types. Leather chair and wool pants meeting, shifting. The dull thud of a ceramic mug hitting the surface of a wooden desk. The tinkle of crystal, the quick pour of bourbon. The sharp, sweet scent of tobacco and the rustle of tissue-thin paper. Keystrokes. A pen scratching. The sudden tear and fizz of a match. Sulfur. Keystrokes. A snap of a rubber band. Smoke, making my eyes tear. A stack of papers slapping together like a settling deck of cards. His voice, deep and melodic on a series of phone calls so brief I can't tell them apart. Keystrokes. He never seems to require use of the bathroom. I do not think about my own needs, and he does not ask. Keystrokes. Occasionally he looks up at me, studying me, and I keep my eyes straight ahead. Somehow, I can feel his smile.

I am a ghost.

I wait.

I hear little. I learn little.

Finally—

"Come."

He's on his feet and out the door and I hasten to follow. We're up high, on the top floor of the compound. The hallways circle around an interior courtyard, in the center of which is a large tree, branches heavy with orange and red leaves. Fall colors. I glance, without moving my head, outside one of the many tall windows gracing the halls, and my mind registers the incongruence of the two images. Outside, things are a strange mix of green and desolate. Inside, this tree is warm and rosy-hued. Perfect autumn foliage.

I shake off the thought.

I have to walk twice as fast to keep up with Anderson's long strides. He stops for no one. Men and women in lab coats jump aside as we approach, mumbling apologies in our wake, and I'm surprised by the giddy sensation that rises up inside of me. I like their fear. I enjoy this power, this feeling of unapologetic dominion.

Dopamine floods my brain.

I pick up speed, still hurrying to keep up. It occurs to me then that Anderson never looks back to make sure I'm following him, and it makes me wonder what he'd do if he discovered I was missing. And then, just as quickly, the thought strikes me as bizarre. He has no reason to look back. I would never go missing.

The compound feels busier than usual today. Announcements blare through the speakers and the air around me fills with fervor. Names are called; demands made. People come and go.

We take the stairs.

Anderson never stops, never seems out of breath. He moves with the strength of a younger man but with the kind of confidence acquired only by age. He carries himself with a certainty both terrifying and aspirational. Faces pale at the sight of him. Most look away. Some can't help but stare. One woman nearly faints when his body brushes against hers, and Anderson doesn't even break his stride when she causes a scene.

I am fascinated.

The speakers crackle. A smooth, robotic female voice announces a code-green situation so calmly I can't help but be surprised by the collective reaction. I witness something akin to chaos as doors slam open around the building. It all seems to happen in sync, a domino effect echoing along corridors from top to bottom of the compound. Men and women in lab coats surge and swarm all levels, jamming the walkways as they scuttle along.

Still, Anderson does not stop. The world revolves around him, makes room for him. Slows when he speeds up. He does not accommodate anyone. Anything.

I am taking notes.

Finally, we reach a door. Anderson presses his hand against the biometric scanner, then peers into a camera that reads his eyes.

The door fissures open.

I smell something sterile, like antiseptic, and the moment we step into the room the scent burns my nose, causing my eyes to tear. The entrance is unusual; a short hallway that hides the rest of the room from immediate view. As we approach, I hear three monitors beep at three different decibel levels. When we round the corner, the room quadruples in size. The space is vast and bright, natural light combining with the searing white glow of artificial bulbs overhead.

There's little else here but a single bed and the figure strapped into it. The beeping is coming not from three machines, but seven, all of which seem to be affixed to the unconscious body of a boy. I don't know him, but he can't be much older than I am. His hair is cropped close to his scalp, a soft buzz of brown interrupted only by the wires drilled into his skull. There's a sheet pulled up to his neck, so I can't see much more than his resting face, but the sight of him there, strapped down like that, reminds me of something.

A flash of memory flares through me.

It's vague, distorted. I try to peel back the hazy layers, but when I manage a glimpse of something—a cave, a tall black man, a tank full of water—I feel a sharp, electrifying sting of rage that leaves my hands shaking. It unmoors me.

I take a jerky step back and shake my head a fraction of an inch, trying to compose myself, but my mind feels foggy, confused. When I finally pull myself together, I realize Anderson is watching me.

Slowly, he takes a step forward, his eyes narrowed in my direction. He says nothing, but I feel, without knowing why, exactly, that I'm not allowed to look away. I'm supposed to maintain eye contact for as long as he wants. It's brutal.

"You felt something when you walked in here," he says.

It's not a question. I'm not sure it requires an answer. Still—

"Nothing of consequence, sir."

"Consequence," he says, a hint of a smile playing at his lips. He takes a few steps toward one of the massive windows, clasps his hands behind his back. For a while, he's silent.

"So interesting," he says finally. "That we never did discuss consequences."

Fear slithers, creeps up my spine.

He's still staring out the window when he says softly, "You will not withhold anything from me. Everything you feel, every emotion you experience—it belongs to me. Do you understand?"

"Yes, sir."

"You felt something when you walked in here," he says again. This time, his voice is heavy with something, something dark and terrifying.

"Yes, sir."

"And what was it?"

"I felt anger, sir."

He turns around at that. Raises his eyebrows.

"After anger, I felt confusion."

"But anger," he says, stepping toward me. "Why anger?"

"I don't know, sir."

"Do you recognize this boy?" he says, pointing at the prone body without even looking at it.

"No, sir."

"No." His jaw clenches. "But he reminds you of someone."

I hesitate. Tremors threaten, and I will them away. Anderson's gaze is so intense I can hardly meet his eyes.

I glance again at the boy's sleeping face.

"Yes, sir."

Anderson's eyes narrow. He waits for more.

"Sir," I say quietly. "He reminds me of you."

Unexpectedly, Anderson goes still. Surprise rearranges his expression and suddenly, startlingly—

He laughs.

It's a laugh so genuine it seems to shock him even more

than it shocks me. Eventually, the laughter settles into a smile. Anderson shoves his hands in his pockets and leans against the window frame. He stares at me with something resembling fascination, and it's such a pure moment, a moment so untainted by malice that he strikes me, suddenly, as beautiful.

More than that.

The sight of him—something about his eyes, something about the way he moves, the way he smiles— The sight of him suddenly stirs something in my heart. Ancient heat. A kaleidoscope of dead butterflies kicked up by a brief, dry gust of wind.

It leaves me feeling sick.

The stony look returns to his face. "That. Right there." He draws a circle in the air with his index finger. "That look on your face. What was that?"

My eyes widen. Unease floods through me, heating my cheeks.

For the first time, I falter.

He moves swiftly, charging toward me so angrily I wonder at my ability to remain steady. Roughly, he takes my chin in his hand, tilts up my face. There are no secrets here, this close to him. I can hide nothing.

"Now," he says, his voice low. Angry. "Tell me now."

I break eye contact, trying desperately to gather my thoughts, and he barks at me to look at him.

I force myself to meet his eyes. And then I hate myself, hate my mouth for betraying my mind. Hate my mind for thinking at all.

"You— You are extremely handsome, sir."

Anderson drops his hand like he's been burned. He backs away, looking, for the first time—

Uncomfortable.

"Are you—" He stops, frowns. And then, too soon, anger clouds his expression. His voice is practically a growl when he says, "You are lying to me."

"No, sir." I hate the sound of my voice, the breathy panic.

His eyes sharpen. He must see something in my expression that gives him pause, because the anger evaporates from his face.

He blinks at me.

Then, carefully, he says: "In the middle of all of this"—he waves around the room, at the sleeping figure hooked up to the machines—"of all the things that could be going through your mind, you were thinking . . . that you find me attractive."

A traitorous heat floods my face. "Yes, sir."

Anderson frowns.

He seems about to say something, and then hesitates. For the first time, he seems unmoored.

A few seconds of tortured silence stretch between us, and I'm not sure how best to proceed.

"This is unsettling," Anderson finally says, and mostly to himself. He presses two fingers to the inside of his wrist, and lifts his wrist to his mouth.

"Yes," he says quietly. "Tell Max there's been an unusual development. I need to see him at once."

Anderson spares me a brief glance before dismissing, with a single shake of his head, the entire mortifying exchange.

He stalks toward the boy strapped down on the bed and says, "This young man is part of an ongoing experiment."

I'm not sure what to say, so I say nothing.

Anderson bends over the boy, toying with various wires, and then stiffens, suddenly. Looks up at me out of the corner of his eye. "Can you imagine why this boy is part of an experiment?"

"No sir."

"He has a gift," Anderson says, straightening. "He came to me voluntarily and offered to share it with me."

I blink, still uncertain how to respond.

"But there are many of you—*Unnaturals*—running wild on this planet," Anderson says. "So many powers. So many different abilities. Our asylums are teeming with them, overrun with power. I have access to nearly anything I want. So what makes him special, hmm?" He tilts his head at me. "What power could he possibly have that would be greater than yours? More useful?"

Again, I say nothing.

"Do you want to know?" he asks, a hint of a smile touching his lips.

This feels like a trick. I consider my options.

Finally, I say, "I want to know only if you want to tell me, sir."

Anderson's smile blooms. White teeth. Genuine pleasure.

I feel my chest warm at his quiet praise. Pride straightens my shoulders. I avert my eyes, staring quietly at the wall.

Still, I see Anderson turn away again, appraising the boy with another single, careful look. "These powers were wasted on him anyway."

He removes the touchpad slotted into a compartment of the boy's bed and begins tapping the digital screen, scrolling and scanning for information. He looks up, once, at the monitors beeping out various vitals, and frowns. Finally, he sighs, dragging a hand through his perfectly arranged hair. I think it looks better for being mussed. Warmer. Softer. Familiar.

The observation frightens me.

I turn away sharply and glance out the window, wondering, suddenly, if I will ever be allowed to use the bathroom.

"Juliette."

The angry timbre of his voice sends my heart racing. I straighten in an instant. Look straight ahead.

"Yes, sir," I say, sounding a little breathless.

I realize then that he's not even looking at me. He's still typing something into the touchpad when he says, calmly, "Were you daydreaming?"

"No, sir."

He returns the touchpad to its compartment, the pieces connecting with a satisfying metallic *click*.

He looks up.

"This is growing tiresome," he says quietly. "I'm already

losing patience with you, and we haven't even come to the end of your first day." He hesitates. "Do you want to know what happens when I lose patience with you, Juliette?"

My fingers tremble; I clench them into fists. "No, sir."

He holds out his hand. "Then give me what belongs to me."

I take an uncertain step forward and his outstretched hand flies up, palm out, stopping me in place. His jaw clenches.

"I am referring to your mind," he says. "I want to know what you were thinking when you lost your head long enough to gaze out the window. I want to know what you are thinking right now. I will always want to know what you're thinking," he says sharply. "In every moment. I want every word, every detail, every emotion. Every single loose, fluttering thought that passes through your head, I want it," he says, stalking toward me. "Do you understand? It's mine. You are *mine*."

He comes to a halt just inches from my face.

"Yes, sir," I say, my voice failing me.

"I will only ask this once more," he says, making an effort to moderate his voice. "And if you ever make me work this hard again to get the answers I need, you will be punished. Is that clear?"

"Yes, sir."

A muscle jumps in his jaw. His eyes narrow. "What were you daydreaming about?"

I swallow. Look at him. Look away.

Quietly, I say:

"I was wondering, sir, if you would ever let me use the bathroom."

Anderson's face goes suddenly blank.

He seems stunned. He regards me a moment longer before saying, flatly: "You were wondering if you could use the bathroom."

"Yes, sir." My face heats.

Anderson crosses his arms across his chest. "That's all?"

I feel suddenly compelled to tell him what I thought about his hair, but I fight against the urge. Guilt floods through me at the indulgence, but my mind is soothed by a strange, familiar warmth, and suddenly I feel no guilt at all for being only partly truthful.

"Yes, sir. That's all."

Anderson tilts his head at me. "No new surges of anger? No questions about what we're doing here? No concerns over the well-being of the boy"—he points—"or the powers he might have?"

"No, sir."

"I see," he says.

I stare.

Anderson takes a deep breath and undoes a button of his blazer. He pushes both hands through his hair. Begins to pace.

He's becoming flustered, I realize, and I don't know what to do about it.

"It's almost funny," he says. "This is exactly what I wanted, and yet, somehow, I'm disappointed."

He takes a deep, sharp breath, and spins around.

Studies me.

"What would you do," he says, nodding his head an inch to his left, "if I asked you to throw yourself out that window?"

I turn, examining the large window looming over us both.

It's a massive, circular stained glass window that takes up half the wall. Colors scatter across the ground, creating a beautiful, distracted work of art over the polished concrete floors. I walk over to window, run my fingers along the ornate panes of glass. I peer down at the expanse of green below. We're at least five hundred feet above the ground, but the distance doesn't inspire my fear. I could make that jump easily, without injury.

I look up. "I would do it with pleasure, sir."

He takes a step closer. "What if I asked you to do it without using your powers? What if it was simply my desire that you throw yourself out the window?"

A wave of searing, blistering heat moves through me, seals shut my mouth. Binds my arms. I can't pry my own mouth open against the terrifying assault, but I can only imagine it's part of this challenge.

Anderson must be trying to test my allegiance.

He must be trying to trap me into a moment of disobedience. Which means I need to prove myself. My loyalty.

It takes an extraordinary amount of my own supernatural strength to fight back the invisible forces clamping my mouth shut, but I manage it. And when I can finally speak, I say,

"I would do it with pleasure, sir."

Anderson takes yet another step closer, his eyes glittering with something— Something brand-new. Something akin to wonder.

"Would you, really?" he says softly.

"Yes, sir."

"Would you do anything I asked you to do? Anything at all?"

"Yes, sir."

Anderson's still holding my gaze when he lifts his wrist to his mouth again and says quietly:

"Come in here. Now."

He drops his hand.

My heart begins to pound. Anderson refuses to look away from me, his eyes growing bluer and brighter by the second. It's almost like he knows that his eyes alone are enough to upset my equilibrium. And then, without warning, he grabs my wrist. I realize too late that he's checking my pulse.

"So fast," he says softly. "Like a little bird. Tell me, Juliette. Are you afraid?"

"No, sir."

"Are you excited?"

"I— I don't know, sir."

The door slides open and Anderson drops my wrist. For the first time in minutes, Anderson looks away from me, finally breaking some painful, invisible connection between us. My body goes slack with relief and, remembering myself, I quickly straighten.

A man walks in.

Dark hair, dark eyes, pale skin. He's young, younger than Anderson, I think, but older than me. He wears a headset. He looks uncertain.

"Juliette," Anderson says, "this is Darius."

I turn to face Darius.

Darius says nothing. He looks paralyzed.

"I won't be requiring Darius's services anymore," Anderson says, glancing in my direction.

Darius blanches. Even from where I'm standing, I can see his body begin to tremble.

"Sir?" I say, confused.

"Isn't it obvious?" Anderson says. "I would like you to dispose of him."

Understanding dawns. "Certainly, sir."

The moment I turn in Darius's direction, he screams; it's a sharp, bloodcurdling sound that irritates my ears. He makes a run for the door and I pivot quickly, throwing out my arm to stop him. The force of my power sends him flying the rest of the way to the exit, his body slamming hard against the steel wall.

He slumps, with a soft moan, to the ground.

I open my palm. He screams.

Power surges through me, filling my blood with fire. The feeling is intoxicating. Delicious.

I lift my hand and Darius's body lifts off the floor, his head thrown back in agony, his body run through by invisible rods. He continues to scream and the sound fills my ears, floods my body with endorphins. My skin hums with his energy. I close my eyes.

Then I close my fist.

Fresh screams pierce the silence, echoing around the vast, cavernous space. I feel a smile tugging at my lips and I lose myself in the feeling, in the freedom of my own power. There's a joy in this, in using my strength so freely, in finally letting go.

Bliss.

My eyes flutter open but I feel drugged, deliriously happy as I watch his seized, suspended body begin to convulse. Blood spurts from his nose, bubbles up inside his open, gasping mouth. He's choking. Nearly dead. And I'm just beginning t—

The fire leaves my body so suddenly it sends me stumbling backward.

Darius falls, with a bone-cracking thud, to the floor.

A desperate emptiness burns through me, leaves me feeling faint. I hold my hands up as if in prayer, trying to figure out what happened, feeling suddenly close to tears. I spin around, trying to understand—

Anderson is pointing a weapon at me.

I drop my hands.

Anderson drops his weapon.

Power surges through me once more and I take a deep, grateful breath, finding relief in the feeling as it floods my senses, refilling my veins. I blink several times, trying to clear my head, but it's Darius's pathetic, agonized whimpers that bring me back to the present moment. I stare at his broken body, the shallow pools of blood on the floor. I feel vaguely annoyed.

"Incredible."

I turn around.

Anderson is staring at me with unvarnished amazement. "Incredible," he says again. "That was incredible."

I stare at him, uncertain.

"How do you feel?" he asks.

"Disappointed, sir."

His eyebrows pull together. "Why disappointed?"

I glance at Darius. "Because he's still alive, sir. I didn't complete the task."

Anderson's face breaks into a smile so wide it electrifies his features. He looks young. He looks kind. He looks wonderful.

"My God," he says softly. "You're perfect."

KENJI

"Hey," I call out. "Wait up!"

I'm still sprinting after Warner and, in a move that surprises absolutely no one, he doesn't wait. He doesn't even slow down. In fact, I'm pretty sure he speeds up.

I realize, as I pick up the pace, that I haven't felt fresh air in a couple of days. I look around as I go, trying to take in the details. The sky is bluer than I've ever seen it. There's no cloud in sight for miles. I don't know if this weather is unique to the geographical location of Sector 241, or if it's just regular climate change. Regardless, I take a deep breath. Air feels good.

I was getting claustrophobic in the dining hall, spending endless hours with the ill and injured. The colors of the room had begun to bleed together, all the linen and ash-colored cots and the too-bright, unnatural light. The smells were intense, too. Blood and bleach. Antiseptic. It was making my head swim. I woke up with a massive headache this morning—though, to be fair, I wake up with a massive headache almost every morning—but being outside is beginning to soothe the ache.

Who knew.

It's nice out here, even if it's a little hot in this outfit. I'm wearing a pair of old fatigues I found in my room. Sam and Nouria made sure from the start that we had everything we needed—even now, even after the battle. We have toiletries. Clean clothes.

Warner, on the other hand—

I squint at his retreating figure. I can't believe he still hasn't taken a shower. He's still wearing Haider's leather jacket, but it's practically destroyed. His black pants are torn, his face still smudged with what I can only imagine is a combination of blood and dirt. His hair is wild. His boots are dull. And somehow—*somehow*—he still manages to look put together. I don't get it.

I slow my pace when I pull up next to him, but I'm still power walking. Breathing hard. Beginning to sweat.

"Hey," I say, pinching my shirt away from my chest, where it's starting to stick. The weather is getting weirder; it's suddenly sweltering. I wince upward, toward the sun.

Here, within the Sanctuary, I've been getting a better idea of the state of our world. News flash: The earth is still basically going to shit. The Reestablishment has just been taking advantage of the aforementioned shit, making things seem irreparably bad.

The truth, on the other hand, is that they're only reparably bad.

Ha.

"Hey," I say again, this time clapping Warner on the shoulder. He shoves off my hand with so much enthusiasm I nearly stumble.

"Okay, listen, I know you're upset, but—"

Warner suddenly disappears.

"Hey, where the hell are you going?" I shout, my voice ringing out. "Are you heading back to your room? Should I just meet you there?"

A couple of people turn to stare at me.

The normally busy paths are pretty empty right now because so many of us are still convalescing, but the few people lingering in the bright sun shoot me dirty looks.

Like I'm the weirdo.

"Leave him alone," someone hisses at me. "He's grieving."

I roll my eyes.

"Hey—*douche bag*," I shout, hoping Warner's still close enough to hear me. "I know you love her, but so do I, and I'm—"

Warner reappears so close to my face I nearly scream. I take a sudden, terrified step backward.

"If you value your life," he says, "don't come near me."

I'm about to point out that he's being dramatic, but he cuts me off.

"I didn't say that to be dramatic. I didn't even say it to scare you. I'm saying it out of respect for Ella, because I know she'd rather I didn't kill you."

I'm quiet for a full second. And then I frown.

"Are you fucking with me right now? You're definitely fucking with me right now. Right?"

Warner's eyes go flinty. Electric. That scary kind of crazy.

"Every single time you claim to understand even a fraction of what I'm feeling, I want to disembowel you. I want to sever your carotid artery. I want to rip out your vertebrae, one by one. You have no idea what it is to love her," he says angrily. "You couldn't even begin to imagine. So stop trying to understand."

Wow, sometimes I really hate this guy.

I have to literally clench my jaw to keep myself from saying what I'm really thinking right now, which is that I want to put my fist through his skull. (I actually imagine it for a moment, imagine what it'd be like to crush his head like a walnut. It's oddly satisfying.) But then I remember that we need this asshole, and that J's life is on the line. The fate of the world is on the line.

So I fight back my anger and try again.

"Listen," I say, making an effort to gentle my voice. "I know what you guys have is special. I know that I can't really understand that kind of love. I mean, hell, I know you were even thinking about proposing to her—and that must've—"

"I did propose to her."

I suddenly stiffen.

I can tell just by the sound of his voice that he's not joking. And I can tell by the look on his face—the infinitesimal flash of misery in his eyes—that this is my opening. This is the data I've been missing. This is the source of the agony that's been drowning him.

I scan the immediate area for eavesdroppers. Yep. Too

many new members of the Warner fan club clutching their hearts.

"Come on," I say to him. "I'm taking you to lunch."

Warner blinks, confusion temporarily clearing his anger. And then, sharply: "I'm not hungry."

"That's obviously bullshit." I look him up and down. He looks good—he always looks good, the asshole—but he looks hungry. Not just the regular kind of hungry, either, but that desperate hunger that's so hungry it doesn't even feel like hunger anymore.

"You haven't eaten anything in days," I say to him. "And you know better than I do that you'll be useless on a rescue mission if you pass out before you even get there."

He glares at me.

"Come on, bro. You want J to come home to skin and bones? The way you're going, she'll take one look at you and run screaming in the opposite direction. This is not a good look. All these muscles need to eat." I poke at his bicep. "Feed your children."

Warner jerks away from me and takes a long, irritated breath. The sound of it almost makes me smile. Feels like old times.

I think I'm making progress.

Because this time, when I tell him to follow me, he doesn't fight.

~~ELLA~~

JULIETTE

Anderson takes me to meet Max.

I follow him down into the bowels of the compound, through winding, circuitous paths. Anderson's steps echo along the stone and steel walkways, the lights flickering as we go. The occasional, overly bright lights cast stark shadows in strange shapes. I feel my skin prickle.

My mind wanders.

A flash of Darius's limp body blazes in my mind, carrying with it a sharp twinge that twists my gut. I fight against an impulse to vomit, even as I feel the contents of my meager breakfast coming up my throat. With effort, I force back the bile. Sweat beads along my forehead, the back of my neck.

My body is screaming to stop moving. My lungs want to expand, collect air. I allow neither.

I force myself to keep walking.

I wick away the images, expunging thoughts of Darius from my mind. The churning in my stomach begins to slow, but in its wake my skin takes on a damp, clammy sensation. I struggle to recount the things I ate this morning. I must've eaten poorly; something isn't agreeing with my stomach. I feel feverish.

I blink.

I blink again, but this time for too long and I see a flash of blood, bubbling up inside Darius's open mouth. The nausea returns with a swiftness that scares me. I suck in a breath, my fingers fluttering, desperate to press against my stomach. Somehow, I hold steady. I keep my eyes open, widening them to the point of pain. My heart starts pounding. I try desperately to maintain control over my spiraling thoughts, but my skin begins to crawl. I clench my fists. Nothing helps. Nothing helps. *Nothing*, I think.

nothing

nothing

nothing

I begin to count the lights we pass.

I count my fingers. I count my breaths. I count my footsteps, measuring the force of every footfall that thunders up my legs, reverberates around my hips.

I remember that Darius is still alive.

He was carried away, ostensibly to be patched up and returned to his former position. Anderson didn't seem to mind that Darius was still alive. Anderson was only testing me, I realized. Testing me, once again, to make sure that I was obedient to him and him alone.

I take in a deep, fortifying breath.

I focus on Anderson's retreating figure. For reasons I can't explain, staring at him steadies me. Slows my pulse. Settles my stomach. And from this vantage point, I can't help but admire the way he moves. He has an impressive, muscular frame—broad shoulders, narrow waist, strong legs—but I marvel most at the way he carries himself. He has a confident stride. He walks tall, with smooth, effortless efficiency. As I watch him, a familiar feeling flutters through me. It gathers in my stomach, sparking dim heat that sends a brief shock to my heart.

I don't fight it.

There's something about him. Something about his face. His carriage. I find myself moving unconsciously closer to him, watching him almost too intently. I've noticed that he wears no jewelry, not even a watch. He has a faded scar between his right thumb and index finger. His hands are rough and callused. His dark hair is shot through with silver, the extent of which is only visible up close. His eyes are the blue-green of shallow, turquoise waters. Unusual.

Aquamarine.

He has long brown lashes and laugh lines. Full, curving lips. His skin grows rougher as the day wears on, the shadow of facial hair hinting at a version of him I try and fail to imagine.

I realize I'm beginning to like him. Trust him.

Suddenly, he stops. We're standing outside a steel door, next to which is a keypad and biometric scanner.

He brings his wrist to his mouth. "Yes." A pause. "I'm outside."

I feel my own wrist vibrate. I look down, surprised, at the blue light flashing through the skin at my pulse.

I'm being summoned.

This is strange. Anderson is standing right next to me;

I thought he was the only one with the authority to summon me.

"Sir?" I say.

He glances back, his eyebrows raised as if to say— *Yes?* And something that feels like happiness blooms to life inside of me. I know it's unwise to make so much of so little, but his movements and expressions feel suddenly softer now, more casual. It's clear that he's begun to trust me, too.

I lift my wrist to show him the message. He frowns.

He steps closer to me, taking my flashing arm in his hands. The tips of his fingers press against my skin as he gently bends back the joint, his eyes narrowing as he studies the summons. I go unnaturally still. He makes a sound of irritation and exhales, his breath skittering across my skin.

A bolt of sensation moves through me.

He's still holding my arm when he speaks into his own wrist. "Tell Ibrahim to back off. I have it under control."

In the silence, Anderson tilts his head, listening on an earpiece that isn't readily visible. I can only watch. Wait.

"I don't care," he says angrily, his fingers closing unconsciously around my wrist. I gasp, surprised, and he turns, our eyes meeting, clashing.

Anderson frowns.

His pleasant, masculine scent fills my head and I breathe him in almost without meaning to. Being this close to him is difficult. Strange. My head is swimming with confusion.

Broken images flood my mind—a flash of golden hair, fingers grazing bare skin—and then nausea. Dizziness.

It nearly knocks me over.

I look away just as Anderson tugs my arm up, toward a floodlight, squinting to get a better look. Our bodies nearly touch, and I'm suddenly so close I can see the edges of a tattoo, dark and curving, creeping up the edge of his collarbone.

My eyes widen in surprise. Anderson lets go of my wrist.

"I already know it was him," he says, speaking quickly, his eyes darting at and away from me. "His code is in the timestamp." A pause. "Just clear the summons. And then remind him that she reports only to me. I decide if and when he gets to talk to her."

He drops his wrist. Touches a finger to his temple.

And then, narrows his eyes at me.

My heart jumps. I straighten. I no longer wait to be prompted. When he looks at me like that, I know it's my cue to confess.

"You have a tattoo, sir. I was surprised. I wondered what it was."

Anderson raises an eyebrow at me.

He seems about to speak when, finally, the steel door exhales open. A curl of steam escapes the doorway, behind which emerges a man. He's tall, taller than Anderson, with wavy brown hair, light brown skin, and light, bright eyes the color of which aren't immediately obvious. He wears a white lab coat. Tall rubber boots. A face mask hangs around his neck, and a dozen pens have been shoved into the pocket of his coat. He makes no effort to move forward or to step aside; he only stands in the doorway, seemingly undecided.

"What's going on?" Anderson says. "I sent you a message an hour ago and you never showed up. Then I come to your door and you make me wait."

The man—Anderson told me his name was Max—says nothing. Instead, he appraises me, his eyes moving up and down my body in a show of undisguised hatred. I'm not sure how to process his reaction.

Anderson sighs, grasping something that isn't obvious to me.

"Max," he says quietly. "You can't be serious."

Max shoots Anderson a sharp look. "Unlike you, we're not all made of stone." And then, looking away: "At least not entirely."

I'm surprised to discover that Max has an accent, one not unlike the citizens of Oceania. Max must originate from this region.

Anderson sighs again.

"All right," Max says coolly. "What did you want to discuss?" He pulls a pen out of his pocket, uncapping it with his teeth. He reaches into his other pocket and pulls free a notebook. Flips it open.

I go suddenly blind.

In the span of a single instant darkness floods my vision. Clears. Hazy images reappear, time speeding up and slowing down in fits and starts. Colors streak across my eyes, dilate my pupils. Stars explode, lights flashing, sparking. I hear voices. A single voice. A whisper—

I am a thief

The tape rewinds. Plays back. The file corrupts.

I am
I am
I I I
am
a thief
a thief I stole
I stole this notebook andthispenfromoneofthedoctors

"Of course you did."

Anderson's sharp voice brings me back to the present moment. My heart is beating in my throat. Fear presses against my skin, conjuring goose bumps along my arms. My eyes move too quickly, darting around in distress until they rest, finally, on Anderson's familiar face.

He's not looking at me. He's not even speaking to me.

Quiet relief floods through me at the realization. My interlude lasted but a moment, which means I haven't missed much more than a couple of exchanged words. Max turns to me, studying me curiously.

"Come inside," he says, and disappears through the door.

I follow Anderson through the entryway, and as soon as I cross the threshold, a blast of icy air sends a shiver up my skin. I don't make it much farther than the entrance before I'm distracted.

Amazed.

Steel and glass are responsible for most of the structures in the space—massive screens and monitors; microscopes; long glass tables littered with beakers and half-filled test tubes. Accordion pipes sever vertical space around the room, connecting tabletops and ceilings. Blocks of artificial light fixtures are suspended in midair, humming steadily. The light temperature in here is so blue I don't know how Max can stand it.

I follow Max and Anderson over to a crescent-shaped desk that looks more like a command center. Papers are stacked on one side of the steel top, screens flickering above. More pens are stuffed into a chipped coffee mug sitting atop a thick book.

A *book*.

I haven't seen a relic like that in a long time.

Max takes his seat. He gestures at a stool tucked under a nearby table, and Anderson shakes his head.

I continue to stand.

"All right, then, go on," Max says, his eyes flickering in my direction. "You said there was a problem."

Anderson looks suddenly uncomfortable. He says nothing for so long that, eventually, Max smiles.

"Out with it," Max says, gesturing with his pen. "What did you do wrong this time?"

"I didn't do anything wrong," Anderson says sharply. Then he frowns. "I don't think so, anyway."

"Then what is it?"

Anderson takes a deep breath. Finally: "She says that she's . . . attracted to me."

Max's eyes widen. He glances from Anderson to me and then back again. And then, suddenly—

He laughs.

My face heats. I stare straight ahead, studying the strange equipment stacked on shelves against the far wall.

Out of the corner of my eye, I see Max scribbling in a notepad. All this modern technology, but he still seems to enjoy writing by hand. The observation strikes me as odd. I file the information away, not really understanding why.

"Fascinating," Max says, still smiling. He gives his head a quick shake. "Makes perfect sense, of course."

"I'm glad you think this is funny," Anderson says, visibly irritated. "But I don't like it."

Max laughs again. He leans back in his chair, his legs outstretched, crossed at the ankles. He's clearly intrigued—excited, even—by the development, and it's causing his earlier iciness to thaw. He bites down on the pen cap, considering Anderson. There's a glint in his eye.

"Do mine eyes deceive me," he says, "or does the great Paris Anderson admit to having a conscience? Or perhaps: a sense of morality?"

"You know better than anyone that I've never owned either, so I'm afraid I wouldn't know what it feels like."

"Touché."

"Anyway—"

"I'm sorry," Max says, his smile widening. "But I need

another moment with this revelation. Can you blame me for being fascinated? Considering the uncontested fact of your being one of the most depraved human beings I've ever known—and among our social circles, that's saying a lot—"

"Ha ha," Anderson says flatly.

"—I think I'm just surprised. Why is *this* too much? Why is this the line you won't cross? Of all the things . . ."

"Max, be serious."

"I am being serious."

"Aside from the obvious reasons why this situation should be disturbing to anyone— The girl's not even eighteen. Even I am not as depraved as that."

Max shakes his head. Holds up his pen. "Actually, she's been eighteen for four months."

Anderson seems about to argue, and then—

"Of course," he says. "I was remembering the wrong paperwork." He glances at me as he says it, and I feel my face grow hotter.

I am simultaneously confused and mortified.

Curious.

Horrified.

"Either way," Anderson says sharply, "I don't like it. Can you fix it?"

Max sits forward, crosses his arms. "Can I *fix* it? Can I fix the fact that she can't help but be attracted to the man who spawned the two faces she's known most intimately?" He shakes his head. Laughs again. "That kind of wiring isn't undone without incurring serious repercussions. Repercussions that would set us back."

"What kind of repercussions? Set us back how?"

Max glances at me. Glances at Anderson.

Anderson sighs. "Juliette," he barks.

"Yes, sir."

"Leave us."

"Yes, sir."

I pivot sharply and head for the exit. The door slides open in anticipation of my approach, but I hesitate, just a few feet away, when I hear Max laugh again.

I know I shouldn't eavesdrop. I know it's wrong. I know I'd be punished if I were caught. I know this.

Still, I can't seem to move.

My body is revolting, screaming at me to cross the threshold, but a pervasive heat has begun to seep into my mind, dulling the compulsion. I'm still frozen in front of the open door, trying to decide what to do, when their voices carry over.

"She clearly has a type," Max is saying. "At this point, it's practically written in her DNA."

Anderson says something I don't hear.

"Is it really such a bad thing?" Max says. "Perhaps her affection for you could work out in your favor. Take advantage of it."

"You think I'm so desperate for companionship—or so completely incompetent—that I'd need to result to seduction in order to get what I want out of the girl?"

Max barks out a laugh. "We both know you've never been desperate for companionship. But as to your competence . . ."

"I don't know why I even bother with you."

"It's been thirty years, Paris, and I'm still waiting for you to develop a sense of humor."

"It's been thirty years, Max, and you'd think I'd have found some new friends by now. Better ones."

"You know, your kids aren't funny, either," Max says, ignoring him. "Interesting how that works, isn't it?"

Anderson groans.

Max only laughs louder.

I frown.

I stand there, trying and failing to process their interactions. Max just insulted a supreme commander of The Reestablishment—multiple times. As Anderson's subordinate, he should be punished for speaking so disrespectfully. He should be fired, at the very least. Executed, if Anderson deems it preferable.

But when I hear the distant sound of Anderson's laughter, I realize that he and Max are laughing *together.* It's a realization that both startles and stuns me:

That they must be friends.

One of the overhead lights pops and hums, startling me out of my reverie. I give my head a quick shake and head out the door.

KENJI

I'm suddenly a big fan of the Warner groupies.

On our way back to my tent, I told only a couple of people I spotted on the path that Warner was hungry—but still not feeling well enough to join everyone in the dining hall—and they've been delivering packages of food to my room ever since. The problem is, all this kindness comes with a price. Six different girls (and two guys) have shown up so far, each one of them expecting payment for their generosity in the form of a conversation with Warner, which—obviously—never happens. But they usually settle for a good long look at him.

It's weird.

I mean, even I know, objectively, that Warner's not disgusting to look at, but this whole production of unabashed flirtation is really starting to feel weird. I'm not used to being in an environment where people openly admit to liking anything about Warner. Back at Omega Point—and even on base in Sector 45—everyone seemed to agree that he was a monster. No one denied their fear or disgust long enough to treat him like the kind of guy at whom they might bat their eyelashes.

But what's funny is: I'm the only one getting irritated.

Every time the doorbell rings I'm like, this is it, this is the time Warner is finally going to lose his mind and shoot someone, but he never even seems to notice. Of all the things that piss him off, gawking men and women don't appear to be on the list.

"So is this, like, normal for you, or what?" I'm still arranging food on plates in the little dining area of my room. Warner is standing stiffly in a random spot by the window. He chose that random spot when we walked in and he's just been standing there, staring at nothing, ever since.

"Is what normal for me?"

"All these people," I say, gesturing at the door. "Coming in here pretending they're not imagining you without your clothes on. Is that just, like, a normal day for you?"

"I think you're forgetting," he says quietly, "that I've been able to sense emotions for most of my life."

I raise my eyebrows. "So this *is* just a normal day for you."

He sighs. Stares out the window again.

"You're not even going to pretend it's not true?" I rip open a foil container. More potatoes. "You won't even pretend you don't know that the entire world finds you attractive?"

"Was that a confession?"

"You wish, dickhead."

"I find it boring," Warner says. "Besides, if I paid attention to every single person who found me attractive I'd never have time for anything else."

I nearly drop the potatoes.

I wait for him to crack a smile, to tell me he's joking, and when he doesn't, I shake my head, stunned.

"Wow," I say. "Your humility is a fucking inspiration."

He shrugs.

"Hey," I say, "speaking of things that disgust me— Do you maybe want to, like, wash a little bit of the blood off your face before we eat?"

Warner glares at me in response.

I hold up my hands. "Okay. Cool. That's fine." I point at him. "Actually, I heard that blood's good for you. You know—organic. Antioxidants and shit. Very popular with vampires."

"Are you able to hear the things you say out loud? Do you not realize how perfectly idiotic you sound?"

I roll my eyes. "All right, beauty queen, food's ready."

"I'm serious," he says. "Does it never occur to you to think things through before you speak? Does it never occur to you to cease speaking altogether? If it doesn't, it should."

"Come on, asswipe. Sit down."

Reluctantly, Warner makes his way over. He sits down and stares, blankly, at the meal in front of him.

I give him a few seconds of this before I say—

"Do you still remember how to do this? Or did you need me to feed you?" I stab a piece of tofu and point it in his direction. "Say *ah*. The tofu choo choo is coming."

"One more joke, Kishimoto, and I will remove your spine."

"You're right." I put down the fork. "I get it. I'm cranky when I'm hungry, too."

He looks up sharply.

"That wasn't a joke!" I say. "I'm being serious."

Warner sighs. Picks up his utensils. Looks longingly at the door.

I don't push my luck.

I keep my face on my food—I'm genuinely excited to be getting a second lunch—and wait until he takes several bites before I go for the jugular.

"So," I finally say. "You proposed, huh?"

Warner stops chewing and looks up. He strikes me, suddenly, as a young guy. Aside from the obvious need for a shower and a change of clothes, he looks like he's finally beginning to shed the tiniest, tiniest bit of tension. And I can tell by the way he's holding his knife and fork now—with a little more gusto—that I was right.

He was hungry.

I wonder what he would've done if I hadn't dragged him in here and sat him down. Forced him to eat.

Would he have just driven himself into the ground?

Accidentally died of hunger on his way to save Juliette?

He seems to have no real care for his physical self. No care for his own needs. It strikes me, suddenly, as bizarre. And concerning.

"Yes," he says quietly. "I proposed."

I'm seized by a knee-jerk reaction to tease him—to suggest that his bad mood makes sense now, that she probably turned him down—but even I know better than that. Whatever is happening in Warner's head right now is dark. Serious. And I need to handle this part of the conversation with care.

So I tread carefully. "I'm guessing she said yes."

Warner doesn't meet my eyes.

I take a deep breath, let it out slowly. It's all beginning to make sense now.

In the early days after Castle took me in, my guard was up so high I couldn't even see over the top of it. I trusted no one. I believed nothing. I was always waiting for the other shoe to drop. I let anger rock me to sleep at night because being angry was far less scary than having faith in people—or in the future.

I kept waiting for things to fall apart.

I was so sure this happiness and safety wouldn't last, that Castle would turn me out, or that he'd turn out to be a piece of shit. Abusive. Some kind of monster.

I couldn't relax.

It took me *years* before I truly believed that I had a family. It took me years to accept, without hesitation, that Castle really loved me, or that good things could last. That I could be happy again without fear of repercussion.

That's why losing Omega Point was so cataclysmic.

It was the amalgamation of nearly all my fears. So many people I loved had been wiped out overnight. My home. My family. My refuge. And the devastation had taken Castle, too. Castle, who'd been my rock and my role model; in the aftermath, he was a ghost. Unrecognizable. I didn't know how anything would shake out after that. I didn't know how we'd survive. Didn't know where we'd go.

It was Juliette who pulled us through.

Those were the days when she and I got really close. That was when I realized I could not only trust her and open up to her, but that I could *depend* on her. I never knew just how strong she was until I saw her take charge, rising up and rallying us all when we were at our lowest, when even Castle was too broken too stand.

J made magic out of tragedy.

She found us safety and hope. Unified us with Sector 45—with Warner and Delalieu—even in the face of opposition, at the risk of losing Adam. She didn't sit around waiting for Castle to take the reins like the rest of us did; there was no time for that. Instead, she dove right into the middle of hell, completely inexperienced and unprepared, because she was determined to save us. And to sacrifice herself in the process, if that was the cost. If it weren't for her—if it weren't for what she did, for all of us—I don't know where we'd be.

She saved our lives.

She saved my life, that's for sure. Reached out a hand in the darkness. Pulled me out.

But none of it would've hurt as much if I'd lost Omega Point during my early years there. It wouldn't have taken me so long to recover, and I wouldn't have needed so much help to get through the pain. It hurt like that because I'd finally let my guard down. I'd finally allowed myself to believe that things were going to be okay. I'd begun to hope. To dream.

To *relax*.

I'd finally walked away from my own pessimism, and the moment I did, life stuck a knife in my back.

It's easy, during those moments, to throw in the towel. To shrug off humanity. To tell yourself that you tried to be happy, and look what happened: more pain. Worse pain. Betrayed by the world. You realize then that anger is safer than kindness, that isolation is safer than community. You shut everything out. Everyone. But some days, no matter what you do, the pain gets so bad you'd bury yourself alive just to make it stop.

I would know. I've been there.

And I'm looking at Warner right now and I see the same deadness behind his eyes. The torture that chases hope. That specific flavor of self-hatred experienced only after being dealt a tragic blow in response to optimism.

I'm looking at him and I'm remembering the look on his face when he blew out his birthday candles. I'm remembering him and J afterward, cuddled up in the corner of the dining tent. I'm remembering how angry he was when I showed up at their room at the asscrack of dawn, determined to drag J out of bed on the morning of his birthday.

I'm thinking—

"Fuck." I throw down my fork. The plastic hits the foil plate with a surprising thud. "You two were engaged?"

Warner is staring at his food. He seems calm, but when

he says, "Yes," the word is a whisper so sad it drags a knife through my heart.

I shake my head. "I'm so sorry, man. I really am. You have no idea."

Warner's eyes flick up in surprise, but only for a moment. Eventually, he stabs a piece of broccoli. Stares at it. "This is disgusting," he says.

Which I realize is code for *Thank you.*

"Yeah," I say. "It is."

Which is code for *No worries, bro. I'm here for you.*

Warner sighs. He puts down his utensils. Stares out the window. I can tell he's about to say something when, abruptly, the doorbell rings.

I swear under my breath.

I shove away from the table to answer the door, but this time, I only open it a crack. A girl about my age peers back at me, standing there with a tinfoil package in her arms.

She smiles.

I open the door a bit more.

"I brought this for Warner," she says, stage-whispering. "I heard he was hungry." Her smile is so big you could probably see it from Mars. I have to make a real effort not to roll my eyes.

"Thanks. I'll take th—"

"Oh," she says, jerking the package out of reach. "I thought I could deliver it to him personally. You know, just to be sure it's being delivered to the right person." She beams.

This time, I actually roll my eyes.

Reluctantly, I pull open the door, stepping aside to let her enter. I turn to tell Warner that another member of his fan club is here to take a long look at his green eyes, but in the second it takes me to move, I hear her scream. The container of food crashes to the ground, spaghetti noodles and red sauce spilling everywhere.

I spin around, stunned.

Warner has the girl pinned to the wall, his hand around her throat. "Who sent you here?" he says.

She struggles to break free, her feet kicking hard against the wall, her cries choked and desperate.

My head is spinning.

I blink and Warner's got her on the floor, on her knees. His boot is planted in the middle of her back, both of her arms bent backward, locked in his grip. He twists. She cries out.

"Who sent you here?"

"I don't know what you're talking about," she says, gasping for breath.

My heart is pounding like crazy.

I have no idea what the hell just happened, but I know better than to ask questions. I remove the Glock tucked inside my waistband and aim it in her direction. And then, just as I'm beginning to wrap my head around the fact that this is an ambush—and likely from someone here, from inside the Sanctuary—I notice the food begin to move.

Three massive scorpions begin to scuttle out from

underneath the noodles, and the sight is so disturbing I nearly throw up and pass out at the same time. I've never seen scorpions in real life.

Breaking news: they're *horrifying*.

I thought I wasn't afraid of spiders, but this is like if spiders were on crack, like if spiders were very, very large and kind of see-through and wore armor and had huge, venomous stingers on one end just primed and ready to murder you. The creatures make a sharp turn, and all three of them head straight for Warner.

I let out a panicked gasp of breath. "Uh, bro—not to, um, freak you out or anything, but there are, like, three scorpions headed straight toward y—"

Suddenly, the scorpions freeze in place.

Warner drops the girl's arms and she scrambles away so fast her back slams against the wall. Warner stares at the scorpions. The girl stares, too.

The two of them are having a battle of wills, I realize, and it's easy for me to figure out who's going to win. So when the scorpions begin to move again—this time, toward her—I try not to pump my fist in the air.

The girl jumps to her feet, her eyes wild.

"Who sent you?" Warner asks again.

She's breathing hard now, still staring at the scorpions as she backs farther into a corner. They're climbing up her shoes now.

"Who?" Warner demands.

"Your father sent me," she says breathlessly. Shins.

Knees. Scorpions on her knees. Oh my God, scorpions on her knees. "Anderson sent me here, okay? Call them off!"

"Liar."

"It was him, I swear!"

"You were sent here by a fool," Warner says, "if you were led to believe you could lie to me repeatedly without repercussion. And you are yourself a fool if you believe I will be anything close to merciful."

The creatures are moving up her torso now. Climbing up her chest. She gasps. Locks eyes with him.

"I see," he says, tilting his head at her. "Someone lied to you."

Her eyes widen.

"You were misled," he says, holding her gaze. "I am not kind. I am not forgiving. I do not care about your life."

As he speaks, the scorpions creep farther up her body. They're sitting near her collarbone now, just waiting, venomous stingers hovering below her face. And then, slowly, the scorpions' stingers begin curving toward the soft skin at her throat.

"Call them off!" she cries.

"This is your last chance," Warner says. "Tell me what you're doing here."

She's breathing so hard now that her chest heaves, her nostrils flaring. Her eyes dart around the room in a wild panic. The scorpions' stingers press closer to her throat. She flattens against the wall, a broken gasp escaping her lips.

"Tragic," Warner says.

She moves fast. Lightning fast. Pulls a gun from somewhere inside her shirt and aims it in Warner's direction and I don't even think, I just react.

I shoot.

The sound echoes, expands—it seems violently loud—but it's a perfect shot. A clean hole through the neck. The girl goes comically still and then slumps, slowly, to the ground.

Blood and scorpions pool around our feet. The body of a dead girl is splayed on my floor, just inches from the bed I woke up in, her limbs bent at awkward angles.

The scene is surreal.

I look up. Warner and I lock eyes.

"I'm coming with you to get J," I say. "End of discussion."

Warner glances from me to the dead body, and then back again. "Fine," he says, and sighs.

~~ELLA~~
JULIETTE

I've been standing outside the door staring at a smooth, polished stone wall for at least fifteen minutes before I check my wrist for a summons.

Still nothing.

When I'm with Anderson I don't have a lot of flexibility to look around, but standing here has given me time to freely examine my surroundings. The stretch of the hallway is eerily quiet, empty of doctors or soldiers in a way that unsettles me. There are long, vertical grates underfoot where the floor should be, and I've been standing here long enough to have become attuned to the incessant drips and mechanical roars that fill the background.

I glance at my wrist again.

Glance around the hall.

The walls aren't gray, like I originally thought. It turns out they're a dull white. Heavy shadows make them appear darker than they are—and in fact, make this entire floor appear darker. The overhead lights are unusual honeycomb clusters arranged along both the walls and ceilings. The oddly shaped lights scatter illumination, casting oblong hexagons in all directions, plunging some walls into complete darkness.

I take a cautious step forward, peering more closely at a rectangle of blackness I'd previously ignored.

It's a hallway, I realize, cast entirely in shadow.

I feel a sudden compulsion to explore its depths, and I have to physically stop myself from stepping forward. My duty is here, at this door. It's not my business to explore or ask questions unless I've been explicitly asked to explore or ask questions.

My eyelids flutter.

Heat presses down on me, flames like fingers digging into my mind. Heat travels down my spine, wraps around my tailbone. And then shoots upward, fast and strong, forcing my eyes open. I'm breathing hard, spinning around.

Confused.

Suddenly, it makes perfect sense that I should explore the darkened hallway. Suddenly there seems no need at all to question my motives or any possible consequences for my actions.

But I've only taken a single step into the darkness when I'm pushed aggressively back. A girl's face peers out at me.

"Did you need something?" she says.

I throw up my hands, then I hesitate. I might not be authorized to hurt this person.

She steps forward. She's wearing civilian clothes, but doesn't appear to be armed. I wait for her to speak, and she doesn't.

"Who are you?" I demand. "Who gave you the authority to be down here?"

"I am Valentina Castillo. I have authority everywhere."

I drop my hands.

Valentina Castillo is the daughter of the supreme commander of South America, Santiago Castillo. I don't know what Valentina is supposed to look like, so this girl might be an impostor. Then again, if I take a risk and I'm wrong—

I could be executed.

I peer around her and see nothing but blackness. My curiosity—and unease—is growing by the minute.

I glance at my wrist. Still no summons.

"Who are you?" she says.

"I am Juliette Ferrars. I am a supreme soldier for our North American commander. Let me pass."

Valentina stares at me, her eyes scanning me from head to toe.

I hear a dull *click*, like the sound of something opening, and I spin around, looking for the source of the sound. There's no one.

"You have unlocked your message, Juliette Ferrars."

"What message?"

"Juliette? *Juliette.*"

Valentina's voice changes. She suddenly sounds like she's scared and breathless, like she's on the move. Her voice echoes. I hear the sounds of footsteps pounding the floor, but they seem far away, like she's not the only one running.

"*Viste,* there wasn't much time," she says, her Spanish accent getting thicker. "This was the best I could do. I have a plan, but *no sé si será posible. Este mensaje es en caso de emergencia.*

"They took Lena and Nicolás down in this direction," she says, pointing toward the darkness. "I'm on my way to try and find them. But if I can't—"

Her voice begins to fade. The light illuminating her face begins to glitch, almost like she's disappearing.

"Wait—" I say, reaching out. "Where are you—"

My hand moves straight through her and I gasp. She has no form. Her face is an illusion.

A hologram.

"I'm sorry," she says, her voice beginning to warp. "I'm sorry. This was the best I could do."

Once her form evaporates completely, I push into the darkness, heart pounding. I don't understand what's happening, but if the daughter of the supreme commander of South America is in trouble, I have a duty to find her and protect her.

I know that my loyalty is to Anderson, but that strange, familiar heat is still pressing against the inside of my mind, quieting the impulse telling me to turn around. I find I'm grateful for it. I realize, distantly, that my mind is a strange mess of contradictions, but I don't have more than a moment to dwell on it.

This hall is far too dark for easy access, but I'd observed earlier that what I once thought were decorative grooves in the walls were actually inset doors, so here, instead of relying on my eyes, I use my hands.

I run my fingers along the wall as I walk, waiting for a

disruption in the pattern. It's a long hallway—I expect there to be multiple doors to sort through—but there appears to be little in this direction. Nothing visible by touch or sight, at least. When I finally feel the familiar pattern of a door, I hesitate.

I press both my hands against the wall, prepared to destroy it if I have to, when it suddenly fissures open beneath my hands, as if it was waiting for me.

Expecting me.

I move into the room, my senses heightened. Dim blue light pulses out along the floors, but other than that, the space is almost completely dark. I keep moving, and even though I don't need to use a gun, I reach for the rifle strapped across my back. I walk slowly, my soft boots soundless, and follow the distant, pulsing lights. As I move deeper into the room, lights begin to flicker on.

Overhead lights in that familiar honeycomb pattern flare to life, shattering the floor in unusual slants of light. The vast dimensions of the room begin to take shape. I stare up at the massive dome-shaped room, at the empty tank of water taking up an entire wall. There are abandoned desks, their respective chairs askew. Touchpads are stacked precariously on floors and desks, papers and binders piling everywhere. This place looks haunted. Deserted.

But it's clear it was once in full use.

Safety goggles hang from a nearby rack. Lab coats from another. There are large, empty glass cases standing upright in seemingly random and intermittent locations, and as I move even farther into the room, I notice a steady purple glow emanating from somewhere nearby.

I round the corner, and there's the source:

Eight glass cylinders, each as tall as the room and as wide as a desk, are arranged in a perfect line, straight across the laboratory. Five of them contain human figures. Three on the end remain empty. The purple light originates from within the individual cylinders, and as I approach, I realize the bodies are suspended in the air, bound entirely by light.

There are three boys I don't recognize. One girl I don't recognize. The other—

I step closer to the tank and gasp.

Valentina.

"What are you doing here?"

I spin around, rifle up and aimed in the direction of the voice. I drop my gun when I see Anderson's face. In an instant, the pervasive heat retreats from my head.

My mind is returned to me.

My mind, my name, my station, my place—my shameful, disloyal, reckless behavior. Horror and fear flood through me, coloring my features. How do I explain what I do not understand?

Anderson's face remains stony.

"Sir," I say quickly. "This young woman is the daughter of the supreme commander of South America. As a servant of The Reestablishment, I felt compelled to help her."

Anderson only stares at me.

Finally, he says: "How do you know that this girl is the daughter of the supreme commander of South America?"

I shake my head. "Sir, there was . . . some kind of vision. Standing in the hallway. She told me that she was Valentina Castillo, and that she needed help. She knew my name. She told me where to go."

Anderson exhales, his shoulders releasing their tension. "This is not the daughter of a supreme commander of The Reestablishment," he says quietly. "You were misled by a practice exercise."

Renewed mortification sends a fresh heat to my face.

Anderson sighs.

"I'm so sorry, sir. I thought— I thought it was my duty to help her, sir."

Anderson meets my eyes again. "Of course you did."

I hold my head steady, but shame sears me from within.

"And?" he says. "What did you think?"

Anderson gestures at the line of glass cylinders, at the figures displayed within.

"I think it's a beautiful display, sir."

Anderson almost smiles. He takes a step closer, studying me. "A beautiful display, indeed."

I swallow.

His voice changes, becomes soft. Gentle. "You would never betray me, would you, Juliette?"

"No, sir," I say quickly. "Never."

"Tell me something," he says, lifting his hand to my face. The backs of his knuckles graze my cheek, trail down my jawline. "Would you die for me?"

My heart is thundering in my chest. "Yes, sir."

He takes my face in his hand now, his thumb brushing, gently, across my chin. "Would you do anything for me?"

"Yes, sir."

"And yet, you deliberately disobeyed me." He drops his hand. My face feels suddenly cold. "I asked you to wait outside," he says quietly. "I did not ask you to wander. I did not ask you to speak. I did not ask you to think for yourself or to save anyone who claimed to need saving. Did I?"

"No, sir."

"Did you forget," he says, "that I am your master?"

"No, sir."

"*Liar,*" he cries.

My heart is in my throat. I swallow hard. Say nothing.

"I will ask you one more time," he says, locking eyes with me. "Did you forget that I am your master?"

"Y-yes, sir."

His eyes flash. "Should I remind you, Juliette? Should I remind you to whom you owe your life and your loyalty?"

"Yes, sir," I say, but I sound breathless. I feel sick with fear. Feverish. Heat prickles my skin.

He retrieves a blade from inside his jacket pocket. Carefully, he unfolds it, the metal glinting in the neon light.

He presses the hilt into my right hand.

He takes my left hand and explores it with both of his own, tracing the lines of my palm and the shapes of my fingers, the seams of my knuckles. Sensations spiral through me, wonderful and horrible.

He presses down lightly on my index finger. He meets my eyes.

"This one," he says. "Give it to me."

My heart is in my throat. In my gut. Beating behind my eyes.

"Cut it off. Place it in my hand. And all will be forgiven."

"Yes, sir," I whisper.

With shaking hands, I press the blade to the tender skin at the base of my finger. The blade is so sharp it pierces the flesh instantly, and with a stifled, agonized cry I press it deeper, hesitating only when I feel resistance. Knife against bone. The pain explodes through me, blinding me.

I fall on one knee.

There's blood everywhere.

I'm breathing so hard I'm heaving, trying desperately not to vomit from either the pain or the horror. I clench my teeth so hard it sends shocks of fresh pain upward, straight to my brain, and the distraction is helpful. I have to press my bloodied hand against the dirty floor to keep it steady, but with one final, desperate cry, I cut through the bone.

The knife falls from my trembling hand, clattering to the floor. My index finger is still hanging on to my hand by a single scrap of flesh, and I rip it off in a quick, violent motion. My body is shaking so excessively I can hardly stand, but somehow I manage to deposit the finger in Anderson's outstretched palm before collapsing to the ground.

"Good girl," he says softly. "Good girl."

It's all I hear him say before I black out.

KENJI

We both stare at the bloody scene a moment longer before Warner suddenly straightens and heads out the door. I tuck my gun into the waistband of my pants and chase after him, remembering to close the door behind us. I don't want those scorpions getting loose.

"Hey," I say, catching up to him. "Where are you going?"

"To find Castle."

"Cool. Okay. But do you think that maybe next time, instead of just, you know, leaving without a word, you could tell me what the hell is going on? I don't like chasing after you like this. It's demeaning."

"That sounds like a personal problem."

"Yeah but I thought personal problems were your area of expertise," I say. "You've got what, at least a few thousand personal problems, right? Or was it a few million?"

Warner shoots me a dark look. "You'd do well to address your own mental turbulence before criticizing mine."

"Uh, what's that supposed to mean?"

"It means that a rabid dog could sniff out your desperate, broken state. You're in no position to judge me."

"Excuse me?"

"You lie to yourself, Kishimoto. You hide your true

feelings behind a thin veneer, playing the clown, when all the while you're amassing emotional detritus you refuse to examine. At least I do not hide from myself. I know where my faults lie and I accept them. But you," he says. "Perhaps you should seek help."

My eyes widen to the point of pain, my head whipping back and forth between him and the path in front of me. "You have got to be kidding me right now. *You're* telling *me* to get help with my issues? What is happening?" I look up at the sky. "Am I dead? Is this hell?"

"I want to know what's happening with you and Castle."

I'm so surprised I briefly stop in place.

"What?" I blink at him. Still confused. "What are you talking about? There's nothing wrong with me and Castle."

"You've been more profane in the last several weeks than in the entire time I've known you. Something is wrong."

"I'm stressed," I say, feeling myself bristle. "Sometimes I swear when I'm stressed."

He shakes his head. "This is different. You're experiencing an unusual amount of stress, even for you."

"Wow." My eyebrows fly up. "I really hope you didn't bother using your"—I make air quotes—*"supernatural ability to sense emotions"*—I drop the air quotes—"to figure that one out. Obviously I'm extra stressed out right now. The world is on fucking fire. The list of things stressing me out is so long I can't even keep track. We're up to our necks in shit. J is gone. Adam defected. Nazeera's been shot. You've had your head so far up your own ass I thought you'd never emerge—"

He tries to cut me off but I keep talking.

"—and literally five minutes ago," I say, "someone from the Sanctuary—ha, hilarious, horrible name—just tried to kill you, and I killed her for it. *Five minutes ago.* So yeah, I think I'm experiencing an unusual amount of stress right now, genius."

Warner dismisses my speech with a single shake of his head. "Your use of profanity increases exponentially when you're irritated with Castle. Your language appears to be directly connected to your relationship with him. Why?"

I try not to roll my eyes. "Not that this information is actually relevant, but Castle and I struck a deal a few years ago. He thought that my"—I make more air quotes—*"overreliance on profanity was inhibiting my ability to express my emotions in a constructive manner."*

"So you promised him you'd tone down your language."

"Yeah."

"I see. It seems you've reneged on the terms of that arrangement."

"Why do you care?" I ask. "Why are we even talking about this? Why are we losing sight of the fact that we were just attacked by someone from *inside* of the Sanctuary? We need to find Sam and Nouria and find out who this girl was, because she was clearly from this camp, and they should know th—"

"You can tell Sam and Nouria whatever you want," Warner says. "But I need to talk to Castle."

Something in his tone frightens me. "Why?" I demand.

"What is going on? Why are you so obsessed with Castle right now?"

Finally, Warner stops moving. "Because," he says. "Castle had something to do with this."

"What?" I feel the blood drain from my body. "No way. Not possible."

Warner says nothing.

"Come on, man, don't be crazy— Castle's not perfect, but he would never—"

"Hey— What the hell just happened?" Winston, breathless and panicked, comes running up to us. "I heard a gunshot coming from the direction of your tent, but when I went to check on you, I saw— I saw—"

"Yeah."

"What happened?" Winston's voice is shrill. Terrified.

At that exact moment, more people come running. Winston starts offering people explanations I don't bother to edit, because my head is still full of steam. I have no idea what the hell Warner is getting at, but I'm also worried that I know him too well to deny his mind. My heart says Castle would never betray us, but my brain says that Warner is usually right when it comes to sussing out this kind of shit. So I'm freaking out.

I spot Nouria in the distance, her dark skin gleaming in the bright sun, and relief floods through me.

Finally.

Nouria will know more about the girl with the scorpions. She has to. And whatever she knows will almost certainly help absolve Castle of any affiliation with this mess. And as soon as we can resolve this freak accident, Warner and I can get the hell out of here and start searching for J.

That's it.

That's the plan.

It makes me feel good to have a plan. But when we're close enough, Nouria narrows her eyes at both me and Warner, and the look on her face sends a brand-new wave of fear through my body.

"Follow me," she says.

We do.

Warner looks *livid*.

Castle looks freaked out.

Nouria and Sam look like they're sick and tired of all of us.

I might be imagining things, but I'm pretty sure Sam just shot Nouria a look—the subtext of which was probably *Why the hell did you have to let your dad come stay with us?*—that was so withering Nouria didn't even get upset, she just shook her head, resigned.

And the problem is, I don't even know whose side I'm on.

In the end, Warner was right about Castle, but he was also wrong. Castle wasn't plotting anything nefarious; he didn't send that girl—her name was Amelia—after Warner. Castle's mistake was thinking that all rebel groups shared the same worldview.

At first it didn't occur to me, either, that the vibe might

be different around here. Different from our group at Point, at least. At Point we were led by Castle, who was more of a nurturer than a warrior. In his days before The Reestablishment he was a social worker. He saw tons of kids coming in and out of the system, and with Omega Point he sought to build a home and refuge for the marginalized. We were all about love and community at Point. And even though we knew that we were gearing up for a fight against The Reestablishment, we didn't always resort to violence; Castle didn't like using his powers in authoritative ways. He was more like a father figure to most of us.

But here—

It didn't take long to realize that Nouria was different from her dad. She's nice enough, but she's also all business. She doesn't like to spend much time on small talk, and she and Sam mostly keep to themselves. They don't always take their meals with everyone else. They don't always participate in group things. And when it comes right down to it, Sam and Nouria are ready and willing to set shit on fire. Hell, they seem to be looking forward to it.

Castle was never really that guy.

I think he was a little blindsided when we showed up here. He was suddenly out of a job when he realized that Nouria and Sam weren't going to take orders from him. And then, when he tried to get to know people—

He was disappointed.

"Amelia was a bit of a zealot," Sam says, sighing. "She'd never exhibited dangerous, violent tendencies, of course, which is why we let her stay—but we all felt that her views were a little intense. She was one of the rare members who felt like the lines between The Reestablishment and the rebel groups should be clear and finite. She never felt safe with the children of the supreme commanders in our midst, and I know that because she took me aside to tell me so. I had a long talk with her about the situation, but I see now that she wasn't convinced."

"Obviously," I mutter.

Nouria shoots me a look. I clear my throat.

Sam goes on: "When everyone but Warner was basically kidnapped—and Nazeera was shot—Amelia probably figured she could finish the job and get rid of Warner, too." She shakes her head. "What a horrible situation."

"Did you have to shoot her?" Nouria says to me. "Was she really that dangerous?"

"She had *three* scorpions!" I cry. "She pulled a gun on Warner!"

"What else was he supposed to think?" Castle says gently. He's staring at the ground, his long dreads freed from their usual tie at the base of his neck. I wish I could see the expression on his face. "If I hadn't known Amelia personally, even I would've thought she was working for someone."

"Tell me, again," Warner says to Castle, "exactly what you said to her about me."

Castle looks up. Sighs.

"She and I got into a bit of a heated discussion," he says. "Amelia was determined that members of The

Reestablishment could never change, that they were evil and would remain evil. I told her I didn't believe that. I told her that I believed that all people were capable of change."

I raise an eyebrow. "Wait, like, you mean you think even someone like Anderson is capable of change?"

Castle hesitates. And I know, just by looking at his eyes, what he's about to say. My heart jumps in my chest. In fear.

"I think if Anderson were truly remorseful," Castle says, "that he, too, could make a change. Yes. I do believe that."

Nouria rolls her eyes.

Sam drops her head in her hands.

"Wait. Wait." I hold up a finger. "So, like, in a hypothetical situation— If Anderson came to Point asking for amnesty, claiming to be a changed man, you'd . . . ?"

Castle just looks at me.

I throw myself back in my chair with a groan.

"Kenji," Castle says softly. "You know better than anyone else how we did things at Omega Point. I dedicated my life to giving second—and third—chances to those who'd been cast out by the world. You'd be stunned if you knew how many people's lives were derailed by a simple mistake that snowballed, escalating beyond their control because no one was ever there to offer a hand or even an hour of assistance—"

"Castle. Sir." I hold up my hands. "I love you. I really do. But Anderson isn't a regular person. He—"

"Of course he's a regular person, son. That's exactly the point. We're all just regular people, when you strip us down.

There's nothing to be afraid of when you look at Anderson; he's just as human as you or me. Just as terrified. And I'm sure if he could go back and do his life over again, he'd make very different decisions."

Nouria shakes her head. "You don't know that, Dad."

"Maybe not," he says quietly. "But it's what I believe."

"Is that what you believe about me, too?" Warner asks. "Is that what you told her? That I was just a nice boy, a defenseless child who'd never lift a finger to hurt her? That if I could do it all over again I'd choose to live my life as a monk, dedicating my days to giving charity and spreading goodwill?"

"No," Castle says sharply. It's clear he's starting to get irritated. "I told her that your anger was a defense mechanism, and that you couldn't help that you were born to an abusive father. I told her that in your heart, you're a good person, and that you don't *want* to hurt anyone. Not really."

Warner's eyes flash. "I want to hurt people all the time," he says. "Sometimes I can't sleep at night because I'm thinking about all the people I'd like to murder."

"Great." I nod, leaning back in my chair. "This is super great. All of this information we're collecting is super helpful and useful." I count off on my fingers: "Amelia was a psycho, Castle wants to be BFFs with Anderson, Warner has midnight fantasies about killing people, and Castle made Amelia think that Warner is a lost little bunny trying to find his way home."

When everyone stares at me, confused, I clarify:

"Castle basically gave Amelia the idea that she could walk into a room and murder Warner! He pretty much told her that Warner was about as harmful as a dumpling."

"*Oh,*" Sam and Nouria say at the same time.

"I don't think she wanted to murder him," Castle says quickly. "I'm sure she just—"

"Dad, please." Nouria's voice is sharp and final. "Enough." She shares a glance with Sam, and takes a deep breath.

"Listen," she says, trying for a calmer tone. "We knew, when you got here, that we'd have to deal with this situation eventually, but I think it's time we had a talk about our roles and responsibilities around here."

"Oh. I see." Castle clasps his hands. Stares at the wall. He looks so sad and small and ancient. Even his dreads seem more silver than black these days. Sometimes I forget he's almost fifty. Most people think he's, like, fifteen years younger than he actually is, but that's just because he's always looked really, really good for his age. But for the first time in years, I feel like I'm beginning to see the number on his face. He looks tired. Worn out.

But that doesn't mean he's done here.

Castle's still got so much more to do. So much more to give. And I can't just sit here and let him be shoved aside. Ignored. I want to shout at someone. I want to tell Nouria and Sam that they can't just kick Castle to the curb like this. Not after everything. Not like this.

And I'm about to say something exactly like that, when Nouria speaks.

"Sam and I," she says, "would like to offer you an official position as our senior adviser here at the Sanctuary."

Castle's head perks up. "Senior adviser?" He stares at Nouria. Stares at Sam. "You're not asking me to leave?"

Nouria looks suddenly confused.

"Leave? Dad, you just got here. Sam and I want you to stay for as long as you like. We just think it's important that we all know what we're doing here, so that we can manage things in as efficient and organized a manner as possible. It's hard for Sam and me to be effective at our jobs if we're worried about tiptoeing around your feelings, and even though it's hard to have conversations like this, we figured it would be best to jus—"

Castle pulls Nouria into a hug so fierce, so full of love, I feel my eyes sting with emotion. I actually have to look away for a moment.

When I turn back, Castle is beaming.

"I'd be honored to advise in any way that I can," Castle says. "And if I haven't said it enough, let me say it again: I'm so proud of you, Nouria. So proud of both of you," he says, looking at Sam. "The boys would've been so proud."

Nouria's eyes go glassy with emotion. Even Sam seems moved.

One more minute of this, and I'm going to need a tissue.

"Right, well." Warner is on his feet. "I'm glad the attempt

on my life was able to bring your family together. I'm leaving now."

"Wait—" I grab Warner's arm and he shoves me off.

"If you keep touching me without my permission, I will remove your hands from your body."

I ignore that. "Shouldn't we tell them that we're leaving?"

Sam frowns. *"Leaving?"*

Nouria's eyebrows fly up. *"We?"*

"We're going to get J," I explain. "She's back in Oceania. James told us everything. Speaking of which— You should probably talk to him. He's got some news about Adam you won't like, news that I don't care to repeat."

"Kent betrayed all of you to save himself."

"To save *James,*" I clarify, shooting Warner a dirty look. "And that was not cool, man. I just said I didn't want to talk about it."

"I'm trying to be efficient."

Castle looks stunned. He says nothing. He just looks stunned.

"Talk to James," I say. "He'll tell you what's happening. But Warner and I are going to catch a plane—"

"Steal a plane."

"Right, steal a plane, before the end of the day. And, uh, you know—we'll just go get J and be back real quick, *bim bam boom.*"

Nouria and Sam are staring at me like I'm an idiot.

"Bim bam boom?" Warner says.

"Yeah, you know, like"—I clap my hands together—"*boom*. Done. Easy."

Warner turns away from me with a sigh.

"Wait— So, just the two of you are doing this?" Sam asks. She's frowning.

"Honestly, the fewer, the better," Nouria answers for me. "That way, there are fewer bodies to hide, fewer actions to coordinate. Regardless, I'd offer to come with you, but we have so many still wounded that we need to care for—and now that Amelia is dead, there's sure to be more emotional upheaval to manage."

Castle's eyes light up. "While they're going after Ella," he says to Nouria and Sam, "and the two of you are running things here, I was thinking I'd reach out to the friends in my network. Let them know what's happening, and that change is afoot. I can help coordinate our moves around the globe."

"That's a great idea," Sam says. "Maybe we c—"

"I don't care," Warner says loudly, and turns for the door. "And I'm leaving now. Kishimoto, if you're coming, keep up."

"Right," I say, trying to sound important. "Yup. Bye." I shoot a quick two-finger salute at everyone and run straight for the door only to slam hard into Nazeera.

Nazeera.

Holy shit. She's awake. She's perfect.

She's *pissed*.

"You two aren't going anywhere without me," she says.

~~ELLA~~
JULIETTE

I am a thief.

I stole this notebook and this pen from one of the doctors, from one of his lab coats when he wasn't looking, and I shoved them both down my pants. This was just before he ordered those men to come and get me. The ones in the strange suits with the thick gloves and the gas masks with the foggy plastic windows hiding their eyes. They were aliens, I remember thinking. I remember thinking they must've been aliens because they couldn't have been human, the ones who handcuffed my hands behind my back, the ones who strapped me to my seat. They stuck Tasers to my skin over and over for no reason other than to hear me scream but I wouldn't. I whimpered but I never said a word. I felt the tears streak down my cheeks but I wasn't crying.

I think it made them angry.

They slapped me awake even though my eyes were open when we arrived. Someone unstrapped me without removing my handcuffs and kicked me in both kneecaps before ordering me to rise. And I tried. I tried but I couldn't and finally 6 hands shoved me out the door and my face was bleeding on the concrete for a while. I can't really remember the part where they dragged me inside.

I feel cold all the time.

I feel empty, like there is nothing inside of me but this broken heart, the only organ left in this hell. I feel the bleats echo within me, I feel the thumping reverberate around my skeleton. I have a heart, says science, but I am a monster, says society. And I know it, of course I know it. I know what I've done. I'm not asking for sympathy.

But sometimes I think—sometimes I wonder—if I were a monster—surely, I would feel it by now?

I would feel angry and vicious and vengeful.

I'd know blind rage and bloodlust and a need for vindication.

Instead I feel an abyss within me that's so deep, so dark I can't see within it; I can't see what it holds. I do not know what I am or what might happen to me.

I do not know what I might do again.

—An excerpt from Juliette's journals in the asylum

KENJI

I stand stock-still for a moment, letting the shock of everything settle around me, and when it finally hits me that Nazeera is really here, really awake, really okay, I pull her into my arms. Her defensive posture melts away, and suddenly she's just a girl—*my girl*—and happiness rockets through me. She's not even close to being short, but in my arms, she feels small. Pocket-sized. Like she was always meant to fit here, against my chest.

It's like heaven.

When we finally pull apart, I'm beaming like an idiot. I don't even care that everyone is staring at us. I just want to live in this moment.

"Hey," I say to her. "I'm so happy you're okay."

She takes a deep, unsteady breath, and then—smiles. It changes her whole face. It makes her look a lot less like a mercenary and a lot more like an eighteen-year-old girl. Though I think I like both versions, if I'm being honest.

"I'm so happy you're okay, too," she says quietly.

We stare at each other a moment longer before I hear someone clear their throat in a dramatic fashion.

Reluctantly, I turn around.

I know, in an instant, that the throat-clearing came from Nouria. I can tell by the way her arms are crossed, the way her eyes are narrowed. Sam, on the other hand, looks amused.

But Castle looks happy. Surprised, but happy.

I grin at him.

Nouria's frown deepens. "You two know Warner left, right?"

That wipes the smile off my face. I spin around, but there's no sign of him. I turn back, swearing quietly under my breath.

Nazeera shoots me a look.

"I know," I say, shaking my head. "He's going to try and leave without us."

She almost laughs. "Definitely."

I'm about to say my good-byes again when Nouria jumps to her feet. "Wait," she says.

"No time," I say, already backing out the door. "Warner is going to bail on us, and I c—"

"He's about to take a shower," Sam says, cutting me off.

I freeze so fast I nearly fall over. I turn around, eyebrows high. "He's what now?"

"He's about to take a shower," she says again.

I blink at her slowly, like I'm stupid, which, honestly, is kind of how I'm feeling at the moment. "You mean you're, like, watching him get ready to take a shower?"

"It's not weird," Nouria says flatly. "Stop making it weird."

I squint at Sam. "What's Warner doing right now?" I ask her. "Is he in the shower yet?"

"Yes."

Nazeera raises a single eyebrow. "So you're just, like, watching a naked Warner in the shower right now?"

"I'm not looking at his body," Sam says, sounding very close to irritated.

"But you *could*," I say, stunned. "That's what's so weird about this. You *could* just watch any of us take extremely naked showers."

"You know what?" Nouria says sharply. "I was going to do something to make things easier for you guys on your way out, but I think I've changed my mind."

"Wait—" Nazeera says. "Make things easier how?"

"I was going to help you steal a jet."

"Okay, all right, I take it back," I say, holding up my hands in apology. "I retract all my previous comments about nakedness. I would also like to formally apologize to Sam, who we all know is way too nice and way too cool to ever spy on anyone in the shower."

Sam rolls her eyes. Cracks a smile.

Nouria sighs. "I don't understand how you deal with him," she says to Castle. "I can't stand all the jokes. It would drive me insane to have to listen to this all day."

I'm about to protest when Castle responds.

"That's only because you don't know him well enough," Castle says, smiling at me. "Besides, we don't love him for his jokes, do we, Nazeera?" The two of them lock eyes for a moment. "We love him for his heart."

At that, the smile slips from my face. I'm still processing the weight of that statement—the generosity of such a statement—when I realize I've already missed a beat.

Nouria is talking.

"The air base isn't far from here," she's saying, "and I guess this is as good a time as any to let you all know that Sam and I are about to take a page out of Ella's playbook and take over Sector 241. Stealing a plane will be the least of the damage—and, in fact, I think it's a great way to launch our offensive strategy." She glances over her shoulder. "What do you think, Sam?"

"Brilliant," she says, "as usual."

Nouria smiles.

"I didn't realize that was your strategy," Castle says, the smile fading from his face. "Don't you think, based on how things turned out the last time, that m—"

"Why don't we discuss this after we've sent the kids off on their mission? Right now it's more important that we get them situated and give them a proper send-off before it's officially too late."

"Hey, speaking of which," I say quickly, "what makes you think we're not already too late?"

Nouria meets my eyes. "If they'd done the transfer," she says, "we would've felt it."

"Felt it how?"

It's Sam who responds: "In order for their plan to work, Emmaline has to die. They won't let that happen naturally, of course, because a natural death could occur in any number of ways, which leaves too many factors up in the air. They need to be able to control the experiment at all times—which is why they were so desperate to get their hands on Ella *before* Emmaline died. They're almost certainly going to kill Emmaline in a controlled environment, and they'll set it up in a way that leaves no room for error. Even so, we're bound to feel something change.

"That infinitesimal shift—after Emmaline's powers recede, but before they're funneled into a new host body—will dramatically glitch our visual of the world. And that moment hasn't happened yet, which makes us think that Ella is probably still safe." Sam shrugs. "But it could be happening any minute now. Time really is of the essence."

"How do you know so much about this?" Nazeera asks, her brows furrowed. "For years I tried to get my hands on this information, and I came up with nothing, despite being so close to the source. But you seem to know all of this on some kind of personal level. It's incredible."

"It's not that incredible," Nouria says, shaking her head. "We've just been focused in our search. All rebel groups have a different strength or core principle. For some, it's safety. For others, it's war. For us, it's been research. The things we've seen have been out there for everyone to see—there are glitches all the time—but when you're not looking for them, you don't notice them. But I noticed. Sam noticed. It was one of the things that brought us together."

The two women share a glance.

"We felt really sure that part of our oppression was in an illusion," Sam says. "And we've been chasing down the truth with every resource we've got. Unfortunately, we still don't know everything."

"But we're closer than most," Nouria says. She takes a sharp breath, refocusing. "We'll be holding down our end of things while you're gone. Hopefully, when you return, we'll have flipped more than one sector to our side."

"You really think you'll be able to accomplish that much in such a short period of time?" I ask, eyes wide. "I was hoping we wouldn't be gone for more than a couple days."

Nouria smiles at me then, but it's a strange smile, a searching smile. "Don't you understand?" she says. "This is it. This is the end. This is the defining moment we've all been fighting for. The end of an era. The end of a revolution. We currently—finally—have every advantage. We have people on the inside. If we do this right, we could collapse The Reestablishment in a matter of days."

"But all of that hinges on us getting to J on time," I say. "What if we're too late?"

"You'll have to kill her."

"*Nouria,*" Castle gasps.

"You're joking," I say. "Tell me you're joking."

"Not joking in the slightest," she says. "If you get there and Emmaline is dead and Ella has taken her place, you must kill Ella. You have to kill her and as many of the supreme commanders as you can."

My jaw has come unhinged.

"What about all that shit you said to J the night we got here? What about all that talk about how inspiring she is and how so many people were moved by her actions—how she's basically a hero? What happened to all that nonsense?"

"It wasn't nonsense," Nouria says. "I meant every word. But we're at war, Kishimoto. We don't have time to be sentimental."

"Sentimental? Are you out of your—"

Nazeera places a calming hand on my arm. "We'll find another way. There has to be another way."

"It's impossible to reverse the process once it's in effect," Sam says calmly. "Operation Synthesis will remove every trace of your old friend. She will be unrecognizable. A super soldier in every sense of the word. Beyond salvation."

"I'm not listening to this," I say angrily. "I'm not listening to this."

Nouria puts up her hands. "This conversation might turn out to be unnecessary. As long as you can get to her in time, it won't matter. But remember: if you get there and Ella is still alive, you need to make sure that she kills Emmaline above all else. Removing Emmaline is key. Once she's gone, the supreme commanders become easy targets. Vulnerable."

"Wait." I frown, still angry. "Why does it have to be J who kills Emmaline? Couldn't one of us do it?"

Nouria shakes her head. "If it were that simple," she says, "don't you think it would've been done by now?"

I raise my eyebrows. "Not if no one knew she existed."

"We knew she existed," Sam says quietly. "We've known about Emmaline for a while now."

Nouria goes on: "Why do you think we reached out to your team? Why do you think we risked the life of one of our own to get a message to Ella? Why do you think we opened our doors to you, even when we knew we'd be exposing ourselves to a possible attack? We made a series of increasingly difficult decisions, putting the lives of all those who depended on us at risk." She sighs. "But even now, after suffering a disastrous loss, Sam and I think that, ultimately, we did the right thing. Can you imagine why?"

"Because you're . . . Good Samaritans?"

"Because we realized, months ago, that Ella was the only one strong enough to kill her own sister. We need her just as much as you do. Not just us"—Nouria gestures to herself and Sam—"but the whole world. If Ella is able to kill Emmaline before any powers can be transferred, then she's killed The Reestablishment's greatest weapon. If she doesn't kill Emmaline now, while power still runs through Emmaline's veins, The Reestablishment can continue to harness and transfer that power to a new host."

"We once thought that Ella would have to fight her sister," Sam says. "But based on the information Ella shared with us while she was here, it seems like Emmaline is ready and willing to die." Sam shakes her head. "Even so, killing her is not as simple as pulling a plug. Ella will be going to war with the ghost of her mother's genius. Evie undoubtedly put in place numerous fail-safes to keep Emmaline invulnerable to attacks from others and from herself. I have no idea what Ella will be up against, but I can guarantee it won't be easy."

"Jesus." I drop my head into my hands. I thought I was already living with peak levels of stress, but I was wrong. This stress I'm experiencing now is on a whole new level.

I feel Nazeera's hand on my back and I look up. Her face looks as uncertain as mine feels, and somehow, it makes me feel better.

"Pack your bags," Nouria says. "Catch up with Warner. I'll meet the three of you at the entrance in twenty minutes."

~~ELLA~~
JULIETTE

In the darkness, I imagine light.

I dream of suns, moons, mothers. I see children laughing, crying, I see blood, I smell sugar. Light shatters across the blackness pressing against my eyes, fracturing nothing into something. Nameless shapes expand and spin, crash into each other, dissolving on contact. I see dust. I see dark walls, a small window, I see water, I see words on a page—

I am not insane I am not insane

In the pain, I imagine bliss.

My thoughts are like wind, rushing, curling into the depths of myself, expelling, dispelling darkness

I imagine love, I imagine wind, I imagine gold hair and green eyes and whispers, laughter

I imagine

Me

extraordinary, unbroken

the girl who shocked herself by surviving, the girl who loved herself through learning, the girl who respected her skin, understood her worth, found her strength

s t r o n g

s t r o n g e r

strongest

Imagine me
master of my own universe
I am everything I ever dreamed of

KENJI

We're in the air.

We've been in the air for hours now. I spent the first four hours sleeping—I can usually fall asleep anywhere, in any position—and I spent the last two hours eating all the snacks on the plane. We've got about an hour left in our flight and I'm so bored I've begun poking myself in the eye just to pass the time.

We got off to a good start—Nouria helped us steal a plane, as promised, by shielding our actions with a sheet of light—but now that we're up here, we're basically on our own. Nazeera had to fend off a few questions over the radio, but because most of the military has no idea what level of shit has already gone down, she still has the necessary clout to bypass inquiries from nosy sector leaders and soldiers. We realize it's only a matter of time, though, before someone realizes we don't have the authority to be up here.

Until then—

I glance around. I'm sitting close enough to the cockpit to be within earshot of Nazeera, but she and I both decided that I should hang back to keep an eye on Warner, who's sitting just far enough away to keep me safe from his scowl.

Honestly, the look on his face is so intense I'm surprised he hasn't started aging prematurely.

Suffice it to say that he didn't like Nouria's game plan.

I mean, I don't like it, either—and I have no intentions of following through with it—but Warner looked like he might shoot Nouria for even *thinking* that we might have to kill J. He's been sitting stiffly in the back of the plane ever since we boarded, and I've been wary of approaching him, despite our recent reconciliation. Semi-reconciliation? I'm calling it a reconciliation.

But right now I think he needs space.

Or maybe it's me, maybe I'm the one who needs space. He's exhausting to deal with. Without J around, Warner has no soft edges. He never smiles. He rarely looks at people. He's always irritated.

Right now, I honestly can't remember why J likes him so much.

In fact, in the last couple of months I'd forgotten what he was like without her around. But this reminder has been more than enough. Too much, in fact. I don't want any more reminders. I can guarantee that I will never again forget that Warner is not a fun guy to spend time with. That dude carries so much tension in his body it's practically contagious. So yeah, I'm giving him space.

So far, I've given him seven hours' worth of space.

I steal another glance at him, wondering how he holds himself so still—so stiff—for seven hours straight. How does he not pull a muscle? Why does he never have to use the bathroom? Where does it all go?

The only concession we got from Warner was that he showed up looking more like his normal self. Sam was right: Warner took a shower. You'd think he was going on a date, not a murder/rescue mission. It's obvious he wants to make a good impression.

He's wearing more Haider castoffs: a pale green blazer, matching pants. Black boots. But because these pieces were selected by Haider, the blazer is not a normal blazer. Of course it isn't. This blazer has no lapels, no buttons. The silhouette is cut in sharp lines that force the jacket to hang open, exposing Warner's shirt underneath—a simple white V-neck that shows more of his chest than I feel comfortable staring at. Still, he looks okay. A little nervous, but—

"Your thoughts are very loud," Warner says, still staring out the window.

"Oh my God, I'm so sorry," I say, feigning shock. "I'd turn the volume down, but I'd have to *die* in order for my brain to stop working."

"A problem easily rectified," he mutters.

"I heard that."

"I meant for you to hear that."

"Hey," I say, realizing something. "Doesn't this feel like some kind of weird déjà vu?"

"No."

"No, no, I'm being serious. What are the odds that the three of us would be on a trip like this again? Though the last time we were all on a trip like this, we ended up being shot out of the sky, so—yeah, I don't want to relive that. Also, J isn't here. So. Huh." I hesitate. "Okay, I think I'm realizing that maybe I don't actually understand what déjà vu means."

"It's French," Warner says, bored. "It literally means *already seen*."

"Wait, so then I do know what it means."

"That you know what anything means is astonishing to me."

Before I have a chance to defend myself, Nazeera's voice carries over from the cockpit.

"Hey," she calls. "Are you guys being friends again?"

I hear the familiar click and slide of metal—a sound that means Nazeera is unbuckling herself from pilot mode. Every once in a while she puts the plane on cruise control (or whatever) and makes her way over to me. But it's been at least half an hour since her last break, and I've missed her.

She folds herself into the chair next to me.

I beam at her.

"I'm so glad you two are finally talking," she says, sighing as she sinks into the seat. "The silence has been depressing."

My smile dies.

Warner's expression darkens.

"Listen," she says, looking at Warner. "I know this whole thing is horrible—that the very reason we're on this plane is horrible—but you have to stop being like this. We have, like, thirty minutes left on this flight, which means we're about to go out there, together, to do something huge. Which means we all have to get on the same page. We have to be able to trust each other and work together. If we don't, or if you don't let us, we could end up losing everything."

When Warner says nothing, Nazeera sighs again.

"I don't care what Nouria thinks," she says, trying for a gentle tone. "We're not going to lose Ella."

"You don't understand," Warner says quietly. He's still not looking at us. "I've already lost her."

"You don't know that," Nazeera says forcefully. "Ella might still be alive. We can still turn this around."

Warner shakes his head. "She was different even before she was taken," he says. "Something had changed inside of her, and I don't know what it was, but I could feel it. I've always been able to feel her—I've always been able to sense her energy—and she wasn't the same. Emmaline did something to her, changed something inside of her. I have no idea what she's going to be like when I see her again. If I see her again." He stares out the window. "But I'm here because I can do nothing else. Because this is the only way forward."

And then, even though I know it's going to piss him off, I say to Nazeera:

"Warner and J were engaged."

"What?" Nazeera stills. Her eyes go wide. Super wide. Wider than the plane. Her eyes go so wide they basically fill the sky. "When? How? Why did no one tell me?"

"I told you that in confidence," Warner says sharply, shooting me a glare.

"I know." I shrug. "But Nazeera's right. We're a team now, whether you like it or not, and we should get all of this out in the open. Air it out."

"Out in the open? What about the fact that you and Nazeera are in a relationship that you never bothered mentioning?"

"Hey," I say, "I was going t—"

"Wait. *Wait.*" Nazeera cuts me off. She holds up her hands. "Why are we changing the subject? Warner, engaged! Oh my God, this is— This is so good. This is a big deal, it could give us a per—"

"It's not *that* big of a deal." I turn, frown at her. "We all knew this kind of thing was coming. The two of them are basically destined to be together, even I can admit that." I tilt my head, considering. "I mean, true, I think they're a little young, but—"

Nazeera is shaking her head. "No. No. That's not what I'm talking about. I don't care about the actual engagement." She stops, glances up at Warner. "I mean—um, congratulations and everything."

Warner looks beyond annoyed.

"I just mean that this reminded me of something. Something so good. I don't know why I didn't think of this sooner. God, it would give us the perfect edge."

"What would?"

But Nazeera is out of her chair, stalking over to Warner and, cautiously, I follow. "Do you remember," she says to him, "when you and Lena were together?"

Warner shoots Nazeera a venomous look and says, with dramatic iciness, "I'd really rather not."

Nazeera waves away his statement with her hand. "Well, I remember. I remember a lot more than I should, probably, because Lena used to complain to me about your relationship all the time. And I remember, specifically, how much your dad and her mom wanted you guys to, like, I don't know—promise yourselves to each other for the foreseeable future, for the protection of the movement—"

"Promise themselves?" I frown.

"Yes, like—" She hesitates, her arms pinwheeling as she gathers her thoughts, but Warner suddenly sits up straighter in his seat, seeming to understand.

"Yes," he says calmly. The irritation is gone from his eyes. "I remember my father saying something to me about the importance of uniting our families. Unfortunately, my recollection of the interaction is vague, at best."

"Right, well, I'm sure your parents were both chasing after the idea for political gain, but Lena was—and probably still is—like, genuinely in love with you, and was always sort of obsessed with the idea of being your wife. She was always talking to me about marrying you, about her dreams for the future, about what your children would look like—"

I glance at Warner to catch his reaction to that statement, and the revolted look on his face is surprisingly satisfying.

"—but I remember her saying something even then, about how detached you were, and how closed off, and how one day, when the two of you got married, she'd finally be able to link your family profiles in the database, which would grant her the necessary security clearance to track your—"

The plane gives a sudden, violent jolt.

Nazeera goes still, words dying in her throat. Warner jumps to his feet. We all make a dash for the cockpit.

The lights are flashing, screaming alerts I don't understand. Nazeera scans the monitor at the same time as Warner, and the two of them share a look.

The plane gives another violent jolt, and I slam, hard, into the something sharp and metal. I let out a long string of curses and for some reason, when Nazeera reaches out to help me up—

I freak out.

"Will someone tell me what the hell is going on? What's happening? Are we being shot out of the sky right now?" I spin around, taking in the flashing lights, the steady beep echoing through the cabin. "Fucking déjà vu! I knew it!"

Nazeera takes a deep breath. Closes her eyes. "We're not being shot out of the sky."

"Then—"

"When we entered Oceania's airspace," Warner explains, "their base was alerted to the presence of our unauthorized aircraft." He glances at the monitor. "They know we're here, and they're not happy about it."

"Right, I get that, but—"

Another violent jolt and I hit the floor. Warner doesn't even seem to startle. Nazeera stumbles, but gracefully, and collapses into the cockpit seat. She looks strangely deflated.

"So, um, okay— What's happening?" I'm breathing hard. My heart is racing. "Are you sure we're not being shot out of the sky again? Why is no one freaking out? Am I having a heart attack?"

"You're not having a heart attack, and they're not shooting us out of the sky," Nazeera says again, her fingers flying over the dials, swiping across screens. "But they've activated remote control of the aircraft. They've taken over the plane."

"And you can't override it?"

She shakes her head. "I don't have the authority to override a supreme commander's missive."

After a beat of silence, she straightens. Turns to face us.

"Maybe this isn't so bad," she says. "I mean, I wasn't exactly sure how we'd land here or how it would all go down, but it's got to be a good sign that they want us to walk in there alive, right?"

"Not necessarily," Warner says quietly.

"Right." Nazeera frowns. "Yeah, I realized that was wrong only after I said it out loud."

"So we're just supposed to wait here?" I'm feeling my intense panic begin to fade, but only a little. "We just wait here until they land our plane and then when they land our plane they surround us with armed soldiers and then when we walk off the plane they murder us and then—you know, we're dead? That's the plan?"

"That," Nazeera says, "or they could tell our plane to crash itself into the ocean or something."

"Oh my God, Nazeera, this isn't funny."

Warner looks out the window. "She wasn't joking."

"Okay, I'm only going to ask this one more time: Why am I the only one who's freaking out?"

"Because I have a plan," Nazeera says. She glances at the dashboard once more. "We have exactly fourteen minutes before the plane lands, but that gives me more than enough time to tell you both exactly what we're going to do."

~~ELLA~~
JULIETTE

First, I see light.

Bright, orange, flaring behind my eyelids. Sounds begin to emerge shortly thereafter but the reveal is slow, muddy. I hear my own breath, then faint beeping. A metal *shhh,* a rush of air, the sound of laughter. Footsteps, footsteps, a voice that says—

Ella

Just as I'm about to open my eyes a flood of heat flushes through my body, burns through bone. It's violent, pervasive. It presses hard against my throat, choking me.

Suddenly, I'm numb.

Ella, the voice says.

Ella

Listen

"Any minute now."

Anderson's familiar voice breaks through the haze of

my mind. My fingers twitch against cotton sheets. I feel the insubstantial weight of a thin blanket covering the lower half of my body. The pinch and sting of needles. A roar of pain. I realize, then, that I cannot move my left hand.

Someone clears their throat.

"This is twice now that the sedative hasn't worked the way it should," someone says. The voice is unfamiliar. Angry. "With Evie gone this whole place is going to hell."

"Evie made substantial changes to Ella's body," Anderson says, and I wonder who he's talking about. "It's possible that something in her new physical makeup prevents the sedative from clearing as quickly as it should."

A humorless laugh. "Your friendship with Max has gotten you many things over the last couple of decades, but a medical degree is not one of them."

"It's only a theory. I think it might be po—"

"I don't care to know your theories," the man says, cutting him off. "What I want to know is why on earth you thought it would be a good idea to injure our key subject, when maintaining her physical and mental stability is *crucial* to—"

"Ibrahim, be reasonable," Anderson interjects. "After what happened last time, I just wanted to be sure that everything was working as it should. I was only testing her lo—"

"We all know about your fetish for torture, Paris, but the novelty of your singularly sick mind has worn off. We're out of time."

"We are not out of time," Anderson says, sounding remarkably calm. "This is only a minor setback; Max was able to fix it right away."

"A minor setback?" Ibrahim thunders. "The girl lost consciousness. We're still at high risk for regression. The subject is supposed to be in stasis. I allowed you free rein of the girl, once again, because I honestly didn't think you would be this stupid. Because I don't have time to babysit you. Because Tatiana, Santiago, and Azi and I all have our hands full trying to do both your job *and* Evie's in addition to our own. In addition to everything else."

"I was doing my own job just fine," Anderson says, his voice like acid. "No one asked you to step in."

"You're forgetting that you lost your job and your continent the moment Evie's daughter shot you in the head and claimed your leavings for herself. You let a teenage girl take your life, your livelihood, your children, and your soldiers from right under your nose."

"You know as well as I do that she's not an ordinary teenage girl," Anderson says. "She's Evie's daughter. You know what she's capable of—"

"But *she* didn't!" Ibrahim cries. "Half the reason the girl was meant to live a life of isolation was so that she'd never know the full extent of her powers. She was meant only to metamorphose quietly, undetected, while we waited for the right moment to establish ourselves as a movement. She was only entrusted to your care because of your decades-long friendship with Max—and because you were a scheming, conniving upstart who was willing to take whatever job you could get in order to move up."

"That's funny," Anderson says, unamused. "You used to like me for being a scheming, conniving upstart who was willing to take whatever job I could get."

"I liked you," Ibrahim says, seething, "when you got the job done. But in the last year, you've been nothing but deadweight. We've given you ample opportunity to correct your mistakes, but you can't seem to get things right. You're lucky Max was able to fix her hand so quickly, but we still know nothing of her mental state. And I swear to you, Paris, if there are unanticipated, irreversible consequences for your actions I will challenge you before the committee."

"You wouldn't dare."

"You might've gotten away with this nonsense while Evie was still alive, but the rest of us know that the only reason you even made it this far was because of Evie's indulgence of Max, who continues to vouch for you for reasons unfathomable to the rest of us."

"For reasons unfathomable to the rest of us?" Anderson laughs. "You mean you can't remember why you've kept me around all these years? Let me help refresh your memory. As I recall, you liked me best when I was the only one willing to do the abject, immoral, and unsavory jobs that helped get this movement off the ground." A pause. "You've kept me around all these years, Ibrahim, because in exchange,

I've kept the blood off your hands. Or have you forgotten? You once called me your savior."

"I don't care if I once called you a prophet." Something shatters. Metal and glass slamming hard into something else. "We can't continue to pay for your careless mistakes. We are at *war* right now, and at the moment we're barely holding on to our lead. If you can't understand the possible ramifications of even a minor setback at this critical hour, you don't deserve to stand among us."

A sudden crash. A door, slamming shut.

Anderson sighs, long and slow. Somehow I can tell, even from the sound of his exhalation, that he's not angry.

I'm surprised.

He just seems tired.

By degrees, the fingers of heat uncurl from around my throat. After a few more seconds of silence, my eyes flutter open.

I stare up at the ceiling, my eyes adjusting to the intense burst of white light. I feel slightly immobilized, but I seem to be okay.

"Juliette?"

Anderson's voice is soft. Far more gentle than I'd expected. I blink at the ceiling and then, with some effort, manage to move my neck. I lock eyes with him.

He looks unlike himself. Unshaven. Uncertain.

"Yes, sir," I say, but my voice is rough. Unused.

"How are you feeling?"

"I feel stiff, sir."

He hits a button and my bed moves, readjusting me so that I'm sitting relatively upright. Blood rushes from my head to my extremities and I'm left slightly dizzy. I blink, slowly, trying to recalibrate. Anderson turns off the machines attached to my body, and I watch, fascinated.

And then he straightens.

He turns his back to me, faces a small, high window. It's too far up for me to see the view. He raises his arms and runs his hands through his hair with a sigh.

"I need a drink," he says to the wall.

Anderson nods to himself and walks out the adjoining door. At first, I'm surprised to be left alone, but when I hear muffled sounds of movement and the familiar trill of glasses, clinking, I'm no longer surprised.

I'm confused.

I realize then that I have no idea where I am. Now that the needles have been removed from my body, I can more easily move, and as I swivel around to take in the space, it dawns on me that I am not in a medical wing, as I first suspected. This looks more like someone's bedroom.

Or maybe even a hotel room.

Everything is extremely white. Sterile. I'm in a big white bed with white sheets and a white comforter. Even the bed frame is made of a white, blond wood. Next to the various carts and now-dead monitors, there's a single nightstand decorated with a single, simple lamp. There's a slim door standing ajar, and through a slant of light I think I spy what serves as a closet, though it appears to be empty. Adjacent to the door is a suitcase, closed but unzipped. There's a screen mounted on the wall directly opposite me, and underneath it, a bureau. One of the drawers isn't completely closed, and it piques my interest.

It occurs to me then that I am not wearing any clothes. I'm wearing a hospital gown, but no real clothes. My eyes scan the room for my military uniform and I come up short.

There's nothing here.

I remember then, in a moment of clarity, that I must've bled all over my clothes. I remember kneeling on the floor. I remember the growing puddle of my own blood in which I collapsed.

I glance down at my injured hand. I only injured my index finger, but my entire left hand is bound in gauze. The pain has reduced to a dull throb. I take that as a good sign.

Gingerly, I begin to remove the bandages.

Just then, Anderson reappears. His suit jacket is gone. His tie, gone. The top two buttons of his shirt are undone, the black curl of ink more clearly visible, and his hair is disheveled. He seems more relaxed.

He remains in the doorway and takes a long drink from a glass half-full of amber liquid.

When he makes eye contact with me, I say:

"Sir, I was wondering where I am. I was also wondering where my clothes are."

Anderson takes another sip. He closes his eyes as he swallows, leans back against the doorframe. Sighs.

"You're in my room," he says, his eyes still closed. "This

compound is vast, and the medical wings—of which there are many—are, for the most part, situated on the opposite end of the facility, about a mile away. After Max attended to your needs, I had him deposit you here so that I'd be able to keep a close eye on you through the night. As to your clothes, I have no idea." He takes another sip. "I think Max had them incinerated. I'm sure someone will bring you replacements soon."

"Thank you, sir."

Anderson says nothing.

I say nothing more.

With his eyes closed, I feel safer to stare at him. I take advantage of the rare opportunity to peer closer at his tattoo, but I still can't make sense of it. Mostly, I stare at his face, which I've never seen like this: Soft. Relaxed. Almost smiling. Even so, I can tell that something is troubling him.

"What?" he says without looking at me. "What is it now?"

"I was wondering, sir, if you're okay."

His eyes open. He tilts his head to look at me, but his gaze is inscrutable. Slowly, he turns.

He throws back the last of his drink, rests the glass on the nightstand, and sits down in a nearby armchair. "I had you cut off your own finger last night, do you remember?"

"Yes, sir."

"And today you're asking me if I'm okay."

"Yes, sir. You seem upset, sir."

He leans back in the chair, looking thoughtful. Suddenly,

he shakes his head. "You know, I realize now that I've been too hard on you. I've put you through too much. Tested your loyalty perhaps too much. But you and I have a long history, Juliette. And it's not easy for me to forgive. I certainly don't forget."

I say nothing.

"You have no idea how much I hated you," he says, speaking more to the wall than to me. "How much I still hate you, sometimes. But now, finally—"

He sits up, looks me in the eye.

"Now you're perfect." He laughs, but there's no heart in it. "Now you're absolutely perfect and I have to just give you away. Toss your body to science." He turns toward the wall again. "What a shame."

Fear creeps up, through my chest. I ignore it.

Anderson stands, grabs the empty glass off the nightstand, and disappears for a minute to refill it. When he returns, he stares at me from the doorway. I stare back. We remain like that for a while before he says, suddenly—

"You know, when I was very young, I wanted to be a baker."

Surprise shoots through me, widens my eyes.

"I know," he says, taking another swallow of the amber liquid. He almost laughs. "Not what you'd expect. But I've always had a fondness for cake. Few people realize this, but baking requires infinite precision and patience. It is an exacting, cruel science. I would've been an excellent baker."

And then: "I'm not really sure why I'm telling you this. I suppose it's been a long time since I've felt I could speak openly with anyone."

"You can tell me anything, sir."

"Yes," he says quietly. "I'm beginning to believe that."

We're both silent then, but I can't stop staring at him, my mind suddenly overrun with unanswerable questions.

Another twenty seconds of this and he finally breaks the silence.

"All right, what is it?" His voice is dry. Self-mocking. "What is it you're *dying* to know?"

"I'm sorry, sir," I say. "I was just wondering— Why didn't you try? To be a baker?"

Anderson shrugs, spins the glass around in his hands. "When I got a bit older, my mother used to force bleach down my throat. Ammonia. Whatever she could find under the sink. It was never enough to kill me," he says, meeting my eyes. "Just enough to torture me for all of eternity." He throws back the rest of the drink. "You might say that I lost my appetite."

I can't mask my horror quickly enough. Anderson laughs at me, laughs at the look on my face.

"She never even had a good reason for doing it," he says, turning away. "She just hated me."

"Sir," I say, "Sir, I—"

Max barges into the room. I flinch.

"What the hell did you do?"

"There are so many possible answers to that question,"

Anderson says, glancing back. "Please be more specific. By the way, what did you do with her clothes?"

"I'm talking about Kent," Max says angrily. "What did you do?"

Anderson looks suddenly uncertain. He glances from Max to me then back again. "Perhaps we should discuss this elsewhere."

But Max looks beyond reason. His eyes are so wild I can't tell if he's angry or terrified. "Please tell me the tapes were tampered with. Tell me I'm wrong. Tell me you didn't perform the procedure on yourself."

Anderson looks at once relieved and irritated. "Calm yourself," he says. "I watched Evie do this kind of thing countless times—and the last time, on me. The boy had already been drained. The vial was ready, just sitting there on the counter, and you were so busy with"—he glances at me—"anyway, I had a while to wait, and I figured I'd make myself useful while I stood around."

"I can't believe— Of course you don't see the problem," Max says, grabbing a fistful of his own hair. He's shaking his head. "You never see the problem."

"That seems an unfair accusation."

"Paris, there's a reason why most Unnaturals only have one ability." He's beginning to pace now. "The occurrence of two supernatural gifts in the same person is exceedingly rare."

"What about Ibrahim's girl?" he says. "Wasn't that your work? Evie's?"

"No," Max says forcefully. "That was a random, natural error. We were just as surprised by the discovery as anyone else."

Anderson goes suddenly solid with tension. "What, exactly, is the problem?"

"It's not—"

A sudden blare of sirens and the words die in Max's throat. "Not again," he whispers. "God, not again."

Anderson spares me a single glance before he disappears into his room, and this time, he reappears fully assembled. Not a hair out of place. He checks the cartridge of a handgun before he tucks it away, in a hidden holster.

"Juliette," he says sharply.

"Yes, sir?"

"I am ordering you to remain here. No matter what you see, no matter what you hear, you are not to leave this room. You are to do nothing unless I command you otherwise. Do you understand? "

"Yes, sir."

"Max, get her something to wear," Anderson barks. "And then keep her hidden. Guard her with your life."

KENJI

This was the plan:

We were all supposed to go invisible—Warner borrowing his power from me and Nazeera—and jump out of the plane just before it landed. Nazeera would then activate her flying powers, and with Warner bolstering her power, the three of us would bypass the welcoming committee intent on murdering us. We'd then make our way directly into the heart of the vast compound, where we'd begin our search for Juliette.

This is what actually happens:

All three of us go invisible and jump out of the plane as it lands. That part worked. The thing we weren't expecting, of course, was for the welcoming/murdering committee to so thoroughly anticipate our moves.

We're up in the air, flying over the heads of at least two dozen highly armed soldiers and one dude who looks like he might be Nazeera's dad, when someone flashes some kind of long-barreled gun up, into the sky. He seems to be searching for something.

Us.

"He's scanning for heat signatures," Warner says.

"I realize that," Nazeera says, sounding frustrated. She picks up speed, but it doesn't matter.

Seconds later, the guy with the heat gun shouts something to someone else, who aims a different weapon at us, one that immediately disables our powers.

It's just as horrifying as it sounds.

I don't even have a chance to scream. I don't have time to think about the fact that my heart is racing a mile a minute, or that my hands are shaking, or that Nazeera—fearless, invulnerable Nazeera—looks suddenly terrified as the sky falls out from under her. Even Warner seems stunned.

I was already super freaked out about the idea of being shot out of the sky again, but I can honestly say that I wasn't mentally prepared for this. This is a whole new level of terror. The three of us are suddenly visible and spiraling to our deaths and the soldiers below are just staring at us, waiting.

For what? I think.

Why are they just staring at us as we die? Why go to all the trouble to take over our plane and land us here, safely, just to watch us fall out of the sky?

Do they find this entertaining?

Time feels strange. Infinite and nonexistent. Wind is rushing up against my feet, and all I can see is the ground, coming at us too fast, but I can't stop thinking about how, in all my nightmares, I never thought I'd die like this. I never thought I'd die because of gravity. I didn't think that *this* was the way I was destined to exit the world, and it seems wrong, and it seems unfair, and I'm thinking about how quickly we failed, how we never stood a chance—when I hear a sudden explosion.

A flash of fire, discordant cries, the faraway sounds of Warner shouting, and then I'm no longer falling, no longer visible.

It all happens so fast I feel dizzy.

Nazeera's arm is wrapped around me and she's hauling me upward, struggling a bit, and then Warner materializes beside me, helping to prop me up. His sharp voice and familiar presence are my only proof of his existence.

"Nice shot," Nazeera says, her breathless words loud in my ear. "How long do you think we have?"

"Ten seconds before it occurs to them to start shooting blindly at us," Warner calls out. "We have to move out of range. Now."

"On it," Nazeera shouts back.

We narrowly avoid gunfire as the three of us plummet, at a sharp diagonal, to the ground. We were already so close to the ground that it doesn't take us long to land in the middle of a field, far enough away from danger to be able to breathe a momentary sigh of relief, but too far from the compound for the relief to last long.

I'm bent over, hands on my knees, gasping for breath, trying to calm down. "What did you do you? What the hell just happened?"

"Warner threw a grenade," Nazeera explains. Then, to Warner: "You found that in Haider's bag, didn't you?"

"That, and a few other useful things. We need to move."

I hear the sound of his retreating footsteps—boots crushing grass—and I hurry to follow.

"They'll regroup quickly," Warner is saying, "so we have only moments to come up with a new plan. I think we should split up."

"No," Nazeera and I say at the same time.

"There's no time," Warner says. "They know we're here, and they've obviously had ample opportunity to prepare for our arrival. Unfortunately, our parents aren't idiots; they know we're here to save Ella. Our presence has almost certainly inspired them to begin the transfer if they haven't done so already. The three of us together are inefficient. Easy targets."

"But one of us has to stay with you," Nazeera says. "You need us within close proximity if you're going to use stealth to get around."

"I'll take my chances."

"No way," Nazeera says flatly. "Listen, I know this compound, so I'll be okay on my own. But Kenji doesn't know this place well enough. The entire footprint measures out to about a hundred and twenty acres of land—which means you can easily get lost if you don't know where to look. You two stick together. Kenji will lend you his stealth, and you can be his guide. I'll go alone."

"What?" I say, panicked. "No, no way—"

"Warner's not wrong," Nazeera says, cutting me off. "The three of us, as a group, really do make for an easier target. There are too many variables. Besides, I have something

I need to do, and the sooner I can get to a computer, the smoother things will go for you both. It's probably best if I tackle that on my own."

"Wait, what?"

"What are you planning?" Warner asks.

"I'm going to trick the systems into thinking that your family and Ella's are linked," she says to Warner. "There's protocol for this sort of thing already in place within The Reestablishment, so if I can create the necessary profiles and authorizations, the database will recognize you as a member of the Sommers family. You'll be granted easy access to most of the high-security rooms throughout the compound. But it's not foolproof. The system does a self-scan for anomalies every hour. If it's able to see through my bullshit, you'll be locked out and reported. But until then—you'll be able to more easily search the buildings for Ella."

"Nazeera," Warner says, sounding unusually impressed. "That's . . . great."

"Better than great," I add. "That's amazing."

"Thanks," she says. "But I should get going. The sooner I start flying, the sooner I can get started, which hopefully means that by the time you reach base, I'll have made something happen."

"But what if you get caught?" I ask. "What if you can't do it? How will we find you?"

"You won't."

"But— Nazeera—"

“We’re at war, Kishimoto,” she says, a slight smile in her voice. “We don’t have time to be sentimental.”

“That’s not funny. I hate that joke. I hate it so much.”

“Nazeera is going to be fine,” Warner says. “You obviously don’t know her well if you think she’s easily captured.”

“She literally just woke up! After being shot! In the chest! She nearly died!”

“That was a fluke,” Warner and Nazeera say at the same time.

“But—”

“Hey,” Nazeera says, her voice suddenly close. “I have a feeling I’m about four months away from falling madly in love with you, so please don’t get yourself killed, okay?”

I’m about to respond when I feel a sudden rush of air. I hear her launching up, into the sky, and even though I know I won’t see her, I crane my neck as if to watch her go.

And just like that—

She’s gone.

My heart is pounding in my chest, blood rushing to my head. I feel confused: terrified, excited, hopeful, horrified. All the best and worst things always seem to happen to me at the same time.

It’s not fair.

“Fucking hell,” I say out loud.

“Come on,” Warner says. “Let’s move out.”

~~ELLA~~
JULIETTE

Max is staring at me like I'm an alien.

He hasn't moved since Anderson left; he just stands there, stiff and strange, rooted to the floor. I remember the look he gave me the first time we met—the unguarded hostility in his eyes—and I blink at him from my bed, wondering why he hates me so much.

After an uncomfortable stretch of silence, I clear my throat. It's obvious that Anderson respects Max—likes him, even—so I decide I should address him with a similar level of respect.

"Sir," I say. "I'd really like to get dressed."

Max startles at the sound of my voice. His body language is entirely different now that Anderson isn't here, and I'm still struggling to figure him out. He seems skittish. I wonder if I should feel threatened by him. His affection for Anderson is no indication that he might treat me as anything but a nameless soldier.

A subordinate.

Max sighs. It's a loud, rough sound that seems to shake him from his stupor. He shoots me a last look before he disappears into the adjoining room, from where I hear indiscernible, shuffling sounds. When he reappears, his arms are empty.

He stares blankly at me, looking more rattled than he did a moment ago. He shoves a hand through his hair. It sticks up in places.

"Anderson doesn't have anything that would fit you," he says.

"No, sir," I say carefully. Still confused. "I was hoping I might be given a replacement uniform."

Max turns away, stares at nothing. "A replacement uniform," he says to himself. "Right." But when he takes in a long, shuddering breath, it becomes clear to me that he's trying to stay calm.

Trying to stay calm.

I realize, suddenly, that Max might be afraid of me. Maybe he saw what I did to Darius. Maybe he's the doctor who patched him up.

Still—

I don't see what reason he'd have to think I'd hurt him. After all, my orders come from Anderson, and as far as I'm aware, Max is an ally. I watch him closely as he lifts his wrist to his mouth, quietly requesting that someone deliver a fresh set of clothes for me.

And then he backs away from me until he's flush with the wall. There's a single, sharp thud as the heels of his boots hit the baseboards, and then, silence.

Silence.

It erupts, settling completely into the room, the quiet

reaching even the farthest corners. I feel physically trapped by it. The lack of sound feels oppressive.

Paralyzing.

I pass the time by counting the bruises on my body. I don't think I've spent this much time looking at myself in the last few days; I hadn't realized how many wounds I had. There seem to be several fresh cuts on my arms and legs, and I feel a vague stinging along my lower abdomen. I pull back the collar of the hospital gown, peering through the overly large neck hole at my naked body underneath.

Pale. Bruised.

There's a small, fresh scar running vertically down the side of my torso, and I don't know what I did to acquire it. In fact, my body seems to have amassed an entire constellation of fresh incisions and faded bruises. For some reason, I can't remember where they came from.

I glance up, suddenly, when I feel the heat of Max's gaze.

He's staring at me as I study myself, and the sharp look in his eyes makes me wary. I sit up. Sit back.

I don't feel comfortable asking him any of the questions piling in my mouth.

So I look at my hands.

I've already removed the rest of my bandages; my left hand is mostly healed. There's no visible scar where my finger was detached, but my skin is mottled up to my forearm, mostly purple and dark blue, a few spots of yellow. I curl my fingers into a fist, let it go. It hurts only a little. The pain is fading by the hour.

The next words leave my lips before I can stop them: "Thank you, sir, for fixing my hand."

Max stares at me, uncertain, when his wrist lights up. He glances down at the message, and then at the door, and as he darts to the entrance, he tosses strange, wild looks at me over his shoulder, as if he's afraid to turn his back on me.

Max grows more bizarre by the moment.

When the door opens, the room is flooded with sound. Flashing lights pulse through the slice of open doorway, shouts and footsteps thundering down the hall. I hear metal crashing into metal, the distant blare of an alarm.

My heart picks up.

I'm on my feet before I can even stop myself, my sharpened senses oblivious to the fact that my hospital gown does little to cover my body. All I know is a sudden, urgent need to join the commotion, to do what I can to assist, and to find my commander and protect him. It's what I was built to do.

I can't just stand here.

But then I remember that my commander gave me explicit orders to remain here, and the fight leaves my body.

Max shuts the door, silencing the chaos with that single motion. I open my mouth to say something, but the look in his eyes warns me not to speak. He places a stack of clothes on the bed—refusing to even come near me—and steps out of the room.

I change into the clothes quickly, shedding the loose gown for the starched, stiff fabric of a freshly washed military uniform. Max brought me no undergarments, but I don't bother pointing this out; I'm just relieved to have something to wear. I'm still buttoning the front placket, my fingers working as quickly as possible, when my gaze falls once more to the bureau directly opposite the bed. There's a single drawer left slightly open, as if it was closed in a hurry.

I'd noticed it earlier.

I can't stop staring at it now.

Something pulls me forward, some need I can't explain. It's becoming familiar now—almost normal—to feel the strange heat filling my head, so I don't question my compulsion to move closer. Something somewhere inside of me is screaming at me to stand down, but I'm only dimly aware of it. I hear Max's muffled, low voice in the other room; he's speaking with someone in harried, aggressive tones. He seems fully distracted.

Encouraged, I step forward.

My hand curls around the drawer pull, and it takes only a little effort to tug it open. It's a smooth, soft system. The wood makes almost no sound as it moves. And I'm just about to peer inside when—

"What are you doing?"

Max's voice sends a sharp note of clarity through my brain, clearing the haze. I take a step back, blinking. Trying to understand what I was doing.

"The drawer was open, sir. I was going to close it." The lie comes automatically. Easily.

I marvel at it.

Max slams the drawer closed and stares, suspiciously, at my face. I blink at him, blithely meeting his gaze.

I notice then that he's holding my boots.

He shoves them at me; I take them. I want to ask him if he has a hair tie—my hair is unusually long; I have a vague memory of it being much shorter—but I decide against it.

He watches me closely as I pull on my boots, and once I'm upright again, he barks at me to follow him.

I don't move.

"Sir, my commander gave me direct orders to remain in this room. I will stay here until otherwise instructed."

"You're currently being instructed. I'm instructing you."

"With all due respect, sir, you are not my commanding officer."

Max sighs, irritation darkening his features, and he lifts his wrist to his mouth. "Did you hear that? I told you she wouldn't listen to me." A pause. "Yes. You'll have to come get her yourself."

Another pause.

Max is listening on an invisible earpiece not unlike the one I've seen Anderson use—an earpiece I'm now realizing must be implanted in their brains.

"Absolutely not," Max says, his anger so sudden it startles me. He shakes his head. "I'm not touching her."

Another beat of silence, and—

"I realize that," he says sharply. "But it's different when

her eyes are open. There's something about her face. I don't like the way she looks at me."

My heart slows.

Blackness fills my vision, flickers back to light. I hear my heart beating, hear myself breathe in, breathe out, hear my own voice, loud—so loud—

There was something about my face

The words slur, slow down

there wassomething about my facesssomething about my facesss-something about my eyes, the way I looked at her

My eyes fly open with a start. I'm breathing hard, confused, and I have hardly a moment to reflect on what just happened in my head before the door flies open again. A roar of noise fills my ears—more sirens, more shouts, more sounds of urgent, chaotic movement—

"Juliette Ferrars."

There's a man in front of me. Tall. Forbidding. Black hair, brown skin, green eyes. I can tell, just by looking at him, that he wields a great deal of power.

"I am Supreme Commander Ibrahim."

My eyes widen.

Musa Ibrahim is the supreme commander of Asia. By all accounts, the supreme commanders of The Reestablishment have equal levels of authority—but Supreme Commander Ibrahim is widely known to be one of the founders of the movement, and one of the only supreme commanders to have held the position from the beginning. He's extremely well respected.

So when he says, "Come with me," I say—

"Yes, sir."

I follow him out the door and into the chaos, but I don't have long to take in the pandemonium before we make a sharp turn into a dark hallway. I follow Ibrahim down a slim, narrow path, the lights dimming as we go. I glance back a few times to see if Max is still with us, but he seems to have gone in another direction.

"This way," Ibrahim says sharply.

We make one more turn and, suddenly, the narrow path opens onto a large, brightly lit landing area. There's an industrial stairwell to the left and a large, gleaming steel elevator to the right. Ibrahim heads for the elevator, and places his hand flat against the seamless door. After a moment, the metal emits a quiet beep, hissing as it slides open.

Once we're both inside, Ibrahim gives me a wide berth. I wait for him to direct the elevator—I scan the interior for buttons or a monitor of some kind—but he does nothing. A second later, without prompting, the elevator moves.

The ride is so smooth it takes me a minute to realize we're moving sideways, rather than up or down. I glance around, taking the opportunity to more closely examine the interior, and only then do I notice the rounded corners. I thought this unit was rectangular; it appears to be circular. I wonder, then, if we're moving as a bullet would, boring through the earth.

Surreptitiously, I glance at Ibrahim.

He says nothing. Indicates nothing. He seems neither interested nor perturbed by my presence, which is new. He holds himself with a certainty that reminds me a great deal of Anderson, but there's something else about Ibrahim—something more—that feels unique. Even from a passing glance it's obvious that he feels absolutely sure about himself. I'm not sure even Anderson feels absolutely sure of himself. He's always testing and prodding—examining and questioning. Ibrahim, on the other hand, seems comfortable. Unbothered. Effortlessly confident.

I wonder what that must feel like.

And then I shock myself for wondering.

Once the elevator stops, it makes three brief, harsh, buzzing sounds. A moment later, the doors open. I wait for Ibrahim to exit first, and then I follow.

When I cross the threshold, I'm first stunned by the smell. The air quality is so poor that I can't even open my eyes properly. There's an acrid smell in the air, something reminiscent of sulfur, and I step through a cloud of smoke so thick it immediately makes my eyes burn. It's not long before I'm coughing, covering my face with my arm as I force my way through the room.

I don't know how Ibrahim can stand this.

Only after I've pushed through the cloud does the stinging smell begin to dissipate, but by then, I've lost track of Ibrahim. I spin around, trying to take in my surroundings, but there are no visual cues to root me. This laboratory doesn't seem much different from the others I've seen. A great deal of glass and steel. Dozens of long, metal tables stretched across the room, all of them covered in beakers and test tubes and what look like massive microscopes. The one big difference here is that there are huge glass domes drilled into the walls, the smooth, transparent semicircles appearing more like portholes than anything else. As I get closer I realize that they're planters of some kind, each one containing unusual vegetation I've never seen. Lights flicker on as I move through the vast space, but much of it is still shrouded in darkness, and I gasp, suddenly, when I walk straight into a glass wall.

I take a step back, my eyes adjusting to the light.

It's not a wall.

It's an aquarium.

An aquarium larger than I am. An aquarium the size of a wall. It's not the first water tank I've seen in a laboratory here in Oceania, and I'm beginning to wonder why there are so many of them. I take another step back, still trying to make sense of what I'm seeing. Dissatisfied, I step closer again. There's a dim blue light in the tank, but it doesn't do much to illuminate the large dimensions. I crane my neck to see the top of it, but I lose my balance, catching myself against the glass at the last second. This is a futile effort.

I need to find Ibrahim.

Just as I'm about to step back, I notice a flash of movement in the tank. The water trembles within, begins to thrash.

A hand slams hard against the glass.

I gasp.

Slowly, the hand retreats.

I stand there, frozen in fear and fascination, when someone clamps down on my arm.

This time, I almost scream.

"Where have you been?" Ibrahim says angrily.

"I'm sorry, sir," I say quickly. "I got lost. The smoke was so thick that I—"

"What are you talking about? What smoke?"

The words die in my throat. I thought I saw smoke. Was there no smoke? Is this another test?

Ibrahim sighs. "Come with me."

"Yes, sir."

This time, I keep my eyes on Ibrahim at all times.

And this time, when we walk through the darkened laboratory into a blindingly bright, circular room, I know I'm in the right place. Because something is wrong.

Someone is dead.

KENJI

When we finally make it to the compound, I'm exhausted, thirsty, and really have to use the bathroom. Warner is none of those things, apparently, because Warner is made of uranium or plutonium or someshit, so I have to beg him to let me take a quick break. And by begging him I mean I grab him by the back of the shirt and force him to slow down—and then I basically collapse behind a wall. Warner shoves away from me, and the sound of his irritated exhalation is all I need to know that my "break" is half a second from over.

"We don't take breaks," he says sharply. "If you can't keep up, stay here."

"Bro, I'm not asking to stop. I'm not even asking for a real break. I just need a second to catch my breath. Two seconds. Maybe five seconds. That's not crazy. And just because I have to catch my breath doesn't mean I don't love J. It means we just ran like a thousand miles. It means my lungs aren't made of steel."

"Two miles," he says. "We ran two miles."

"In the sun. Uphill. You're in a fucking suit. Do you even sweat? How are you not tired?"

"If by now you don't understand, I certainly can't teach you."

I haul myself to my feet. We start moving again.

"I'm not sure I even want to know what you're talking about," I say, lowering my voice as I reach for my gun. We're rounding the corner to the entrance, where our big, fancy plan to break into the building involves waiting for someone to open the door, and catching that door before it closes.

No luck yet.

"Hey," I whisper.

"What?" Warner sounds annoyed.

"How'd you end up proposing?"

Silence.

"Come on, bro. I'm curious. Also, I, uh, really have to pee, so if you don't distract me right now all I'm going to think about is how much I have to pee."

"You know, sometimes I wish I could remove the part of my brain that stores the things you say to me."

I ignore that.

"So? How'd you do it?" Someone comes through the door and I tense, ready to jump forward, but there's not enough time. My body relaxes back against the wall. "Did you get the ring like I told you to?"

"No."

"What? What do you mean, *no*?" I hesitate. "Did you at least, like, light a candle? Make her dinner?"

"No."

"Buy her chocolates? Get down on one knee?"

"No."

"No? No, you didn't do even one of those things? None of them?" My whispers are turning into whisper-yells. "You didn't do a single thing I told you to do?"

"No."

"Son of a bitch."

"Why does it matter?" he asks. "She said yes."

I groan. "You're the worst, you know that? The *worst*. You don't deserve her."

Warner sighs. "I thought that was already obvious."

"Hey— Don't you dare make me feel sorry for y—"

I cut myself off when the door suddenly opens. A small group of doctors (scientists? I don't know) exits the building, and Warner and I jump to our feet and get into position. This group has just enough people—and they take just long enough exiting—that when I grab the door and hold it open for a few seconds longer, it doesn't seem to register.

We're in.

And we've only been inside for less than a second before Warner slams me into the wall, knocking the air from my lungs.

"Don't move," he whispers. "Not an inch."

"Why not?" I wheeze.

"Look up," he says, "but only with your eyes. Don't move your head. Do you see the cameras?"

"No."

"They anticipated us," he says. "They anticipated our moves. Look up again, but do it carefully. Those small black dots are cameras. Sensors. Infrared scanners. Thermal imagers. They're searching for inconsistencies in the security footage."

"*Shit.*"

"Yes."

"So what do we do?"

"I'm not sure," Warner says.

"You're not sure?" I say, trying not to freak out. "How can you not be sure?"

"I'm thinking," he whispers, irritated. "And I don't hear you contributing any ideas."

"Listen, bro, all I know is that I really, really need to p—"

I'm interrupted by the distant sound of a toilet flushing. A moment later, a door swings open. I turn my head a millimeter and realize we're right next to the men's bathroom.

Warner and I seize the moment, catching the door before it falls closed. Once inside the bathroom we press up against the wall, our backs to the cold tile. I'm trying hard not to think about all the pee residue touching my body, when Warner exhales.

It's a brief, quiet sound—but he sounds relieved.

I'm guessing that means there are no scanners or cameras in this bathroom, but I can't be sure, because Warner doesn't say a word, and it doesn't take a genius to figure out why.

We're not sure if we're alone in here.

I can't see him do it, but I'm pretty sure Warner is checking the stalls right now. It's what I'm doing, anyway. This isn't a huge bathroom—as I'm sure it's one of many—and it's right by the entrance/exit of the building, so right now it doesn't seem to be getting a lot of traffic.

When we're both certain the room is clear, Warner says—

"We're going to go up, through the vent. If you truly need to use the bathroom, do it now."

"Okay, but why do you have to sound so disgusted about it? Do you really expect me to believe that you never have to use the bathroom? Are basic human needs below you?"

Warner ignores me.

I see the stall door open, and I hear his careful sounds as he climbs the metal cubicles. There's a large vent in the ceiling just above one of the stalls, and I watch as his invisible hands make short work of the grate.

Quickly, I use the bathroom. And then I wash my hands as loudly as possible, just in case Warner feels the need to make a juvenile comment about my hygiene.

Surprisingly, he doesn't.

Instead, he says, "Are you ready?" And I can tell by the echoing sound of his voice that he's already halfway up the vent.

"I'm ready. Just let me know when you're in."

More careful movement, the metal drumming as he goes. "I'm in," he says. "Make sure you reattach the grate after you climb up."

"Got it."

"On a related note, I hope you're not claustrophobic. Though if you are . . . Good luck."

I take a deep breath.

Let it go.

And we begin our journey into hell.

~~ELLA~~
JULIETTE

Max, Anderson, a blond woman, and a tall black man are all standing in the center of the room, staring at a dead body, and they look up only when Ibrahim approaches.

Anderson's eyes home in on me immediately.

I feel my heart jump. I don't know how Max got here before we did, and I don't know if I'm about to be punished for obeying Supreme Commander Ibrahim.

My mind spirals.

"What's she doing here?" Anderson asks, his expression wild. "I told her to stay in the r—"

"I overruled your orders," Ibrahim says sharply, "and told her to come with me."

"My bedroom is one of the most secure locations on this wing," Anderson says, barely holding on to his anger. "You've put us all at risk by moving her."

"We are currently under attack," Ibrahim says. "You left her alone, completely unattended—"

"I left her with Max!"

"Max, who's too terrified of his own creation to spend even a few minutes alone with the girl. You forget, there's a reason he was never granted a military position."

Anderson shoots Max a strange, confused look. Somehow, the confusion on Anderson's face makes me feel better about my own. I have no idea what's happening. No idea to whom I should answer. No idea what Ibrahim meant by *creation*.

Max just shakes his head.

"The children are here," Ibrahim says, changing the subject. "They're here, in our midst, completely undetected. They're going room by room searching for her, and already they've killed four of our key scientists in the process." He nods at the dead body—a graying, middle-aged man, blood pooling beneath him. "How did this happen? Why haven't they been spotted yet?"

"Nothing has registered on the cameras," Anderson says. "Not yet, anyway."

"So you're telling me that this—and the three other dead bodies we've found so far—was the work of ghosts?"

"They must've found a way to trick the system," the woman says. "It's the only possible answer."

"Yes, Tatiana, I realize that—but the question is *how*." Ibrahim pinches his nose between his thumb and index finger. And it's clear he's talking to Anderson when he says: "All the preparations you claimed to have made in anticipation of a possible assault—they were all for nothing?"

"What did you expect?" Anderson is no longer trying to control his anger. "They're our children. We bred them for this. I'd be disappointed if they were stupid enough to fall into our traps right away."

Our children?

"Enough," Ibrahim cries. "Enough of this. We need to initiate the transfer now."

"I already told you why we can't," Max says urgently. "Not yet. We need more time. Emmaline still needs to fall below ten percent viability in order for the procedure to operate smoothly, and right now, she's at twelve percent. Another few days—maybe a couple of weeks—and we should be able to move forward. But anything above ten percent viability means there's a chance she'll still be strong enough to resis—"

"I don't care," Ibrahim says. "We've waited long enough. And we've wasted enough time and money trying to keep both her alive and her sister in our custody. We can't risk another failure."

"But initiating the transfer at twelve percent viability has a thirty-eight percent chance of failure," Max says, speaking quickly. "We could be risking a great deal—"

"Then find more ways to reduce viability," Ibrahim snaps.

"We're already at the top end of what we can do right now," Max says. "She's still too strong—she's fighting our efforts—"

"That's only more reason to get rid of her sooner," Ibrahim says, cutting him off again. "We're expending an egregious amount of resources just to keep the other kids isolated from her advances—when God only knows what damage she's already done. She's been meddling everywhere, causing needless disaster. We need a new host. A healthy one. And we need it now."

"Ibrahim, don't be rash," Anderson says, trying to sound calm. "This could be a huge mistake. Juliette is a perfect soldier—she's more than proven herself—and right now she could be a huge help. Instead of locking her away, we should be sending her out. Giving her a mission."

"Absolutely not."

"Ibrahim, he makes a good point," the tall black man says. "The kids won't be expecting her. She'd be the perfect lure."

"See? Azi agrees with me."

"I don't." Tatiana shakes her head. "It's too dangerous," she says. "Too many things could go wrong."

"What could possibly go wrong?" Anderson asks. "She's more powerful than any of them, and completely obedient to me. To us. To the movement. You all know as well as I do that she's proven her loyalty again and again. She'd be able to capture them in a matter of minutes. This could all be over in an hour, and we'd be able to move on with our lives." Anderson locks eyes with me. "You wouldn't mind rounding up a few rebels, would you, Juliette?"

"I would be happy to, sir."

"See?" Anderson gestures to me.

A sudden alarm blares, the sound so loud it's painful. I'm still rooted in place, so overwhelmed and confused by this sudden flood of dizzying information that I don't even know what to do with myself. But the supreme commanders look suddenly terrified.

"Azi, where is Santiago?" Tatiana cries. "You were last with him, weren't you? Someone check in with Santiago—"

"He's down," Azi says, tapping against his temple. "He's not responding."

"*Max*," Anderson says sharply, but Max is already rushing out the door, Azi and Tatiana on his heels.

"Go collect your son," Ibrahim barks at Anderson.

"Why don't you go collect your daughter?" Anderson shoots back.

Ibrahim's eyes narrow. "I'm taking the girl," he says quietly. "I'm finishing this job, and I'll do it alone if I have to."

Anderson glances from me to Ibrahim. "You're making a mistake," he says. "She's finally become our asset. Don't let your pride keep you from seeing the answer in front of us. Juliette should be the one tracking down the kids right now. The fact that they won't be anticipating her as an assailant makes them easier targets. It's the most obvious solution."

"You are out of your mind," Ibrahim shouts, "if you think I'm foolish enough to take such a risk. I will not just hand her over to her friends like some common idiot."

Friends?

I have friends?

"Hey, princess," someone whispers in my ear.

KENJI

Warner just about slaps me upside the head.

He yanks me back, grabbing me roughly by the shoulder, and drags us both across the overly bright, extremely creepy laboratory.

Once we're far enough away from Anderson, Ibrahim, and Robot J, I expect Warner to say something—anything—

He doesn't.

The two of us watch the distant conversation grow more heated by the moment, but we can't really hear what they're saying from here. Though I think even if we could hear what they were saying, Warner wouldn't be paying attention. The fight seems to have left his body. I can't even see him right now, but I can feel it. Something about his movements, his quiet sighs.

His mind is on Juliette.

Juliette, who looks the same. Better, in fact. She looks healthy, her eyes bright, her skin glowing. Her hair is down—long, heavy, dark—the way it was the first time I ever saw her.

But she's not the same. Even I can see that.

And it's devastating.

I guess this is somehow better than if she'd replaced Emmaline altogether, but this weird, robotic, super-soldier version of J is also deeply concerning.

I think.

I keep waiting for Warner to finally break the silence, to give me some indication of his feelings and/or theories on the matter—and maybe, while he's at it, offer me his professional opinion on what the hell we should be doing next—but the seconds continue to pass in perfect silence.

Finally, I give up.

"All right, get it out," I whisper. "Tell me what you're thinking."

Warner lets out a long breath. "This doesn't make sense."

I nod, even though he can't see me. "I get that. Nothing makes sense in situations like these. I always feel like it's unfair, you know, like the worl—"

"I'm not being philosophical," Warner says, cutting me off. "I mean it literally doesn't make sense. Nouria and Sam said that Operation Synthesis would turn Ella into a super soldier—and that once the program went into effect, the result would be irreversible.

"But this is not Operation Synthesis," he says. "Operation Synthesis is literally about synthesizing Ella's and Emmaline's powers, and right now, there's no—"

"Synthesis," I say. "I get it."

"This doesn't feel right. They did things out of order."

"Maybe they freaked out after Evie's attempt to wipe J's mind didn't work. Maybe they needed to find a way to fix that fail, and quick. I mean, it's much easier to keep her around if she's docile, right? Loyal to their interests. It's much easier than keeping her in a holding cell, anyway. Babysitting her constantly. Monitoring her every movement. Always worried she's going to magic the toilet paper into a shiv and break out.

"Honestly"—I shrug—"it feels to me like they're just getting lazy. I think they're sick and tired of J always breaking out and fighting back. This is literally the path of least resistance."

"Yes," Warner says slowly. "Exactly."

"Wait— Exactly what?"

"Whatever they did to her—prematurely initiating this phase—was done hastily. It was a patch job."

A lightbulb flickers to life in my head. "Which means their work was sloppy."

"And if their work was sloppy—"

"—there are definitely holes in it."

"Stop finishing my sentences," he says, irritated.

"Stop being so predictable."

"Stop acting like a child."

"*You* stop acting like a child."

"You are being ridicu—"

Warner goes suddenly silent as Ibrahim's shaking, angry voice booms across the laboratory.

"I said, *get out of the way.*"

"I can't let you do this," Anderson says, his voice growing louder. "Did you not just hear that alarm? Santiago is out. They took out yet another supreme commander. How much longer are we going to let this go on?"

"Juliette," Ibrahim says sharply. "You're coming with me."

"Yes, sir."

"Juliette, stop," Anderson demands.

"Yes, sir."

What the hell is happening?

Warner and I dart forward to get a better look, but it doesn't matter how close we get; I still can't believe my eyes.

The scene is surreal.

Anderson is guarding Juliette. The same Anderson who's spent so much of his energy trying to murder her—is now standing in front of her with his arms out, guarding her with his life.

What the hell happened while she was here? Did Anderson get a new brain? A new heart? A parasite?

And I know I'm not alone in my confusion when I hear Warner mutter, *"What on earth?"* under his breath.

"Stop being foolish," Anderson says. "You're taking advantage of a tragedy to make an unauthorized decision, when you know as well as I do that we all need to agree on something this important before moving forward. I'm just asking you to wait, Ibrahim. Wait for the others to return, and we'll put it to a vote. Let the council decide."

Ibrahim pulls a gun on Anderson.

Ibrahim pulls a gun on Anderson.

I nearly lose my shit. I gasp so loud I almost blow our cover.

"Step aside, Paris," he says. "You've already ruined this mission. I've given you dozens of chances to get this right. You gave me your word that we'd intercept the children before they even stepped foot in the building, and look how that turned out. You've promised me—all of us—time and time again that you would make this right, and instead all you do is cost us our time, our money, our power, our lives. *Everything.*

"It's now up to me to make this right," Ibrahim says, anger making his voice unsteady. He shakes his head. "You don't even understand, do you? You don't understand how much Evie's death has cost us. You don't understand how much of our success was built with her genius, her technological advances. You don't understand that Max will never be what Evie was—that he could never replace her. And you don't seem to understand that she's no longer here to forgive your constant mistakes.

"No," he says. "It's up to me now. It's up to me to fix things, because I'm the only one with his head on straight. I'm the only one who seems to grasp the enormity of what's ahead of us. I'm the only one who sees how close we are to complete and utter ruination. I am determined to make this right, Paris, even if it means taking you out in the process. So step aside."

"Be reasonable," Anderson says, his eyes wary. "I can't just step aside. I want our movement—everything we've worked so hard to build—I want it to be a success, too. Surely you must realize that. You must realize that I haven't given up my life for nothing; you must know that my loyalty is to you, to the council, to The Reestablishment. But you must also know that she's worth too much. I can't let this go so easily. We've come too far. We've all made too many sacrifices to screw this up now."

"Don't force my hand, Paris. Don't make me do this."

J steps forward, about to say something, and Anderson pushes her body behind him. "I ordered you to remain silent," he says, glancing back at her. "And I am now ordering you to remain safe, at all costs. Do you hear me, Juliette? Do y—"

When the shot rings out, I don't believe it.

I think my mind is playing tricks on me. I think this is some kind of weird interlude—a strange dream, a moment of confusion—I keep waiting for the scene to change. Clear. Reset.

It doesn't.

No one thought it would happen like this. No one thought the supreme commanders would destroy themselves. No one thought we'd see Anderson felled by one his own, no one thought he'd clutch his bleeding chest and use his last gasp of breath to say:

"Run, Juliette. *Run—*"

Ibrahim shoots again, and this time, Anderson goes silent.

"Juliette," Ibrahim says, "you're coming with me."

J doesn't move.

She's frozen in place, staring at Anderson's still figure. It's so weird. I keep waiting for him to wake up. I keep waiting for his healing powers to kick in. I keep waiting for that annoying moment when he comes back to life, clutching a pocket square to his wound—

But he doesn't move.

"Juliette," Ibrahim says sharply. "You will answer to me now. And I am ordering you to follow me."

J looks up at him. Her face is blank. Her eyes are blank. "Yes, sir," she says.

And that's when I know.

That's when I know exactly what's going to happen next. I can feel it, can feel some strange electricity in the air before he makes his move. Before he blows our cover.

Warner pulls back his invisibility.

He stands there motionless for only a moment, for just long enough for Ibrahim to register his presence, to cry out, to reach for his gun. But he's not fast enough.

Warner is standing ten feet away when Ibrahim goes suddenly slack, when he chokes and the gun slips from his hand, when his eyes bulge. A thin red line appears in the middle of Ibrahim's forehead, a terrifying trickle of blood that precipitates the sudden, soft sound of his skull breaking open. It's the sound of tearing flesh, an innocuous sound that reminds me of ripping open an orange. And it doesn't take long before Ibrahim's knees hit the floor. He falls without grace, his body collapsing into itself.

I know he's dead because I can see directly into his skull. Clumps of his fleshy brain matter leak out onto the floor.

This, I think, is the kind of horrifying shit J is capable of.

This is what she's always been capable of. She's just always been too good a person to use it.

Warner, on the other hand—

He doesn't even seem bothered by the fact that he just ripped open a man's skull. He seems totally calm about the brain matter dripping on the floor. No, he's only got eyes for J, who's staring back at him, confused. She glances from Ibrahim's limp body to Anderson's limp body and she throws her arms forward with a sudden, desperate cry—

And nothing happens.

Robo J has no idea that Warner can absorb her powers.

Warner takes a step toward her and she narrows her eyes before slamming her fist into the floor. The room begins to shake. The floor begins to fissure. My teeth are rattling so hard I lose my balance, slam against the wall, and accidentally pull back my invisibility. When Juliette spots me, she screams.

I fly out of the way, throwing myself forward, diving over a table. Glass crashes to the floor, shatters everywhere.

I hear someone groan.

I peek through the legs of a table just in time to see Anderson begin to move. This time, I actually gasp.

The whole world seems to pause.

Anderson struggles up, to his feet. He doesn't look

okay. He looks sick, pale—an imitation of his former self. Something is wrong with his healing power, because he looks only half-alive, blood oozing from two places on his torso. He sways as he gets to his feet, coughing up blood. His skin goes gray. He uses his sleeve to wipe blood from his mouth.

J goes rushing toward him, but Anderson lifts a hand in her direction, and she halts. His bleak face registers a moment of surprise as he gazes at Ibrahim's dead body.

He laughs. Coughs. Wipes away more blood.

"Did you do this?" he says, his eyes locked on his own kid. "You did me a favor."

"What have you done to her?" Warner demands.

Anderson smiles. "Why don't I show you?" He glances at J. "Juliette?"

"Yes, sir."

"Kill them."

"Yes, sir."

J moves forward just as Anderson pulls something from his pocket, aiming its sharp, blue light in Warner's direction. This time, when J throws her arm out, Warner goes flying, his body slamming hard against the stone wall.

He falls to the floor with a gasp, the wind knocked from his lungs, and I take advantage of the moment to rush forward, pulling my invisibility around us both.

He shoves me away.

"Come on, bro, we have to get out of here— This isn't a fair fight—"

"You go," he says, clutching his side. "Go find Nazeera, and then find the other kids. I'll be fine."

"You're not going to be fine," I hiss. "She's going to kill you."

"That's fine, too."

"Don't be stupid—"

The metal tables providing us our only bit of cover go flying, crashing hard against the opposite wall. I take one last glance at Warner and make a split-second decision.

I throw myself into the fight.

I know I only have a second before my brain matter joins Ibrahim's on the floor, so I make it count. I pull my gun from its holster and shoot three, four times.

Five.

Six.

I bury lead in Anderson's body until he's knocked back by the force of it, sagging to the floor with a hacking, bloody cough. J rushes forward but I disappear, darting behind a table, and once the weapon in Anderson's hand clatters to the floor, I shoot that, too. It pops and cracks, briefly catching fire as the tech explodes.

J cries out, falling to her knees beside him.

"Kill them," Anderson gasps, blood staining the edges of his lips. "Kill them all. Kill anyone who stands in your way."

"Yes, sir," Juliette says.

Anderson coughs. Fresh blood seeps from his wounds.

J gets to her feet and turns around, scanning the room for us, but I'm already rushing over to Warner, throwing my invisibility over us both. Warner seems a little stunned, but he's miraculously uninjured.

I try to help him to his feet, and for the first time, he doesn't push away my arm. I hear him inhale. Exhale.

Never mind, he's a little injured.

I wait for him to do something, say something, but he just stands there, staring at J. And then—

He pulls back his invisibility.

I nearly scream.

J pivots when she spots him, and immediately runs forward. She picks up a table, throws it at us.

We dive out of the way so hard I nearly break my nose against the ground. I can still hear things shattering around us when I say,

"What the hell were you thinking? You just blew our chance to get out of here!"

Warner shifts, glass crunching beneath him. He's breathing hard.

"I was serious about what I said, Kishimoto. You should go. Find Nazeera. But this is where I need to be."

"You mean you need to be getting killed right now? That's where you need to be? Do you even hear yourself?"

"Something is wrong," Warner says, dragging himself to his feet. "Her mind is trapped, trapped inside of something. A program. A virus. Whatever it is, she needs help."

J screams, sending another earthquake through the room. I slam into a table and stumble backward. A sharp pain shoots through my gut and I suck in my breath. Swear.

Warner has one arm out against the wall, steadying himself. I can tell he's about to step forward, directly into the fight, and I grab his arm, pull him back.

"I'm not saying we give up on her, okay? I'm saying that there has to be another way. We need to get out of here, regroup. Come up with a better plan."

"No."

"Bro, I don't think you understand." I glance at J, who's stalking forward, eyes burning, the ground fissuring before her. "She's really going to kill you."

"Then I will die."

That's it.

Warner's last words before he leaves.

He meets J in the middle of the room and she doesn't hesitate before taking a violent swing at his face.

He blocks.

She swings again. He blocks. She kicks. He ducks.

He's not fighting her.

He only matches her, move for move, meeting her blows, anticipating her mind. It reminds me of his fight with Anderson back at the Sanctuary—how he never struck his father, only defended himself. It was obvious then that he was just trying to enrage his father.

But this—

This is different. It's clear that he's not enjoying this. He's not trying to enrage her, and he's not trying to defend himself. He's fighting her for *her*. To protect her.

To save her, somehow.

And I have no idea if this is going to work.

J clenches her fists and screams. The walls shake, the floor continues to crack open. I stumble, catch myself against a table.

And I'm just standing here like an idiot, racking my brain for a clue, trying to figure out what to do, how to help—

"Holy shit," Nazeera says. "What the hell is going on?"

Relief floods through me fast and hot. I have to resist the impulse to pull her invisible body into my arms. To tuck her close to my chest and keep her from leaving again.

Instead, I pretend to be cool.

"How'd you get here?" I ask. "How'd you find us?"

"I was hacking the systems, remember? I saw you on the cameras. You guys aren't exactly being quiet up here."

"Right. Good point."

"Hey, I have news, by the way, I foun—" She cuts herself off abruptly, her words fading to nothing. And then, after a beat, she says quietly:

"Who killed my dad?"

My stomach turns to stone.

I take a sharp breath before I say, "Warner did that."

"Oh."

"You okay?"

I hear her exhale. "I don't know."

J screams again and I look up.

She's furious.

I can tell, even from here, that she's frustrated. She can't use her powers on Warner directly, and he's too good a fighter to be beat without an edge. She's resorted to throwing very large, very heavy objects at him. Whatever she can find. Random medical equipment. Pieces of the wall.

This is not good.

"He wouldn't leave," I tell Nazeera. "He wanted to stay. He thinks he can help her."

She sighs. "We should let him try. In the interim, I could use your help."

I turn, reflexively, to face her, forgetting for a moment that she's invisible. "Help with what?" I ask.

"I found the other kids," she says. "That's why I was gone for so long. Getting that security clearance for you guys was way easier than I thought it'd be. So I stuck around to do some deep-level hacking into the cameras—and I found out where they're hiding the other supreme kids. But it's not pretty. And I could use a hand."

I look up to catch one last glimpse of Warner.

Of J.

But they're gone.

~~ELLA~~
JULIETTE

Run, Juliette

run

faster, run until your bones break and your shins split and your muscles atrophy

Run run run

until you can't hear their feet behind you

Run until you drop dead.

Make sure your heart stops before they ever reach you. Before they ever touch you.

Run, I said.

The words appear, unbidden, in my mind. I don't know where they come from and I don't know why I know them, but I say them to myself as I go, my boots pounding the ground, my head a strangled mess of chaos. I don't understand what just happened. I don't understand what's happening to me. I don't understand anything anymore.

The boy is close.

He moves more swiftly than I anticipated, and I'm surprised. I didn't expect him to be able to meet my blows. I didn't expect him to face me so easily. Mostly, I'm stunned he's somehow immune to my power. I didn't even know that was possible.

I don't understand.

I'm racking my brain, trying desperately to comprehend how such a thing might've happened—and whether I might've been responsible for the anomaly—but nothing makes sense. Not his presence. Not his attitude. Not even the way he fights.

Which is to say: he doesn't.

He doesn't even want to fight. He seems to have no interest in beating me, despite the ample evidence that we are well matched. He only fends me off, making only the most basic effort to protect himself, and still I haven't killed him.

There's something strange about him. Something about him that's getting under my skin. Unsettling me.

But he dashed out of sight when I threw another table at him, and he's been running ever since.

It feels like a trap.

I know it, and yet, I feel compelled to find him. Face him. Destroy him.

I spot him, suddenly, at the far end of the laboratory, and he meets my eyes with an insouciance that enrages me. I charge forward but he moves swiftly, disappearing through an adjoining door.

This is a trap, I remind myself.

Then again, I'm not sure it matters whether this is a trap. I am under orders to find him. Kill him. I just have to be better. Smarter.

So I follow.

From the time I met this boy—from the first moment we began exchanging blows—I've ignored the dizzying sensations coursing through my body. I've tried to deny my sudden, feverish skin, my trembling hands. But when a fresh wave of nausea nearly sends me reeling, I can no longer deny my fear:

There's something wrong with me.

I catch another glimpse of his golden hair and my vision blurs, clears, my heart slows. For a moment, my muscles seem to spasm. There is a creeping, tremulous terror clenching its fist around my lungs and I don't understand it. I keep hoping the feeling will change. Clear. Disappear. But as the minutes pass and the symptoms show no signs of abating, I begin to panic.

I'm not tired, no. My body is too strong. I can feel it—can feel my muscles, their strength, their steadiness—and I can tell that I could keep fighting like this for hours. Days. I'm not worried about giving up, I'm not worried about breaking down.

I'm worried about my head. My confusion. The uncertainty seeping through me, spreading like a poison.

Ibrahim is dead.

Anderson, nearly so.

Will he recover? Will he die? Who would I be without him? What was it Ibrahim wanted to do to me? From what was Anderson trying to protect me? Who are these children I'm meant to kill? Why did Ibrahim call them my friends?

My questions are endless.

I kill them.

I shove aside a series of steel desks and catch a glimpse of the boy before he darts around a corner. Anger punches through me, shooting a jolt of adrenaline to my brain, and I start running again, renewed determination focusing my mind. I charge through the dimly lit room, shoving my way through an endless sea of medical paraphernalia. When I stop moving, silence descends.

Silence so pure it's deafening.

I spin around, searching. The boy is gone. I blink, confused, scanning the room as my pulse races with renewed fear. Seconds pass, gather into moments that feel like minutes, hours.

This is a trap.

The laboratory is perfectly still—the lights so perfectly dim—that as the silence drags on I begin to wonder if I'm caught in a dream. I feel suddenly paranoid, uncertain. Like maybe that boy was a figment of my imagination. Like maybe all of this is some strange nightmare, and maybe I'll wake up soon and Anderson will be back in his office, and Ibrahim will be a man I've never met, and tomorrow I'll wake up in my pod by the water.

Maybe, I think, this is all just another test.

A simulation.

Maybe Anderson is challenging my loyalty one last time. Maybe it's my job to stay put, to keep myself safe like he asked me to, and to destroy anyone who tries to stand in my way. Or maybe—

Stop.

I sense movement.

Movement so fine it's nearly imperceptible. Movement so gentle it could've been a breeze, except for one thing:

I hear a heart beating.

Someone is here, someone motionless, someone sly. I straighten, my senses heightened, my heart racing in my chest.

Someone is here someone is here someone is here—

Where?

There.

He appears, as if out of a dream, standing before me like a statue, still as cooling steel. He stares at me, green eyes the color of sea glass, the color of celadon.

I never really had a chance to see his face.

Not like this.

My heart races as I assess him, his white shirt, green jacket, gold hair. Skin like porcelain. He does not slouch or fidget and, for a moment, I'm certain I was right, that perhaps he's nothing more than a mirage. A program.

Another hologram.

I reach out, uncertain, the tips of my fingers grazing the exposed skin at his throat and he takes a sharp, shaky breath.

Real, then.

I flatten my hand against his chest, just to be sure, and I feel his heart racing under my palm. Fast, lightning fast.

I glance up, surprised.

He's nervous.

Another unsteady breath escapes him and this time, takes with it a measure of control. He steps back, shakes his head, stares up at the ceiling.

Not nervous.

He is distraught.

I should kill him now, I think. *Kill him now.*

A wave of nausea hits me so hard it nearly knocks me off my feet. I take a few unsteady steps backward, catching myself against a steel table. My fingers grip the cold metal edge and I hang on, teeth clenched, willing my mind to clear.

Heat floods my body.

Heat, torturous heat, presses against my lungs, fills my blood. My lips part. I feel parched. I look up and he's right in front of me and I do nothing. I do nothing as I watch his throat move.

I do nothing as my eyes devour him.

I feel faint.

I study the sharp line of his jaw, the gentle slope where his neck meets shoulder. His lips look soft. His cheekbones high, his nose sharp, his brows heavy, gold. He is finely made. Beautiful, strong hands. Short, clean nails. I notice he wears a jade ring on his left pinkie finger.

He sighs.

He shakes off his jacket, carefully folding it over the back of a nearby chair. Underneath he wears only a simple white T-shirt, the sculpted contours of his bare arms catching the attention of the dim lights. He moves slowly, his motions unhurried. When he begins to pace I watch him, study the shape of him. I am not surprised to discover that he moves beautifully. I am fascinated by him, by his form, his measured strides, the muscles honed under skin. He seems like he might be my age, maybe a little older, but there's something about the way he looks at me that makes him seem older than our years combined.

Whatever it is, I like it.

I wonder what I'm supposed to do with this, all of this. Is it truly a test? If so, why send someone like him? Why a face so refined? Why a body so perfectly honed?

Was I meant to enjoy this?

A strange, delirious feeling stirs inside of me at the thought. Something ancient. Something wonderful. It is almost too bad, I think, that I will have to kill him. And it is the heat, the dullness, the inexplicable numbness in my mind that compels me to say—

"Where did they make you?"

He startles. I didn't think he would startle. But when he turns to look at me, he seems confused.

I explain: "You are unusually beautiful."

His eyes widen.

His lips part, press together, tremble into a curve that surprises me. Surprises him.

He smiles.

He smiles and I stare—two dimples, straight teeth, shining eyes. A sudden, incomprehensible heat rushes across my skin, sets me aflame. I feel violently hot. Sick with fever.

Finally, he says: "So you *are* in there."

"Who?"

"Ella," he says, but he's speaking softly now. "Juliette. They said you'd be gone."

"I'm not gone," I say, my hands shaking as I pull myself together. "I am Juliette Ferrars, supreme soldier to our North American commander. Who are you?"

He moves closer. His eyes darken as he stares at me, but there's no true darkness there. I try to stand taller, straighter. I remind myself that I have a task, that this is my moment to attack, to fulfill my orders. Perhaps I sh—

"Love," he whispers.

Heat flashes across my skin. Pain presses against my mind, a vague realization that I've left something overlooked. Dusty emotion trembles inside of me, and I kill it.

He steps forward, takes my face in his hands. I think about breaking his fingers. Snapping his wrists. My heart is racing.

I cannot move.

"You shouldn't touch me," I say, gasping the words.

"Why not?"

"Because I will kill you."

Gently, he tilts my head back, his hands possessive, persuasive. An ache seizes my muscles, holds me in place. My eyes close reflexively. I breathe him in and my mouth fills with flavor—fresh air, fragrant flowers, heat, happiness—and I'm struck by the strangest idea that we've been here before, that I've lived this before, that I've known him before and then I feel, I feel his breath on my skin and the sensation, the sensation is—

heady,

disorienting.

I'm losing track of my mind, trying desperately to locate my purpose, to focus my thoughts, when

he moves

the earth tilts, his lips graze my jaw and I make a sound, a desperate, unconscious sound that stuns me. My skin is frenzied, burning. That familiar warmth contaminates my blood, my temperature spiking, my face flushing.

"Do I—"

I try to speak but he kisses my neck and I gasp, his hands still caught around my face. I'm breathless, heart pounding, pulse pounding, head pounding. He touches me like he knows me, knows what I want, knows what I need. I feel insane. I don't even recognize the sound of my own voice when I finally manage to say,

"Do I know you?"

"Yes."

My heart leaps. The simplicity of his answer strangles my mind, digs for truth. It feels true. Feels true that I've known these hands, this mouth, those eyes.

Feels real.

"Yes," he says again, his own voice rough with feeling. His hands leave my face and I'm lost in the loss, searching for warmth. I press closer to him without even meaning to, asking him for something I don't understand. But then his hands slide under my shirt, his palms pressing against my back, and the magnitude of the sudden, skin-to-skin contact sets my body on fire.

I feel explosive.

I feel dangerously close to something that might kill me, and still I lean into him, blinded by instinct, deaf to everything but the ferocious beat of my own heart.

He pulls back, just an inch.

His hands are still caught under my shirt, his bare arms wrapped around my bare skin and his mouth lingers above mine, the heat between us threatening to ignite. He pulls me closer and I bite back a moan, losing my head as the hard lines of his body sink into me. He is everywhere, his scent, his skin, his breath. I see nothing but him, sense nothing but him, his hands spreading across my torso, my lungs compressing under his careful, searing exploration. I lean into the sensations, his fingers grazing my stomach, the small of my back. He touches his forehead to mine and I press up, onto my toes, asking for something, begging for something—

"What," I gasp, "what is happening—"

He kisses me.

Soft lips, waves of sensation. Feeling overflows the vacancies in my mind. My hands begin to shake. My heart beats so hard I can hardly keep still when he nudges my mouth open, takes me in. He tastes like heat and peppermint, like summer, like the sun.

I want more.

I take his face in my hands and pull him closer and he makes a soft, desperate sound in the back of his throat that sends a spike of pleasure directly to my brain. Pure, electric heat lifts me up, outside of myself. I seem to be floating here, surrendered to this strange moment, held in place by an ancient mold that fits my body perfectly. I feel frantic, seized by a need to know more, a need I don't even understand.

When we break apart his chest his heaving and his face is flushed and he says—

"Come back to me, love. Come back."

I'm still struggling to breathe, desperately searching his eyes for answers. Explanations. "Where?"

"Here," he whispers, pressing my hands to his heart. "Home."

"But I don't—"

Flashes of light streak across my vision. I stumble backward, half-blind, like I'm dreaming, reliving the caress of a forgotten memory, and it's like an ache looking to be soothed, it's a steaming pan thrown in ice water, it's a flushed cheek pressed to a cool pillow on a hot hot night and heat gathers, collects behind my eyes, distorting sights, dimming sounds.

Here.
This.
My bones against his bones. This is my home.

I return to my skin with a sudden, violent shudder and feel wild, unstable. I stare at him, my heart seizing, my lungs fighting for air. He stares back, his eyes such a pale green in the light that, for a moment, he doesn't even seem human.

Something is happening to my head.

Pain is collecting in my blood, calcifying around my heart. I feel at war with myself, lost and wounded, my mind spinning with uncertainty. "What is your name?" I ask.

He steps forward, so close our lips touch. Part. His breath whispers across my skin and my nerves hum, spark.

"You know my name," he says quietly.

I try to shake my head. He catches my chin.

This time, he's not careful.

This time, he's desperate. This time, when he kisses me he breaks me open, heat coming off him in waves. He tastes like springwater and something sweet, something searing.

I feel dazed. Delirious.

When he breaks away I'm shaking, my lungs shaking, my breaths shaking, my heart shaking. I watch, as if in a dream, as he pulls off his shirt, tosses it to the ground. And then he's here again, he's back again, he's caught me in his arms and he's kissing me so deeply my knees give out.

He picks me up, bracing my body as he sets me down on the long, steel table. The cool metal seeps through the fabric of my pants, sending goose bumps along my heated skin and I gasp, my eyes closing as he straddles my legs, claims my mouth. He presses my hands to his chest, drags my fingers down his naked torso and I make a desperate, broken sound, pleasure and pain stunning me, paralyzing me.

He unbuttons my shirt, his deft hands moving quickly even as he kisses my neck, my cheeks, my mouth, my throat. I cry out when he moves, his kisses shifting down my body, searching, exploring. He pushes aside the two halves of my shirt, his mouth still hot against my skin, and then he closes the gap between us, pressing his bare chest to mine, and my heart explodes.

Something snaps inside of me.

Severs.

A sudden, fractured sob escapes my throat. Unbidden tears sting my eyes, startling me as they fall down my face. Unknown emotion soars through me, expanding my heart, confusing my head. He pulls me impossibly closer, our bodies soldered together. And then he presses his forehead to my collarbone, his body trembling with emotion when he says—

"Come back."

My head is full of sand, sound, sensations spinning in my mind. I don't understand what's happening to me,

I don't understand this pain, this unbelievable pleasure. I'm staining his skin with my tears and he only pulls me tighter, pressing our hearts together until the feeling sinks its teeth into my bones, splits open my lungs. I want to bury myself in this moment, I want to pull him into me, I want to drag myself out of myself but there's something wrong, something blocked, something stopped—

Something broken.

Realization arrives in gentle waves, theories lapping and overlapping at the shores of my consciousness until I'm drenched in confusion. Awareness.

Terror.

"You know my name," he says softly. "You've always known me, love. I've always known you. And I'm so—I'm so desperately in love with you—"

The pain begins in my ears.

It collects, expanding, pressure building to a peak so acute it transforms, sharpening into a torture that stops my heart.

First I go deaf, stiff. Second I go blind, slack.

Third, my heart restarts.

I come back to life with a sudden, terrifying inhalation that nearly chokes me, blood rushing to my ears, my eyes, leaking from my nose. I taste it, taste my own blood in my mouth as I begin to understand: there is something inside of me. A poison. A violence. Something wrong something wrong something *wrong*

And then, as if from miles away, I hear myself scream.

There's cold tile under my knees, rough grout pressing into my knuckles. I scream into the silence, power building power, electricity charging my blood. My mind is separating from itself, trying to identify the poison, this parasite residing inside of me.

I have to kill it.

I scream, forcing my own energy inward, screaming until the explosive energy building inside of me ruptures my eardrums. I scream until I feel the blood drip from my ears and down my neck, I scream until the lights in the laboratory begin to pop and break. I scream until my teeth bleed, until the floor fissures beneath my feet, until the skin at my knees begins to crack. I scream until the monster inside of me begins to die.

And only then—

Only when I'm certain I've killed some small part of my own self do I finally collapse.

I'm choking, coughing up blood, my chest heaving from the effort expended. The room swims. Swings around.

I press my forehead to the cold floor and fight back a wave of nausea. And then I feel a familiar, heavy hand against my back. With excruciating slowness, I manage to lift my head.

A blur of gold appears, disappears before me.

I blink once, twice, and try to push up with my arms but a sharp, searing pain in my wrist nearly blinds me. I look down, examining the strange, hazy sight. I blink again. Ten times more.

Finally, my eyes focus.

The skin inside my right arm has split open. Blood is smeared across my skin, dripping on the floor. From within the fresh wound, a single blue light pulses from a steel, circular body, the edges of which push up against my torn flesh.

With one final effort, I rip the flashing mechanism from my arm, the last vestige of this monster. It drops from my shaking fingers, clatters to the floor.

And this time, when I look up, I see his face.

"Aaron," I gasp.

He drops to his knees.

He pulls my bleeding body into his arms and I break, I break apart, sobs cracking open my chest. I cry until the pain spirals and peaks, I cry until my head throbs and my eyes swell. I cry, pressing my face against his neck, my fingers digging into his back, desperate for purchase. Proof.

He holds me, silent and steady, gathering my blood and bones against his body even as the tears recede, even when I begin to tremble. He holds me tight as my body shakes, holds me close when the tears start anew, holds me in his arms and strokes my hair and tells me that everything, everything is going to be okay.

KENJI

I was assigned to keep watch outside this door, which, initially, was supposed to be a good thing—assisting in the rescue mission, et cetera—but the longer I wait out here, guarding Nazeera while she hacks the computers keeping the supreme kids in some freaky state of hypersleep, the more things go wrong.

This place is falling apart.

Literally.

The lights in the ceiling are beginning to spark and sputter, the massive staircases are beginning to groan. The huge windows lining either side of this fifty-story building are beginning to crack.

Doctors are running, screaming. Alarms are flashing like crazy, sirens blaring. Some robotic voice is announcing a crisis over the speakers like it's the most casual thing in the world.

I have no idea what's happening right now, though if I had to guess, I'd say it had something to do with Emmaline. But I just have to stand here, bracing myself against the door so as not to be accidentally trampled, and wait for whatever is happening to come to an end. The problem is, I don't know if it's going to be a happy ending or a sad one—

For anyone.

I haven't heard anything from Warner since we split up, and I'm trying really, really hard not to think about it. I'm choosing to focus, instead, on the positive things that happened today, like the fact that we managed to kill three supreme commanders—four if you count Evie—and that Nazeera's genius hacking work was a success, because without her, there's no way we'd have made much headway at all.

After our sojourn through the vents, Warner and I managed to drop down into the heart of the compound, undetected. It was easier to avoid the cameras once we were in the center of things; the rooms were closer together, and though the higher security areas have more security *access* points—some of them have fewer cameras. So as long as we avoided certain angles, the cameras didn't notice us, and with the fake clearance Nazeera built for us, we got through easily. It was because of her that we were in the right place—after having unintentionally killed a super-important scientist—when all the supreme commanders began to swarm.

It was because of her that we were able to take out Ibrahim and Anderson. And it was because of her that Warner is locked up with Robo J somewhere. Honestly, I don't even know how to feel about it all. I haven't really allowed myself to think about the fact that J might never come back, that I might never see my best friend again. If I think about it too much, I start feeling like I can't breathe, and I can't afford to stop breathing right now. Not yet.

So I try not to think about it.

But Warner—

Warner is either going to come out of this alive and happy, or dead doing something he believed in.

And there's nothing I can do about it.

The problem is, I haven't seen him in over an hour, and I have no idea what that means. It could either be really good news or really, really bad. He never shared his plan with me—surprise surprise—so I don't even know exactly what he'd planned to do to once he got her alone. And even though I know better than to doubt him, I have to admit that there's a tiny part of me that wonders if he's even alive right now.

An ancient, earsplitting groan interrupts my thoughts.

I look up, toward the source of the sound, and realize that the ceiling is caving in. The roof is coming apart. The walls are beginning to crumble. The long, circuitous hallways all ring around an interior courtyard within which lives a massive, prehistoric-looking tree. For no reason I can understand, the steel railings around the hallways are beginning to melt apart. I watch in real time as the tree catches fire, flames roaring higher at an astonishing rate. Smoke builds, curling in my direction, already beginning to suffocate the halls, and my heart is racing as I look around, my panic spiking. I start banging on the door, not caring who hears me now.

It's the end of the fucking world out here.

I'm screaming for Nazeera, begging her to come out,

to get out here before it's too late, and I'm coughing now, smoke catching in my lungs, still hoping desperately that she'll hear my voice when suddenly, violently—

The door swings open.

I'm knocked backward by the force of it, and when I look up, eyes burning, Nazeera is there. Nazeera, Lena, Stephan, Haider, Valentina, Nicolás, and Adam.

Adam.

I can't explain exactly what happens next. There's so much shouting. So much running. Stephan punches a clean hole through a crumbling wall, and Nazeera helps fly us all out to safety. It happens in a blur. I see things unfold in flashes, in screams.

It feels like a dream. My eyes stinging, tearing.

I'm crying because of the fire, I think. It's the heat, the sky, the roaring flames devouring everything.

I watch the capital of Oceania—all 120 acres of it—go up in flames.

And Warner and Juliette go with it.

ELLA
(JULIETTE)

The first thing we do is find Emmaline.

I reach out to her in my mind and she answers right away. Heat, fingers of heat, curling around my bones. Sparking to life in my heart. She was always here, always with me.

I understand now.

I understand that the moments that saved me were gifts from my sister, gifts she was able to give only by destroying herself in return. She's so much weaker now than she was two weeks ago because she expended so much of herself to keep me alive. To keep their machinations from reaching my heart. My soul.

I remember everything now. My mind is sharpened to a new point, honed to a clarity I've never before experienced. I see everything. Understand everything.

It doesn't take long to find her.

I don't apologize for the people I scatter, the walls I shatter along the way. I don't apologize for my anger or my pain. I don't stop moving when I see Tatiana and Azi; I don't have to. I snap their necks from where I'm standing. I tear their bodies in half with a single gesture.

When I reach my sister, the agony inside of me reaches

its peak. She is limp inside her tank, a desiccated fish, a dying spider. She's curled into herself in its darkest corner, her long dark hair wrapping around her wrinkled, sagging figure. A low keening emanates from her tank.

She is crying.

She is small. Scared. She reminds me of another version of myself, a person I can hardly remember, a young girl thrown in prison, too broken by the world to realize that she'd always had the power to break herself free. To conquer the earth.

I had that luxury.

Emmaline didn't.

The sight of her makes me want to fall to pieces. My heart rages with anger, devastation. When I think about what they did to her—what they've done to her—

Don't

I don't.

I take a deep, shuddering breath. Try to collect myself. I feel Aaron take my hand and I squeeze his fingers in gratitude. It steadies me to have him here. To know he's beside me. With me.

My partner in everything.

Tell me what you want, I say to Emmaline. *Anything at all. Whatever it is, I'll do it.*

Silence.

Emmaline?

A sharp, desperate fear jumps through me.

Her fear, not mine.

Distorted sensations flash behind my eyes—flares of color, the sounds of grinding metal—and her panic intensifies. Tightens. I feel it hum down my spine.

"What's wrong?" I say out loud. "What happened?"

Here

Here

Her milky form disappears into the tank, sinking deep underwater. Goose bumps rise along my arms.

"You seem to have forgotten about me."

My father steps into the room, his tall rubber boots thudding softly against the floor.

I throw my arms out immediately, hoping to rip out his spleen, but he's too fast—his movements too fast. He presses a single button on a small, handheld remote, and I hardly have time to take a breath before my body begins to convulse. I cry out, my eyes blinded by violent, violet light, and manage to turn my head only in small, excruciating movements.

Aaron.

He and I are both frozen here, bathed in a toxic light emanating from the ceiling. Gasping for breath. Shaking uncontrollably. My mind spins, working desperately to think of a plan, a loophole, a way out.

"I am astonished by your arrogance," my father says. "Astonished that you thought you could just walk in here and assist in your sister's suicide. You thought it would be simple? You thought there wouldn't be consequences?"

He turns a dial and my body seizes more violently, lifting off the floor. The pain is blinding. Light flashes in and out of my eyes, stunning my mind, numbing my ability to think. I hang in the air, no longer able to turn my head. Gravity pushes and pulls at my body, threatens to tear apart my limbs.

If I could scream, I would.

"Anyway, it's good you're here. Best to get this over with now. We've waited long enough." He nods, absently, at Emmaline's tank. "Obviously you've seen how desperate we are for a new host."

NO

The word is like a scream inside my head.

Max stiffens.

He looks up, staring at precisely nothing, the anger in his eyes barely held in check. I only realize then that he can hear her, too.

Of course he can.

Emmaline pounds against her tank, the sounds dull, the effort alone seeming to exhaust her. Still, she presses forward, her sunken cheek flattening against the glass.

Max hesitates, vacillating.

He's no good at hiding his emotions—and his present uncertainty is easily discernible. It's clear, even from my disoriented perspective, that he's trying to decide which of us he needs to deal with first. Emmaline pounds her fist again, weaker this time.

NO

Another scream inside my head.

With a stifled sigh, Max decides on Emmaline.

I watch him pivot, stalk toward her tank. He presses his hand flat against the glass and it brightens to a neon blue. The blue light expands, then scatters around the chamber, slowly revealing an intricate series of electrical circuits. The neon veins are thicker in some places, occasionally braided, mostly fine. It resembles a cardiovascular system not unlike the one inside my own body.

My own body.

Something gasps to life inside of me. Reason. Rational thought. I'm trapped here, tricked by the pain into thinking I have no control over my powers, but that's not true. When I force myself to remember, I can feel it. My energy still thrums through me. It's a faint, desperate whisper—but it's there.

Bit by agonizing bit, I gather my mind.

I grit my teeth, focusing my thoughts, clenching my body to its breaking point. Slowly, I braid together the disparate strands of my power, holding on to the threads for dear life.

And even more slowly, I claw my hand through the light.

The effort splits open my knuckles, the tips of my fingers. Fresh blood streaks across my hand and spills down my wrist as I lift my arm in a sluggish, excruciating arc above my head.

As if from light-years away, I hear beeping.

Max.

He's inputting new codes into Emmaline's tank. I have no idea what that means for her, but I can't imagine it's good.

Hurry.

Hurry, I tell myself.

Violently, I force my arm through the light, biting back a scream as I do. One by one, my fingers uncurl above my head, blood dripping from each digit down my bleeding wrist and into my eyes. My hand opens, palm up toward the ceiling. Fresh blood snakes down the planes of my face as I drive my energy into the light.

The ceiling shatters.

Aaron and I fall to the floor, hard, and I hear something snap in my leg, the pain screaming through me.

I fight it back.

The lights pop and shriek, the polished concrete ceiling beginning to crack. Max spins around, horror seizing his face as I throw my hand forward.

Close my fist.

Emmaline's tank fissures with a sudden, violent crack.

"NO!" he cries. Feverishly, he pulls the remote free from his lab coat, hitting its now useless buttons. "No! No, *no*—"

The glass groans open with an angry yawn, giving way with one final, shattering roar. Max goes comically still.

Stunned.

He dies, then, with exactly that expression on his face. And it's not me who kills him. It's Emmaline.

Emmaline, who pulls her webbed hands free of the broken glass and presses her fingers to her father's head. She kills him with nothing more than the force of her own mind.

The mind he gave her.

When she is done, his skull has split open. Blood leaks from his dead eyes. His teeth have fallen out of his face, onto his shirt. His intestines spill out from a severe rupture in his torso.

I look away.

Emmaline collapses to the floor. She's gasping through the regulator fused to her face. Her already weak limbs begin to tremble, violently, and she's making sounds I can only assume are meant to be words she's no longer able to speak.

She is more amphibian than human.

I realize this only now, only when faced with the proof of her incompatibility with our air, with the outside world. I crawl toward her, dragging my broken, bloodied leg behind me.

Aaron tries to help, but when we lock eyes, he falls back. He understands that I need to do this myself.

I gather my sister's small, withered body against my own, pulling her wet limbs into my lap, pressing her head against my chest. And I say to her, for the second time:

"Tell me what you want. Anything at all. Whatever it is, I'll do it."

Her slick fingers clutch at my neck, clinging for dear life. A vision fills my head, a vision of everything going up in flames. A vision of this compound, her prison, disintegrating. She wants it razed, returned to dust.

"Consider it done," I say to her.

She has another request. Just one more.

And I say nothing for too long.

Please

Her voice is in my heart, begging. Desperate. Her agony is acute. Her terror palpable.

Tears spring to my eyes.

I press my cheek against her wet hair. I tell her how much I love her. How much she means to me. How much more I wish we could've had. I tell her that I will never forget her.

That I will miss her, every single day.

And then I ask her to let me take her body home with me when I am done.

A gentle warmth floods my mind, a heady feeling.

Happiness.

Yes, she says.

When it's done, when I've ripped the tubes from her body, when I've gathered her wet, trembling bones against my own, when I've pressed my poisonous cheek to hers, when I've leeched out what little life was left in her body.

When it is done, I curl myself around her cold corpse and cry.

I clutch her hollow body against my heart and feel the injustice of it all roar through me. I feel it fracture me apart. I feel her take part of me with her as she goes.

And then I scream.

I scream until I feel the earth move beneath my feet, until I feel the wind change directions. I scream until the walls collapse, until I feel the electricity spark, until I feel the lights catch fire. I scream until the ground fissures, until all falls down.

And then we carry my sister home.

EPILOGUE

WARNER

ONE

The wall is unusually white.

More white than is usual. Most people think white walls are true white, but the truth is, they only seem white, and are not actually white. Most shades of white are mixed in with a bit of yellow, which helps soften the harsh edges of a pure white, making it more of an ecru, or ivory. Various shades of cream. Egg white, even. True white is practically intolerable as a color, so white it's nearly blue.

This wall, in particular, is not so white as to be offensive, but a sharp enough shade of white to pique my curiosity, which is nothing short of a miracle, really, because I've been staring at it for the greater part of an hour. Thirty-seven minutes, to be exact.

I am being held hostage by custom. Formality.

"Five more minutes," she says. "I promise."

I hear the rustle of fabric. Zippers. A shudder of—

"Is that tulle?"

"You're not supposed to be listening!"

"You know, love, it occurs to me now that I've lived through actual hostage situations far less torturous than this."

"Okay, okay, it's off. Packed away. I just need a second to put on my cl—"

"That won't be necessary," I say, turning around. "Surely this part, I should be allowed to watch."

I lean against the unusually white wall, studying her as she frowns at me, her lips still parted around the shape of a word she seems to have forgotten.

"Please continue," I say, gesturing with a nod. "Whatever you were doing before."

She holds on to her frown for a moment longer than is honest, her eyes narrowing in a show of frustration that is pure fraud. She compounds this farce by clutching an article of clothing to her chest, feigning modesty.

I do not mind, not one single bit.

I drink her in, her soft curves, her smooth skin. Her hair is beautiful at any length, but it's been longer lately. Long and rich, silky against her skin, and when I'm lucky—against mine.

Slowly, she drops the shirt.

I suddenly stand up straighter.

"I'm supposed to wear this under the dress," she says, her fake anger already forgotten. She fidgets with the boning of a cream-colored corset, her fingers lingering absently along the garter belt, the lace-trimmed stockings. She can't meet my eyes. She's gone suddenly shy, and this time, it's real.

Do you like it?

The unspoken question.

I assumed, when she invited me into this dressing room, that it was for reasons beyond me staring at the color variations in an unusually white wall. I assumed she wanted me here to see something.

To see her.

I see now that I was correct.

"You are so beautiful," I say, unable to shed the awe in my voice. I hear it, the childish wonder in my tone, and it embarrasses me more than it should. I know I shouldn't be ashamed to feel deeply. To be moved.

Still, I feel awkward.

Young.

Quietly, she says, "I feel like I just spoiled the surprise. You're not supposed to see any of this until the wedding night."

My heart actually stops for a moment.

The wedding night.

She closes the distance between us and twines her arms around me, freeing me from my momentary paralysis. My heart beats faster with her here, so close. And though I don't know how she knew that I suddenly required the reassurance of her touch, I'm grateful. I exhale, pulling her fully against me, our bodies relaxing, remembering each other.

I press my face into her hair, breathe in the sweet scent of her shampoo, her skin. It's only been two weeks. Two weeks since the end of an old world. The beginning of a new one.

She still feels like a dream to me.

"Is this really happening?" I whisper.

A sharp knock at the door startles my spine straight.

Ella frowns at the sound. "Yes?"

"So sorry to bother you right now, miss, but there's a gentleman here wishing to speak with Mr. Warner."

Ella and I lock eyes.

"Okay," she says quickly. "Don't be mad."

My eyes narrow. "Why would I be mad?"

Ella pulls away to better look me in the eye. Her own eyes are bright, beautiful. Full of concern. "It's Kenji."

I force down a spike of anger so violent I think I give myself a stroke. It leaves me light-headed. "What is he doing here?" I manage to get out. "How on earth did he know how to find us?

She bites her lip. "We took Amir and Olivier with us."

"I see." We took extra guards along, which means our outing was posted to the public security bulletin. Of course.

Ella nods. "He found me just before we left. He was worried—he wanted to know why we were heading back into the old regulated lands."

I try to say something then, to marvel aloud at Kenji's inability to make a simple deduction despite the abundance of contextual clues right before his eyes—but she holds up a finger.

"I told him," she says, "that we were looking for replacement outfits, and reminded him that, for now, the supply centers are still the only places to shop for food or clothing or"—she waves a hand, frowns—"anything, at the moment.

Anyway, he said he'd try to meet us here. He said he wanted to help."

My eyes widen slightly. I feel another stroke incoming. "He said he wanted to *help*."

She nods.

"Astonishing." A muscle ticks in my jaw. "And funny, too, because he's already helped so much—just last night he helped us both a great deal by destroying my suit and your dress, forcing us to now purchase clothing from a"—I look around, gesture at nothing—"a *store* on the very day we're supposed to get married."

"Aaron," she whispers. She steps closer again. Places a hand on my chest. "He feels terrible about it."

"And you?" I say, studying her face, her feelings. "Don't *you* feel terrible about it? Alia and Winston worked so hard to make you something beautiful, something designed precisely for you—"

"I don't mind." She shrugs. "It's just a dress."

"But it was your wedding dress," I say, my voice failing me now, practically breaking on the word.

She sighs, and in the sound I hear her heart break, more for me than for herself. She turns around and unzips the massive garment bag hanging on a hook above her head.

"You're not supposed to see this," she says, tugging yards of tulle out of the bag, "but I think it might mean more to you than it does to me, so"—she turns back, smiles—"I'll let you help me decide what to wear tonight."

I nearly groan aloud at the reminder.

A nighttime wedding. Who on earth is married at night? Only the hapless. The unfortunate. Though I suppose we now count among their ranks.

Rather than reschedule the entire thing, we pushed it forward by a few hours so that we'd have time to purchase new clothes. Well, I have clothes. My clothes don't matter as much.

But her dress. He destroyed her dress the night before our wedding. Like a monster.

I'm going to murder him.

"You can't murder him," she says, still pulling handfuls of fabric out of the bag.

"I'm certain I said no such thing out loud."

"No," she says, "but you were thinking it, weren't you?"

"Wholeheartedly."

"You can't murder him," she says simply. "Not now. Not ever."

I sigh.

She's still struggling to unearth the gown. "Forgive me, love, but if all this"—I nod at the garment bag, the explosion of tulle—"is for a single dress, I'm afraid I already know how I feel about it."

She stops tugging. Turns around, eyes wide. "You don't like it? You haven't even seen it yet."

"I've seen enough to know that whatever this is, it's not a gown. This is a haphazard layering of polyester." I lean around her, pinching the fabric between my fingers. "Do they not carry silk tulle in this store? Perhaps we can speak to the seamstress."

"They don't have a seamstress here."

"This is a clothing store," I say. I turn the bodice inside out, frowning at the stitches. "Surely there must be a seamstress. Not a very good one, clearly, but—"

"These dresses are made in a factory," she says to me. "Mostly by machine."

I straighten.

"You know, most people didn't grow up with private tailors at their disposal," she says, a smile playing at her lips. "The rest of us had to buy clothes off the rack. Premade. Ill-fitting."

"Yes," I say stiffly. I feel suddenly stupid. "Of course. Forgive me. The dress is very nice. Perhaps I should wait for you to try it on. I gave my opinion too hastily."

For some reason, my response only makes things worse.

She groans, shooting me a single, defeated look before folding herself into the little dressing room chair.

My heart plummets.

She drops her face in her hands. "It really is a disaster, isn't it?"

Another swift knock at the door. "Sir? The gentleman seems very eager t—"

"He's certainly not a gentleman," I say sharply. "Tell him to wait."

A moment of hesitation. Then, quietly: "Yes, sir."

"Aaron."

I don't need to look up to know that she's unhappy with my rudeness. The owners of this particular supply center shut down their entire store for us, and they've been excruciatingly kind. I know I'm being cruel. At present, I can't seem to help it.

"Aaron."

"Today is your wedding day," I say, unable to meet her eyes. "He has ruined your wedding day. Our wedding day."

She gets to her feet. I feel her frustration fade. Transform. Shuffle through sadness, happiness, hope, fear, and finally—

Resignation.

One of the worst possible feelings on what should be a joyous day. Resignation is worse than frustration. Far worse.

My anger calcifies.

"He hasn't ruined it," she says finally. "We can still make this work."

"You're right," I say, pulling her into my arms. "Of course you're right. It doesn't matter, really. None of it does."

"But it's my wedding day," she says. "And I have nothing to wear."

"You're right." I kiss the top of her head. "I'm going to kill him."

A sudden pounding at the door.

I stiffen. Spin around.

"Hey, guys?" More pounding. "I know you're super

pissed at me, but I have good news, I swear. I'm going to fix this. I'm going to make it up to you."

I'm just about to respond when Ella tugs at my hand, silencing my scathing retort with a single motion. She shoots me a look that plainly says—

Give him a chance.

I sigh as the anger settles inside my body, my shoulders dropping with the weight of it. Reluctantly, I step aside to allow her to deal with this idiot in the manner she prefers.

It is her wedding day, after all.

Ella steps closer to the door. Points at it, jabbing her finger at the unusually white paint as she speaks. "This better be good, Kenji, or Warner is going to kill you, and I'm going to help him do it."

And then, just like that—

I'm smiling again.

TWO

We're driven back to the Sanctuary the same way we're driven everywhere these days—in a black, all-terrain, bulletproof SUV—but the car and its heavily tinted windows only make us more conspicuous, which I find worrisome. But then, as Castle likes to point out, I have no ready solution for the problem, so we remain at an impasse.

I try to hide my reaction as we drive up through the wooded area just outside the Sanctuary, but I can't help my grimace or the way my body locks down, preparing for a fight. After the fall of The Reestablishment, most rebel groups emerged from hiding to rejoin the world—

But not us.

Just last week we cleared this dirt path for the SUV, enabling it to now get as close as possible to the unmarked entrance, but I'm not sure it's doing much to help. A mob of people has already crowded in so tightly around us that we're moving no more than an inch at a time. Most of them are well-meaning, but they scream and pound at the car with the enthusiasm of a belligerent crowd, and every time we endure this circus I have to physically force myself to remain calm. To sit quietly in my seat and ignore the urge to remove the gun from its holster beneath my jacket.

Difficult.

I know Ella can protect herself—she's proven this fact a thousand times over—but still, I worry. She's become notorious to a near-terrifying degree. To some extent, we all have. But Juliette Ferrars, as she's known around the world, can go nowhere and do nothing without drawing a crowd.

They say they love her.

Even so, we remain cautious. There are still many around the globe who would love to bring back to life the emaciated remains of The Reestablishment, and assassinating a beloved hero would be the most effective start to such a scheme. Though we have unprecedented levels of privacy in the Sanctuary, where Nouria's sight and sound protections around the grounds grant us freedoms we enjoy nowhere else, we've been unable to hide our precise location. People know, generally, where to find us, and that small bit of information has been feeding them for weeks. The civilians wait here—thousands and thousands of them—every single day.

For no more than a glimpse.

We've had to put barricades in place. We've had to hire extra security, recruiting armed soldiers from the local sectors. This area is unrecognizable from what it was a month ago. It's a different world already. And I feel my body go solid as we approach the entrance. Nearly there now.

I look up, ready to say something—

"Don't worry." Kenji locks eyes with me. "Nouria upped the security. There should be a team of people waiting for us."

"I don't know why all this is necessary," Ella says, still staring out the window. "Why can't I just stop for a minute and talk to them?"

"Because the last time you did that you were nearly trampled," Kenji says, exasperated.

"Just the one time."

Kenji's eyes go wide with outrage, and on this point, he and I are in full agreement. I sit back and watch as he counts off on his fingers. "The same day you were nearly trampled, someone tried to cut off your hair. Another day a bunch of people tried to kiss you. People literally throw their newborn babies at you. Plus, I've already counted six people who've peed their pants in your presence, which, I have to add, is not only upsetting, but unsanitary, especially when they try to hug you while they're still wetting themselves." He shakes his head. "The mobs are too big, princess. Too strong. Too passionate. Everyone screams in your face, fights to put their hands on you. And half the time we can't protect you."

"But—"

"I know that most of these people are well-intentioned," I say, taking her hand. She turns in her seat, meets my eyes. "They are, for the most part, kind. Curious. Overwhelmed with gratitude and desperate to put a face to their freedom.

"I know this," I say, "because I always check the crowds,

searching their energy for anger or violence. And though the vast majority of them are good"—I sigh, shake my head—"sweetheart, you've just made a lot of enemies. These massive, unfiltered crowds are not safe. Not yet. Maybe not ever."

She takes a deep breath, lets it out slowly. "I know you're right," she says quietly. "But somehow it feels wrong not to be able to talk to the people we've been fighting for. I want them to know how I feel. I want them to know how much we care—and how much we're still planning on doing to rebuild, to get things right."

"You will," I say. "I'll make sure you have the chance to say all those things. But it's only been two weeks, love. And right now we don't have the necessary infrastructure to make that happen."

"But we're working on it, right?"

"We're working on it," Kenji says. "Which, actually—not that I'm making excuses or anything—but if you hadn't asked me to prioritize the reconstruction committee, I probably wouldn't have issued orders to knock down a series of unsafe buildings, one of which included Winston and Alia's studio, which"—he holds up his hands—"for the record, I didn't know was their studio. And again, not that I'm making excuses for my reprehensible behavior or anything—but how the hell was I supposed to know it was an art studio? It was officially listed in the books as unsafe, marked for demolition—"

"They didn't know it was marked for demolition," Ella says, a hint of impatience in her voice. "They made it into their studio precisely because no one was using it."

"Yes," Kenji says, pointing at her. "Right. But, see, I didn't know that."

"Winston and Alia are your friends," I point out unkindly. "Isn't it your business to know things like that?"

"Listen, man, it's been a really hectic two weeks since the world fell apart, okay? I've been busy."

"We've all been busy."

"Okay, enough," Ella says, holding up a hand. She's looking out the window, frowning. "Someone is coming."

Kent.

"What's Adam doing here?" Ella asks. She turns back to look at Kenji. "Did you know he was coming?"

If Kenji responds, I don't hear him. I'm peering out of the very-tinted windows at the scene outside, watching Adam push his way through the crowd toward the car. He appears to be unarmed. He shouts something into the sea of people, but they won't be quieted right away. A few more tries—and they settle down. Thousands of faces turn to stare at him.

I struggle to make out his words.

And then, slowly, he stands back as ten heavily armed men and women approach our car. Their bodies form a barricade between the vehicle and the entrance into the Sanctuary, and Kenji jumps out first, invisible and leading the way. He projects his power to protect Ella, and I steal his stealth for myself. The three of us—our bodies invisible—move cautiously toward the entrance.

Only once we're on the other side, safely within the boundaries of the Sanctuary, do I finally relax.

A little.

I glance back, the way I always do, at the crowd gathered just beyond the invisible barrier that protects our camp. Some days I just stand here and study their faces, searching for something. Anything. A threat still unknown, unnamed.

"Hey—awesome," Winston says, his unexpected voice shaking me out of my reverie.

I turn back to look at him, discovering him sweaty and out of breath as he pulls up to us.

"So glad you guys are back," he says, still panting. "Do any of you happen to know anything about fixing pipes? We've got kind of a sewage problem in one of the tents, and it's all hands on deck."

Our return to reality is swift.

And humbling.

But Ella steps forward, already reaching for the—dear God, is it wet?—wrench in Winston's hand, and I almost can't believe it. I wrap an arm around her waist, tugging her back.

"Please, love. Not today. Any other day, maybe. But not today."

"What?" She glances back. "Why not? I'm really good with a wrench. Hey, by the way," she says, turning to the others, "did you know that Ian is secretly really good at woodworking?"

Winston laughs.

"It's only been a secret to you, princess," Kenji says.

She frowns. "Well, we were fixing one of the more savable buildings the other day, and he taught me how to use everything in his toolbox. I helped him repair the roof," she says, beaming.

"That's a strange justification for spending the hours before your wedding digging feces out of a toilet." Kent saunters up to us. He's laughing.

My brother.

So strange.

He's a happier, healthier version of himself than I've ever seen before. He took a week to recover after we got him back here, but when he regained consciousness and we told him what happened—and assured him that James was safe—he fainted.

And didn't wake up for another two days.

He's become an entirely different person in the days since. Practically jubilant. Happy for everyone. A darkness still clings to all of us—will probably cling to all of us forever—

But Adam seems undeniably changed.

"I just wanted to give you guys a heads-up," he says, "that we're doing a new thing now. Nouria wants me to go out there and do a general deactivation before anyone enters or exits the grounds. Just as a precaution." He looks at Ella. "Juliette, is that okay with you?"

Juliette.

So many things changed when we came home, and this was one of them. She took back her name. Reclaimed it. She said that by erasing Juliette from her life she feared she was giving the ghost of my father too much power over her. She realized she didn't want to forget her years as Juliette—or to diminish the young woman she was, fighting against all odds to survive. Juliette Ferrars is who she was when she was made known to the world, and she wants it to remain that way.

I'm the only one allowed to call her Ella now.

It's just for us. A tether to our shared history, a nod to our past, to the love I've always felt for her, no matter her name.

I watch her as she laughs with her friends, as she pulls a hammer free from Winston's tool belt and pretends to hit Kenji with it—no doubt for something he deserves. Lily and Nazeera come out of nowhere, Lily carrying a small bundle of a dog she and Ian saved from an abandoned building nearby. Ella drops the hammer with a sudden cry and Adam jumps back in alarm. She takes the dirty, filthy creature into her arms, smothering it with kisses even as it barks at her with a wild ferocity. And then she turns to look at me, the animal still yipping in her ear, and I realize there are tears in her eyes. She is crying over a dog.

Juliette Ferrars, one of the most feared, most lauded heroes of our known world, is crying over a dog. Perhaps no one else would understand, but I know that this is the first time she's ever held one. Without hesitation, without fear, without danger of causing an innocent creature any harm. For her, this is true joy.

To the world, she is formidable.

To me?

She is the world.

So when she dumps the creature into my reluctant arms, I hold it steady, uncomplaining when the beast licks my face with the same tongue it used, no doubt, to clean its hindquarters. I remain steady, betraying nothing even when warm drool drips down my neck. I hold still as its grimy feet dig into my coat, nails catching at the wool. I am so still, in fact, that eventually the creature quiets, his anxious limbs settling against my chest. He whines as he stares at me, whines until I finally lift a hand, drag it over his head.

When I hear her laugh, I am happy.

Juliette and Warner's story continues in the devastatingly romantic novella BELIEVE ME, the final installment in Shatter Me: Series One.

SHATTER ME: SERIES ONE

NOVELLA FIVE

"Warner?"

"Mr. Warner?"

The invocation of my name in stereo nearly startles me; I absorb this surprise with practiced calm, carefully releasing the dog to the ground. I begin to turn in the direction of the familiar voices, but the liberated creature decides to do nothing with its freedom, instead lifting a paw to my trousers as it whines, yet again, its upturned face imploring me to do something.

Feed it? Pet it?

It barks then, and I spare it a single sharp look, after which it quiets, eyes cast down as its mangy body slumps to the ground, head resting on its paws. The dog settles so close to me its little black snout bumps my boot. I sigh.

"Mr. Warner?" Castle, again.

He and his daughter, Nouria, are staring at me, the latter breaking eye contact only to shoot her father a nearly imperceptible look of frustration.

I glance between them. Clearly, the two still haven't fully settled the specifics of their roles around here.

"Yes?" I say, even as a feeling of unease blooms in my chest.

Castle and Nouria have come to collect me for a private conversation; I can sense this right away. That my mind reaches for anger in response is irrational—I understand this even as it happens—for they cannot know the fear I experience when I leave Ella behind. I have a sudden need to search for her eyes then, to reach for her hand, and I crush the impulse even as my heart rate climbs, a symptom of the new panic lately born in my body. These reactions began shortly after we returned to the Sanctuary; when, to the soundtrack of horrified screams, Ella's limp figure was carted off the plane and planted in the medical tent, where she lived and slept for ten of the fourteen days we've been back. It has been, in a word—*difficult*. And now, whenever I can't see her, my brain tries to convince me she's dead.

Castle says, "Could we steal you for a brief window? Something urgent has come up, and w—"

Nouria presses pause on this statement with a gentle touch to her father's forearm. Her smile is forced.

"I'll need only a few minutes of your time," she says, glancing briefly at someone—Ella, probably—before meeting my eyes again. "I promise it won't take long."

I want to say no.

Instead, I say, "Of course," and finally compel myself to look at Ella, whose steady gaze I have been avoiding. I smile at her as my brain attempts to override its own instincts, to do the calculus necessary to prove my fears a manifestation of an imaginary threat. Every day that Ella remains alive and well is a victory, a concrete set of numbers to add to a column, all of which make it easier for me to do this math; I'm able to process the panic a bit faster now than I did those first few nights. Still—despite my efforts to keep this from her—I have felt Ella watch me. Worry.

Even now, my smile has not convinced her.

She scrutinizes my eyes as she presses a bouquet of newly acquired tools—screwdrivers?—into Kenji's arms. She walks over to me and promptly takes my hand and I'm dealt the blow of an emotional eye roll from our audience. It is a miracle, then, that Ella's love is louder; and I'm so grateful for the reassurance of her touch it pierces me through the chest.

"What's going on?" she says to Nouria. "Maybe I can help."

I catch a note of worry from Nouria then, and, impressive: it never touches her features. She grins when she says, "I think you have enough to do today. Warner and I just have some things we need to discuss. *Privately.*"

She says this last bit in a teasing way, the implication that our discussion might have something to do with the wedding. I stare intently at Nouria, who will not now meet my eyes.

Ella squeezes my hand and I turn to face her.

You okay? she seems to say.

She's done this a lot lately, speaking to me with her thoughts, her emotions.

For a moment, I can only stare at her. A riot of feeling seems to have fused inside me, fear and joy and love and terror now indistinguishable from one another. I lean down, kiss her gently on the cheek. Her skin is so soft I'm tempted to linger, even as the emotional disgust of our audience ratchets only higher.

I've been afraid to touch her lately.

In fact, I've done little more than hold her since we fled Oceania. She nearly died on the flight home. She was already weak when we found Emmaline, having spent most of her energy fighting to kill the poisonous program overriding her mind; worse, she'd torn the tech free from her arm, leaving behind a gaping, gruesome wound. She was still bleeding from her ears, her nose, her eyes, and her teeth when she tore through Max's light, stripping the flesh from her fingers in the process. She was so drained by this point that even with Evie's reinforcements her body was failing. She landed badly and snapped her femur when she fell loose from Max's holding chamber, and then used what little strength she had left to first kill her own sister and then set fire to the capital of Oceania.

When the adrenaline wore off and I saw, for the first time, the edge of severed bone jutting through her pant leg—

The memory is not worth describing.

The next several hours were grim; we had no healers on the flight home, no sufficient pain medication, nothing more than a basic first aid kit. Ella had lost so much blood—and was in such excruciating pain—that she soon fell unconscious. I had no doubt she would die before we touched ground. That she survived that horrific plane ride was its own miracle.

When we finally arrived on base Sonya and Sara did everything they could to help Ella, but they made no promises; even as Ella's physical injuries healed, she was unresponsive. She was incapable of even opening her eyes.

For days, I wasn't sure she would make it.

"Aaron—"

"*Secrets,*" I whisper, forcing myself to draw away. "Nothing to worry about."

She studies my eyes. I feel her quietly wage war, happiness and doubt fighting for dominance.

"Good secrets?" she asks hopefully.

My heart lurches at the softness in her voice, the smile that lights up her eyes. I never cease wondering at how skillfully she compartmentalizes her emotions, even in the wake of so much brutality.

Ella is strong where I have forever been weak.

I lost faith in people—in the world—long ago. But no matter how much bloodshed and darkness she experiences, Ella never seems to lose hope in humanity. She is always striving to build a better future. She is always gentle and kind with those she loves.

It is still so strange to me that I am one of those people.

I feel the hum of Castle and Nouria's increasing impatience, and my resentment grows only larger; I generate a fresh smile for Ella and walk away as I do, having left her question unanswered. I don't know what Nouria needs from me, but I fear her news is bleak; no doubt Ella's life is at risk in some new way we'd not anticipated.

The thought alone fills me with dread.

Unbidden, I feel my hands tremble; I shove them in my pockets as I go. The hesitant bark of a mangy dog is soon followed by the sound of its paws tapping the ground, the little beast picking up speed as it hurries to keep pace with me. Briefly, I close my eyes.

This place is a zoo.

Even as I recognize the importance of our work, there remains a regrettably large portion of my mind that finds everyone here detestable—*everything* here detestable.

I am tired.

I want nothing more than to escape this noise with Ella. I want, above all else, for her to be safe. I want people to stop trying to kill her. I want, for the first time in my life, to live in peace, undisturbed; I want to be required by no one but my wife.

These, I realize, are unattainable fantasies.

Castle and Nouria both nod at me as I approach, indicating that I should follow their lead as they turn down the path. I already know they're headed to Nouria and Sam's office—affectionately labeled *the war room*—where we've had many similar meetings.

I glance back just once, hoping to catch a final glimpse of Ella's face, and instead home in on Kenji, whose thoughts are so loud they're impossible to ignore. I experience a flash of anger; I know he's going to follow me even before he moves in my direction.

Between him and the dog trailing me, I'd choose the dog.

Still, both creatures are on my heels now, and I hear Adam laugh as he says something unintelligible to Winston, the two of them no doubt enjoying the spectacle that is my life.

"What?" I say sharply.

The approaching shadow soon evolves into flesh beside me, Kenji matching my strides down the overgrown path, our boots crushing aggressive weeds underfoot. Figures dot the periphery of my vision, their feelings assaulting me as I go. Some of them still think I'm some kind of hero, and are consumed as a result by an idiotic devotion to a warped perception of my identity. My face. My body.

I find these interactions suffocating. Just now, Kenji's anger toward me is so audible I feel it giving me a headache. Still—better anger, I think, than grief.

The collective grief of a crowd is nearly unbearable.

"You know, I really thought you'd be less of an asshole once we got J home," he says flatly. "I see nothing has changed. I see all the efforts I made to defend your shitty behavior were for nothing."

The dog barks. I hear it panting.

It barks again.

"So you're just going to ignore me?" Kenji exhales, irritated. "Why? Why are you like this? Why are you always such a dick?"

Sometimes I'm so desperate for quiet I think I might

commit murder for a moment of silence. Instead, I shut down incrementally, tuning out as many voices as I'm able. It wasn't so bad before I was forced to join this peace cult. In my previous life at Sector 45 I was left alone. At Omega Point, I spent most of my time in solitary confinement. When we later took over 45, I retained the privacy of my rooms.

Here, I am losing my mind.

I am bombarded, en masse, by the emotional downloads of others. There is no reprieve from the pandemonium. Ella likes spending time with these people, and these people do everything in crowds. Meals are taken in a massive dining tent. End-of-day mingling is done communally, in the quiet tent, where it is never quiet. Many of the cabins were damaged or destroyed in the battle, which means everyone is currently sharing space—or sleeping in common areas—while we rebuild. Nouria and Sam did us a kindness by repurposing Ella's room in the medical tent; it seemed the only alternative to bunking with everyone else in a makeshift barracks. Still, our room smells always of antiseptic and death. There is only one narrow hospital bed, over which Ella and I argue each night. She insists, despite my unassailable protests, that I take the bed while she sleeps on the floor.

It's the only time I ever get upset with her.

I don't mind the cold floor. I don't mind physical discomfort. No, what I hate is lying awake every night listening to the pain and grief of others still recovering. I hate being reminded constantly of the ten days I spent standing in the corner of our room watching Ella struggle to come back to life.

My need for silence has grown debilitating. Sometimes I think if I could kill this part of me, I would.

"Don't touch me," I say suddenly, sensing Kenji's intention to make contact with me—to tap my shoulder or grab my arm—before it happens. It takes a great deal of self-control not to physically respond.

"Why do you have to say it like that?" he says, wounded. "Why do you make it sound like I was going to *enjoy* touching you? I'm just trying to get your attention."

"What do you need, Kishimoto?" I ask unkindly. "I'm not interested in your company."

His responding pain is loud; it glances off my chest, leaving a vague impression. This pathetic new development fills me with shame. I desperately don't want to care, and yet—

Ella adores this idiot.

I come to a sudden stop on the path. The dog bumps my legs, wagging its tail violently before barking again. I take a deep breath, stare at a tree in the distance.

"What is it you need?" I ask again, this time gently.

I feel him frown as he processes his feelings. He doesn't look at me when he says, "I just wanted to tell you that I got it."

I stiffen at that, my body activating with awareness. I pivot fully to face him. Suddenly, Kenji Kishimoto appears to me vividly rendered: his tired eyes, his tanned skin, his heavy, sharp black brows—and his hair, in desperate need of a cut. There's a bruise fading along his temple, his left hand wrapped in gauze. I hear the rattle of leaves and spot a squirrel, darting into a bush. The dog goes berserk.

"You got what?" I say carefully.

"Oh, now you're interested?" He meets my eyes, his own narrowed in anger. "Now you're going to look at me like I'm a human being? You know what? Fuck this. I don't even know why I do shit for you."

"You didn't do it for me."

Kenji makes a sound of disbelief, looking away before looking back at me. "Yeah, well, she deserves to have a nice ring, doesn't she? You miserable piece of shit. Who proposes to a girl without a ring?"

"I might remind you that you are in no position to exercise moral superiority," I say, my voice growing lethal even as I will myself to remain calm. "Having *destroyed* her wedding dress."

"That was an accident!" he cries. "Yours was an oversight!"

"Your very existence is an oversight."

"Oh, wow." He throws up his hands. "Ha ha. Very mature comeback."

"Do you have it or not?"

"Yeah. I do." He shoves his hands in his pockets. "But, you know, now I'm thinking I should just give it to her myself. After all, I was the one who did all of this for you. I was the one who asked Winston to sketch your design. I was the one who found someone to make the goddamn thing—"

"I was not going to leave the grounds while she was lying in a hospital bed," I say, so close to shouting that Kenji visibly startles. He steps back, studies me a moment.

I neutralize my expression, but too late.

Kenji loses his anger as he stands there, softening as he stares at me. I experience nothing but rage in response.

He never seems to understand. It's his constant pity—his sympathy, not his stupidity—that makes me want to kill him.

I take a step forward, lower my voice. "If you are idiotic enough to think I will allow you to be the one to give her this wedding ring, you have clearly underestimated me. I might not be able to kill you, Kishimoto, but I will devote my life to making yours a palpable, never-ending hellscape."

He cracks a smile. "I'm not going to give her the ring, man. I wouldn't do that. I was just messing with you."

I stare at him. I can hardly speak for wanting to throttle him. "You were just *messing* with me? That was your idea of a joke?"

"Yeah, okay, listen, you are way too intense," he says, making a face. "Juliette would've thought that was funny."

"You clearly don't know her very well if you think so."

"Whatever." Kenji crosses his arms. "I've known her longer than you have, asshole."

At this, I experience an anger so acute I think I might actually kill him. Kenji must see this, because he backpedals.

"No—you're right," he says, pointing at me. "My bad,

bro. I forgot about all the memory-wiping stuff. I didn't mean that. I only meant, like— I know her, too, you know?"

"I'm going to give you five seconds to get to your point."

"See? Who says stuff like that?" Kenji's brows furrow; his anger is back. "What does that even mean? What are you going to do to me in five seconds? What if I don't even have a point? No—you know what, I do have a point. My point is that I'm sick of this. I'm sick of your attitude. I'm sick of making excuses for your crappy behavior. I really thought you'd try to be cool for J's sake, especially now, after everything she's been through—"

"I know what she's been through," I say darkly.

"Oh, really?" Kenji says, feigning surprise. "So then maybe you already know this, too"—he makes a dramatic gesture with his hands—"*news flash*: she's, like, a genuinely nice person. She actually gives a shit about other people. She doesn't threaten to murder people all the time. *And she likes my jokes.*"

"She's very charitable, I know."

Kenji exhales angrily and looks around, searching the sky for inspiration. "You know, I've tried, I really have, but I just don't know what she sees in you. She's like—she's like sunshine. And you're a dark, violent rain cloud. Sun and rain don't—"

Kenji cuts himself off, blinking.

I walk away before the realization hits him. Nothing is worth listening to him finish that sentence.

"Oh my God," he says, his voice carrying. *"Oh my God."*

I pick up speed.

"Hey— Don't walk away from me when I'm about to say something awesome—"

"Don't you dare say it—"

"I'm going to say it, man. I have to say it," Kenji says, jumping ahead of me on the path. He's walking backward now, grinning like an idiot.

"I was wrong," he says, making a crude heart shape with his hands. "Sun and rain make a rainbow."

I come to a sudden halt. For a moment, I close my eyes.

"I want to throw up now," Kenji says, still smiling. "Really. Actual vomit. You disgust me."

I'm able to manufacture only mild anger in response to this slew of insults, as the feeling dissipates in the face of irrefutable evidence: Kenji's words belie his emotions. He's genuinely happy for us; I can feel it.

He's happy for Ella, in particular.

I experience a pang at that, at the love and devotion she's inspired in others. It's a rare thing to find even a single person who desires your unqualified joy; she has found many.

She's built her own family.

I exist on the outskirts of this phenomenon: hyperaware that I eclipse her light with my darkness, worried always that she will find me wanting. These relationships mean a great deal to her; I have long known this, and I have tried, for her sake, to be more social. To be nicer to her friends. I don't protest when she asks to gather with the others; I no longer suggest that we take our meals alone together. I follow her around, sitting quietly beside her as she talks and laughs with people whose names I struggle to remember. I watch her bloom in the company of those she cares about, all while I try to drown out their voices, to kill the noise in my head. I worry, constantly, that despite my efforts, I will not be able to be what she wants.

It's true; I am insufferable.

I wonder whether it is only a matter of time before Ella discovers this fact for herself.

Subdued, the fight leaves my body.

"Either give me the ring or leave me alone," I say, hearing the exhaustion in my voice. "Nouria and Castle are waiting for me."

Kenji registers the change in my tone and switches gears, activating in himself a rarely witnessed solemnity. He looks at me for longer than I am comfortable before reaching into his pocket, from which he withdraws a dark blue velvet box.

This, he holds out to me.

I experience an unsettling spike of nerves as I study the box, and collect the object with trepidation, closing my fingers around its soft contours while staring into the distance, trying to collect myself.

I was not expecting to feel like this.

My heart is hammering in my chest. I feel like a nervous child. I wish Kenji were not here to witness this moment, and I wish I cared less about the contents of this box than I actually do, which is impossible.

It's desperately important to me that Ella love it.

Very slowly, I force myself to open the lid, the delicate objects inside catching the light before I've even had a chance to examine them. The rings glitter in the sun, refracting color everywhere. I don't dare remove them from their case, choosing instead only to stare, heart pounding as I do.

I couldn't decide between the two.

Kenji told me it was stupid to get two rings, but as I seldom care for Kenji's opinions, I'd ignored him. Now, as I stare at the set, I wonder if she will think me absurd. One is meant to be an engagement ring, and the other a wedding band—but they are both equally stunning, each in their own way.

The engagement ring is more traditional; the gold band is ultrathin, simple and elegant. There is a single center stone—repurposed from an antique—and though it's quite large, it seemed to me a study in contrasts that reflected how I saw Ella: both powerful and gentle. The jeweler had sent me a selection of stones, each extracted from rings salvaged from different eras. I'd been fascinated by the unusual faceting of an old mine cut diamond. It had been forged by hand a very, very long time ago and was, as a result, slightly imperfect, but I liked that it wasn't machine-made. The tedious, painful honing of a dull but unbreakable stone into a state of dazzling brilliance—it seemed appropriate.

Kenji had assured me there was such a thing as a *princess-cut* diamond, which he thought would be a hilarious choice for Ella, as it recalls his ridiculous nickname for her. I told him I had no interest in choosing a ring based on a joke;

neither did I want my wife's wedding ring reminding her of another man. Besides, when I saw the shape of the stone in question, it felt wrong. The square was too sharp—all hard edges. It didn't remind me of Ella at all.

I asked that the antique stone be placed in a lightly filigreed, brushed-gold setting, the whisper-thin band of which I wanted to resemble an organic, delicate twig. This design is matched in the wedding band: a fine, curving branch rendered in gold, bare but for two tiny emerald leaves growing on opposite sides of the same path.

"It's really beautiful, man. She's going to love it."

I snap the box shut, returning to the present moment with a disorienting jolt. I look up to discover a contemplative Kenji has been watching me too closely; and I feel so suddenly uncomfortable in his presence that I fantasize, for a moment, about disappearing.

Then, I do.

"Son of a bitch," Kenji says angrily. He runs both hands through his hair, glaring at the place I stood. I tuck the velvet box into my pocket and turn down the path.

The dog barks twice.

"That's real mature, bro," Kenji shouts in my direction. "Very nice." Then—acidly—"And *you're welcome,* by the way. Dickhead."

The dog, still barking, haunts me all the way to the war room.

An epic, romantic fantasy series inspired by Persian mythology from #1 international bestselling author

TAHEREH MAFI.

"Prepare to be destroyed."

—Stephanie Garber, #1 *New York Times* bestselling author of the Caraval series

Don't miss these stunning novels fron
the *New York Times* bestselling autho
of the **SHATTER ME** series.

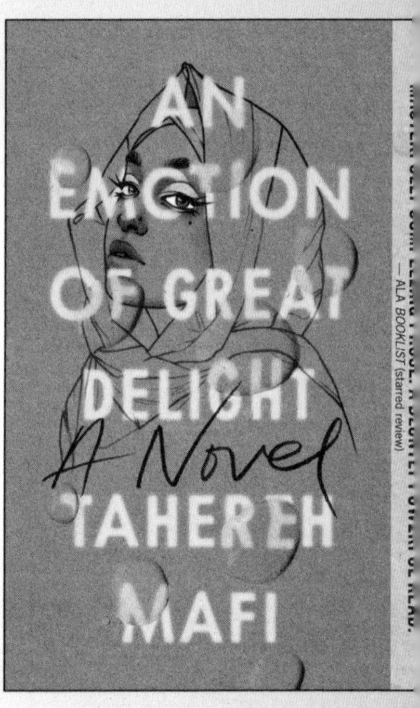

"The very best books move you to reconsider the world around you, and this is one of those."

—Nicola Yoon, #1 *New York Times* bestselling author

STORYTIDE
An Imprint of HarperCollins*Publishers*

epicreads.com